THE PLACE OF DESCENT

A Graham Eliot Novel

THE PLACE OF DESCENT

DOUG POWELL

WhiteFire
PUBLISHING

This is a work of fiction. All characters and events portrayed in this novel are either fictitious or used fictitiously.

THE PLACE OF DESCENT

WhiteFire Publishing
13607 Bedford Rd NE
Cumberland, MD 21502

ISBN: 978-1-946531-34-6 (print)
978-1-946531-35-3 (digital)

ONE

THE DARK OAK GRID OF THE COFFERED CEILING ABOVE GRAHAM ELIOT ensnared his thoughts like an opulent net. He had always struggled with feeling like an observer of his own life rather than the main participant. Olivia used to joke that presence was not his gift. *Wife Wisdom*, she'd called her insights. Now that she was gone, he usually felt like a stranger to himself, a pretender in someone else's life. Especially in his current surroundings.

The private library enveloped him in rare books and manuscripts, imbuing the room with an aroma of history, as if he could smell the words of their ancient authors. A paneled wood door with a pointed arch stood among the shelves, like a portal to the worlds contained in the books. Floor-to-ceiling bookcases filled to capacity created an abstract mosaic of spines that left no room or need for decoration. He tried to imagine a room like this in his own house in Los Angeles, but the idea was absurd given the modest suburban home he kept just a few miles north of Disneyland. He felt both alien and in his element in the midst of the private collection in Münster, Germany.

By rights, it should've been Andrew Singer doing the work. But since his murder—a crime Graham had unexpectedly played a part in solving two years earlier—Graham had taken up the work left undone by Singer. And it was Singer's life he felt he was trespassing on. The vision to create a database of images of every known New Testament manuscript, as well as other ancient manuscripts that contributed to the understanding of the Bible, was Singer's. But it wasn't until after Singer's death that Burkhard Vogel finally agreed to allow the collection his family passed down to be scanned. Singer had tried for years to develop a relationship with Vogel, to gain his trust enough to create extremely high-resolution images using equipment specially designed for the photographing of ancient documents.

Graham turned his attention back to the laptop and calibrated the lights for the multi-spectral camera, changing the tint of the shadows pooling in the sunken squares of the coffer. The angular stand next to him was designed for functionality, with no thought for aesthetics, a design philosophy that stood in harsh contrast to the tastefully appointed room.

He zoomed in on a stroke of ink, checking his focus before capturing the next image. Looking at the manuscript in such detail transformed the words into squiggles of ink, devoid of meaning. As he zoomed out to frame the folio, the minuscule Greek letters became recognizable again. The lowercase style of the letters was typical of manuscripts belonging to the Byzantine text family. Of the 5,800 or so known New Testament manuscripts, ninety percent of them shared this trait. The manuscript had been dated to AD 900 and was cataloged in the index of New Testament manuscripts kept by the Institute for New Testament Textual Research at the University of Münster.

The INTF—after the initials for its German name, *Institut für Neutestamentliche Textforschung*—used the data to create the Greek text that formed the basis of all translations of the New Testament. The final, edited text included an apparatus, or footnotes, that cited the manuscripts used to support the reading of each verse, referring to them by the names and numbers assigned by the INTF. Graham had continued Singer's close relationship with the INTF, and had, in fact, come to Münster at their invitation to deliver a series of lectures. He'd used the opportunity to reach out to Vogel, and to his surprise, Vogel had given him permission to document the manuscript. Why Vogel had changed his mind, he didn't know or care.

Graham read the text on his monitor, a passage from Luke 21.

> *During the day, he was teaching in the temple, but in the evening he would go out and spend the night on what is called the Mount of Olives. Then all the people would come early in the morning to hear him in the temple.*

However, instead of ending the chapter there—as in most Bibles—the text continued beyond verse 38.

> *At dawn he went to the temple again, and all the people were coming to him. He sat down and began to teach them. Then the scribes and the Pharisees brought a woman caught in adultery, making her stand in the center.*

"Discover something of interest, Dr. Eliot?"

Graham had become so entranced by the text that he hadn't heard anyone enter the library and was startled to hear Burkhard Vogel's voice. Small round rims of glasses caught the light as the remainder of Vogel emerged from the shadows. He was a trim, fastidious man in his late fifties, with close-cropped hair and serious, intelligent eyes. The custom-tailored suit rarified him, insulating him from ordinary concerns of the world, his affluence an inherited trait on par with the blond color of his hair.

"I'm just reading the passage of the woman caught in adultery," Graham said. "It's fascinating to see the story in the middle of Luke's Gospel instead of in John 7:53 to 8:11. I remember hearing about this variant in my first class on textual criticism, but I've never actually seen a copy with it."

"Ah, yes. I am pleased you can appreciate it." Vogel's German accent shaped his English, emphasizing consonants in a deliberate precision that mirrored his appearance. "I confess, the particulars are lost on me. I do not read Greek. I am certain there are scholars who must think that is a great injustice—a manuscript of such importance belonging to someone who cannot read it." He smiled apologetically.

Graham chuckled at the truth in the statement. "It could be worse. You could have a Bible in a language you *do* know and not read it."

"Excellent point," Vogel said, arching his brow. "And a problem far too common."

Graham pointed to the screen and moved his finger along a line of text. "Here's where it starts. Goes until the middle of the next folio. But this isn't the only variant. Some copies of John put it in different parts of the book. The one thing all the variations have in common is that they are from the Byzantine text type. The oldest biblical manuscripts don't have it at all."

Vogel bent to look at the pattern of ink, as if closer inspection would fashion them into the words that Graham saw. "Tell me, Dr. Eliot, do you believe the passage belongs in the Bible given that scholars do not know if or where it originally belonged?" He waited until finishing the question before looking to Graham for the answer.

"My opinion is that the pericope—the story—is probably an oral tradition that was passed down and included at a later time. I think it is plausible the story is a real event. It sounds like something Jesus would do. But I do think that if the passage is going to be included in the Bible, then it should be clearly noted where the text is uncertain, like by bracketing the text so that readers know there is an issue with it."

Vogel's face remained a mask. "Do you not believe that doing so would raise more questions than answers, that it will make faithful believers doubt the Word of God?"

"Not at all," Graham said. "I would hope that being clear about it would actually strengthen the faith of believers. Marking what parts of the text are in question would show just how little of the New Testament *is* in question. It should give assurance that we can know what the original writing said and that scholars can identify the parts that might not be original. There are only about five hundred words in the New Testament that are in doubt as to whether they are part of the original text or not. And no essential doctrine is based on them."

Vogel's eyes moved across the manuscript. "I assume that in addition to this passage, the bulk of the remaining uncertain text is the end of Mark."

"Exactly. Mark 16:9–20. The ending of that Gospel is almost certainly not original, but people shouldn't doubt the entire text because of those two passages. They should realize that ninety-nine percent of the New Testament is known with reasonable certainty. And even though the number of New Testament manuscripts has quadrupled over the last hundred and fifty years, not a single new discovery has changed the reading of the text. Every manuscript confirms the text as we have it."

Vogel opened his hands in an empty gesture. "Of course, the interpretation of that text differs—sometimes dramatically."

"That is an understatement," Graham said, wondering what Vogel's view of Scripture was.

"This brings me to another piece of business I would like to discuss with you," Vogel said. "Indulge me, please, and follow me to my study? I would like to show you something."

TWO

VOGEL LED GRAHAM THROUGH THE ARCHED DOOR INTO A STUDY AND took his place behind a large desk that matched the dark wood coffers and shelves. Many of the surrounding cases contained artifacts rather than books, but the shelves directly behind the desk displayed a collection of inscriptions that instantly captured Graham's attention.

On the far left of the shelf, a six-inch-tall stone roughly the shape of Wisconsin-turned-upside-down sat beneath its own soft light. Graham recognized it as Tablet XI of the Gilgamesh Epic. The inscription recorded the Babylonian story of a worldwide flood that shared striking similarities to the biblical story of Noah. However, it had been written more than 1,500 years before Moses wrote Genesis. Several copies of the Gilgamesh Epic had been discovered, the oldest one dating to 2,000 BC. But Graham remembered this seventh century BC copy was the best-preserved version of the story.

To the right, a slightly taller, narrower *L*-shaped stone sat next to it. Graham identified it as Tablet III of the Atrahasis Epic. Like Gilgamesh, the inscription contained the story of a worldwide deluge, though this version belonged to the Mesopotamian culture of nineteenth century BC.

The third inscribed tablet on the shelf was a stone about ten inches wide and eight inches tall that Graham knew was the Sumerian Creation Myth from sixteenth century BC.

Completing the row was an eight-inch-tall, four-sided, rectangular block Graham recognized as the Weld-Blundell Prism. The eighteenth-century BC text contained a list of Sumerian kings that was famously divided to distinguish those who had ruled before the deluge from those who ruled after. The list not only gave the names of the kings, but how long they ruled. Interestingly, the kings before the flood had astonishing long rules, while the kings after the flood had far shorter reigns. The parallel with the biblical differences in lifespans before and after the flood of Noah was inescapable. Several other copies of the Sumerian kings list had been found, but this one was the most famous.

"Museum quality replicas," Vogel said, stating what Graham already knew.

"Still, very impressive," Graham said. "I have seen the originals, of course, at the British Museum. Many times. And the prism, at the Ashmolean at Oxford."

"Have you seen this?" Vogel picked up a picture frame from a small stand on his desk and handed it to Graham.

He stared incomprehensibly at a Chinese character artfully rendered in calligraphy. "No. What does it say?"

"It is the Chinese word for *ship*," Vogel said. "The symbol is formed by combining the characters for 'eight' and 'mouth.'"

"Hmm." Graham squinted thoughtfully. "As in eight people on the ark. And the mouth is the vessel that holds things."

"Fascinating, is it not?" Vogel gestured blindly to the display behind him. "And what is your opinion? Did Moses commit plagiarism? Did he appropriate the story of the flood from other cultures?"

Graham smiled cautiously, again wondering where Vogel's convictions lay. "Some of my professors certainly thought so."

"And you, Dr. Eliot?"

"It's possible," Graham said, undermining the words with a doubtful look on his face. "But I think it is more likely that they are all records of the same event, documented by different cultures. And as you no doubt know, there are many more flood myths besides these. They differ on the details such as the man's name who built the ark, how many people were saved, and why the flood happened. But I believe the variations indicate corruptions of the story. The fundamental catastrophe is the same."

Vogel nodded, though Graham couldn't tell if he was agreeing with his position or simply indicating that he followed the train of thought.

"You believe, then, that the deluge described in the myths was an actual, historical event?"

"Yes, I do." Graham felt as if the conversation had transformed into a test, and he wondered how his direct answer would be received.

Vogel arched his brow. "And do you believe the waters covered the entirety of the earth?"

Graham had come to dread the question after encountering too many Christians who treated the answer as a test of orthodoxy, as if it addressed an essential doctrine of the faith. And the answer invariably led to a debate about the relationship between science and the Bible—a rabbit hole he didn't want to go down at the moment. But he felt an obligation to reply, given the privilege of having access to Vogel's manuscripts, and he heard himself give his stock answer.

"Whether or not a catastrophic flood covered the entire surface of the earth is a question I leave to geologists. I am an Ancient Near East scholar. The text of Genesis leaves the door open to different interpretations that are equally valid. The flood may well have been global, covering the entire earth. But the language of the Bible could also be taken to mean the flood was regional or even local as long as it effected *all* human beings.

"Since that is who is being judged, that is all that is necessary to fulfill the scope of the flood. I lean toward a flood effecting all human beings, but not necessarily the entire globe. I could be wrong on that, but if I am, I would happily admit it. Nothing about my theology or view of Scripture would change, and I would not have done any damage to the text in changing my interpretation."

Vogel smiled approvingly. "Quite judicious. I expected nothing less." He gestured, lifting an empty palm. "And yet, some would call you a heretic for such views."

Graham shrugged. "Someone would call me a heretic no matter what view I took. The global flood crowd would accuse me of compromising the Bible, while on the other, archaeologists who don't share my faith would consider it a scholarly heresy to treat the Bible as historically reliable. At least that particular passage. As long as I have accusations on both sides, I feel I've attained a kind of balance."

Vogel rocked slightly in an inward laugh that quickly subsided. "I wonder if you will be quite as perspicacious about what I want to ask you."

"And what is that?"

Vogel paused, as if gauging Graham's reaction before it happened. "The location of the ark of Noah."

THREE

A HUFF OF LAUGHTER ESCAPED GRAHAM, AND HE IMMEDIATELY wished he had an *undo* button like on his computer, one that could make him *un*laugh.

Vogel's expression remained unchanged, prepared for the response. "I assure you I am quite serious."

"Forgive me," Graham said, sobering. "Surely you know how many times people have claimed to have found Noah's Ark but couldn't offer any real proof."

"I am quite aware of the stories about the ark." Vogel's words sounded heavy, varnished with patience. "I confess that I am an enthusiast on the subject. Have you visited the full-scale replica of the ark in the Netherlands?"

"No, I have not," Graham said, laboring to filter skepticism.

"Pity, that. It is not two hour's drive from here. Quite an impressive exhibit. This ship is fully functioning. I have also visited the one in Kentucky, the Ark Encounter."

"I really have not paid much attention to it."

"No?" Vogel said, tilting his head back. "I take it, then, you have not visited the ark in Hong Kong, either?"

Graham shook his head. "The one owned by the group who was all over the news a few years ago saying they found the ark, right?" He pictured the video purported to have been shot inside of the ark which had been discovered in a crevasse on Mount Ararat in northeast Turkey. The footage aired on several news channels and disseminated online. The images showed a poorly lit, claustrophobic space resembling a mine, with old-looking wooden beams embedded in the ice walls, draped in cobwebs. "You do understand that claim is a hoax, right? The cave entrance shown on the video isn't on the mountain. It's below it. And the guides and carpenters who actually took the wood up the mountain have said under oath that they built the whole thing. They were told they were doing it for a movie set. They didn't know it was a fraud. The whole thing was concocted by an unscrupulous guide who conned Hong Kong investors to hire him to find authentic artifacts for their ark exhibit. The guide had a funny name. Something like—"

"Parachute." Vogel's face remained composed, immune to the criticism. "The wood they used in the fraud proved to be taken from a 3,500-year-old castle in Iran. Not even close to the right age."

"Yes! Parachute," Graham said, relieved Vogel didn't buy into the claim. "But the worst part is that when the investors learned they had been the victims of a hoax, they didn't retract their support. They became co-conspirators. Please do not tell me this has anything to do with them."

"No, no," Vogel said with a dismissive wave. "I was not deceived. It is unfortunate that group has taken the stance they have. Their ark is quite well done. I admit, however, to finding the spectacle of the arks distasteful in the way they reduce the sacred to a tourist attraction. Even more so for being a facsimile, like going to some wretched wax museum. And yet, to see the scale of the ark in person is quite overwhelming."

Graham turned a palm upward. "You just made my point. Part of my problem with looking for the ark is its size. A four-hundred-and-fifty-foot long, seventy-five-foot wide, forty-five-foot-high boat is not exactly a needle in a haystack, even when the haystack is a mountain. I believe the story is true, but I don't believe that it could have survived until now."

"But what of Josephus, Eusebius, Epiphanius, or John Chrysostom?" Vogel kept his voice even as his brow arched condescendingly. "They each record that the landing site was still known in their own times. They report that pilgrims would travel up the mountain to visit the ark and carry away small pieces."

"I vaguely remember they mentioned the ark," Graham said. "But they only documented what the people of the time believed, which was at least twenty-five-hundred years removed from the flood. Place names change in that amount of time. Geography changes. Legends develop. That's one of the reasons why I never really looked into it. The idea of finding the ark is just too implausible. Most books on biblical archaeology don't even address the topic. Noah's Ark is almost strictly the domain of treasure hunters, pseudo-archaeology, and Sunday school."

Vogel bobbed his head, acknowledging the view without agreeing with it. "What is your opinion of Durupinar?"

"Durupinar isn't a serious candidate." Graham didn't even attempt to conceal his smirk. "It's a geological formation made by earthquakes and erosion that just happens to be about the size of the ark. And it's not the right shape; it's an ellipse, which doesn't match the description in the Bible. Also, it's not in the right location. It's not *on* Ararat, just *near* it, down in a valley twenty miles away or something. So even if there were archaeological remains there, you'd have to pick and choose the parts of the Bible to trust in order to make it fit."

"The Turkish authorities appear to disagree with you," Vogel said.

"You mean because of the visitor's center there? They only did that because Ron Wyatt brought so much attention to the site. They're capitalizing on visitors to the area. I doubt very much they were compelled by the argument of an anesthesiologist from Nashville, Tennessee, who saw a picture of it in *Life* magazine and became convinced it was Noah's Ark. It turned Wyatt into an amateur archaeologist—or rather pseudo-archaeologist given that he had no training—and he spent years visiting the place and promoting it. He *did* claim to have mapped a regular pattern of iron deposits on the site he said were left from rivets used in the ark, but no one has ever been able to confirm the deposits, let alone where they came from."

"I take it, then, it is your opinion Wyatt was a fraud?"

"Actually, no." Graham pictured the modest, understated demeanor of a man who didn't seem comfortable in front of the camera despite trying to bring attention to his work. "I think he truly believed in what he was doing and that his goal was to uncover evidence that would corroborate Scripture. He knew the Bible front-to-back. Unfortunately, I think his enthusiasm was stronger than his scholarship, and that made him mistaken about most of the things he claimed. I do, however, think he was right about Mount Sinai, that it's in Saudi Arabia."

Graham momentarily drifted away, remembering how a year earlier, his graduate assistant had disappeared after illegally entering Saudi Arabia to see for himself the mountain Wyatt identified as Sinai. It fell to Graham to rescue him, requiring him to trespass into the country as well. Not only did he find his student, but while he was there, he became convinced that Wyatt's mountain was the best candidate for the true Mount Sinai.

Vogel broke into the memory. "You do not think the ark could have slid down the mountain in the mud and come to rest in a field some miles away from where it landed?"

"I didn't say that." Graham raised a finger in protest. "I said there is no evidence of it at Durupinar."

"I am pleased to hear that." Vogel gave a single, satisfied nod. "I agree with you. Not least of which because I know of three other instances of boat-shaped ellipses in the mud flow around Ararat, albeit smaller."

"As I said, I don't pay much attention to ark research." Graham shrugged, hoping the topic was coming to a close. "As far as I know, there is only one expedition of Ararat that has ever been done by a legitimate archaeologist, and that was Isaac Ross just a couple of years ago. Ross is an acquaintance of mine. And he is an excellent scholar. But to the best of my knowledge, he's never found anything."

Vogel smiled knowingly as he spoke. "I am sympathetic to your view, and yet I cannot say I share it. Especially because of what I am about to show you." He tapped the keyboard on his desk, then switched to the mouse. As he navigated his files, he continued speaking in a distracted, multitasking tone. "My family corporation serves as a defense contractor. We provide access to our satellites. One of them is equipped to provide subsurface imaging from miles away in space. This is military-grade technology, not available to the public. A few weeks ago, it was brought to my attention that one of the satellite operators had used the subsurface radar to do a search for a team of ark hunters who wanted to mount an expedition to Ararat."

Vogel pivoted the monitor so both of them could see the image he had opened. The screen showed a black and white survey grid with undulating curves that whorled like tree rings from a misshapen trunk, indicating changes in elevation. A vertical column of letters showed the coordinates down the left side of the image, and a horizontal row of numbers marked the coordinates along the bottom. Two small black rectangles were plotted on the grid sitting near each other, each highlighted with a red circle. One of the black boxes sat at a forty-five-degree angle so that the two rectangles together had the impression of a clock showing 5:15.

"This is an elevation map of the peak of Mount Ararat." Vogel pointed to a spot on the monitor. "These black rectangles just below the summit delineate the anomalies detected by the subsurface radar."

Graham looked at Vogel, suddenly interested despite his skepticism. "Exactly what do you mean by *anomalies*?"

"The radar detected two places thirty-five feet beneath the ice that indicated organic material not composed of ice, rock, or metal. It was consistent with wood. And yet—as you can see—their shapes are rectilinear, too regular to be naturally occurring. They appear to be man-made objects."

Graham squinted at the screen, as if trying to squeeze more information out of what he was looking at. "Okay. But there are two of them. If I remember correctly, Noah didn't have a fleet of ships. Just one."

"Let me assure you, Dr. Eliot, this is not a joke," Vogel said coldly. He zoomed the image closer to the black rectangles. "Consider this: each piece is approximately two hundred feet long and fifty feet wide. Combined, you have—roughly—the size and dimensions of the ark. As if the ark had broken in two."

FOUR

The news adrenalized Graham, felt as much as heard, blinding him momentarily with implications. "And you said this is recent?"

"No, I said I only learned of it recently." Vogel motioned languidly with one hand, brushing away the question. "The survey itself was done nearly five years ago. Long enough ago for the team who wanted the survey to visit the site twice. However, they have been unable to return to the mountain in the last two years because of terrorist actions in the area. Mount Ararat has been—and remains—closed."

Graham's head bobbed in thought. "That must be the expedition I heard about. They spent the two seasons using chainsaws to cut a shaft into the ice." He tapped a finger on the black boxes on the survey. "This must be what they are trying to reach."

"According to my sources, they sunk a shaft next to the smaller anomaly, approximately thirty feet away. Unfortunately, Ararat's excavation season is quite brief. The mountain is 17,000 feet high, and its weather is bad nearly eleven months out of the year. There is a short season in late summer when the peak can be reached. The window is four to six weeks long, and it takes several days to ascend to the site with equipment."

Graham sat back, arms folded. "I don't understand. Why are you telling me this?"

"I need you to investigate the site." Vogel remained motionless, fixing his eyes on Graham.

"But you just told me there was a team already there," Graham said, instantly conflicted, caught between his interest in the expedition and a dig that was not his to work.

"Yes," Vogel said, "it is true there is a team with a claim to the site.

But currently they are not there. No one is. That is why I am asking you to go."

"Mr. Vogel, is something going on that you are not telling me? You must know it would be unethical for me to investigate someone else's excavation. It would be a kind of espionage."

Vogel nodded with a heavy sigh. "Actually, espionage is exactly the charge that I am trying to avoid. It is why I am asking this of you." He looked blindly across the room, as if selecting his next words from a shelf. "Ararat is so near the borders of Georgia, Armenia, Azerbaijan, and Iran. At the time of World War I, it was part of Russian territory. Armenia, too, was also much larger in the past and included the mountain within its borders. When the Ottoman Empire was dismantled after World War I, the area was set aside for the Kurds. Kurdistan, it was to have been called."

"Like the Palestinians want," Graham said.

"Indeed," Vogel said with a sharp nod. "When modern Turkey was formed in 1923, the promise of the land was rescinded. In 1945, the Kurds petitioned the United Nations for a sovereign state but found no sympathetic ears. To this day, Kurdish rebels are fighting to claim the territory promised their grandfathers. They control the area around the mountain just as much as the Turkish soldiers—perhaps more so. Of course, having this take place at Russia's doorstep only makes an unstable situation more dangerous. As you can imagine, the militaries of each of these countries are sensitive to what happens in the area. Therefore, for one of my satellites to have taken photos of the area gives the appearance that I am a spy for one side over the others. Not only has that accusation been made by Russia, but that was how I came to learn my satellite had been used privately."

Graham shook his head. "That's a difficult position to be put in."

"Quite. And yet—as you have no doubt gathered—it has revealed an unexpected nexus between my interests and my assets. I have personally spoken to the operator of the satellite who did the search, and I am satisfied that his interest was confined to the peak of Ararat and that espionage was not a motive. However, his extracurricular activity has led to my assets in Russia being frozen."

"Surely, there must be a way to prove what the satellite was used for," Graham said. "Activity logs or something. And the operator could testify to his actions."

"Yes, but that could take years," Vogel said. "I am now facing legal action, including extradition. In addition to my personal liberty, the charge threatens my contracts in other parts of the world, and therefore my ability to generate the funds to pursue the furthering of the collection you have come to see and my ability to preserve it. That is why I have asked you here. I need you to visit the site to prove the dig is really what the team of archaeologists say it is. If it is, then it is proof that I did not commit espionage. I will be exonerated."

The admission of the charge and the unusual purpose of the assignment left Graham in silence as he tried to make sense of what he had just heard. Despite the peculiar circumstances, his first objection still stood: the impropriety of trespassing on the work of a colleague.

"Why don't you reach out to Dr. Ross since he's already working the site?"

Vogel shrugged as he once again made his apologetic smile. "Given that he used my equipment without my permission to discover the site, he has not proven himself worthy of my trust. I do not want to legitimize his actions by asking him to come to my defense. And—given my interests—I am sure he would be suspicious of my motives and think that I was trying to appropriate his discovery to claim as my own. You have a more legitimate claim as an academically interested party, and this is within your field of expertise. If Dr. Ross were somehow to become aware of your visit to the site, I would reveal to him what I just revealed to you. Your reputation would be protected. You would be justified as an agent sent to verify the work and protect *my* reputation."

"You are assuming," Graham said, "that I have nothing more pressing that would keep me from going."

Vogel made a forbearing smile. "You are a research professor. You have no teaching duties to return to. In fact, I am willing to award a grant generous enough to fund your research for several years if you are successful."

Graham wondered if he should interpret the offer as a fee or a bribe, and decided it was better to ask more questions than negotiate terms. "And, of course, it does give you an excuse to learn the status of the search for the ark."

"A happy by-product, to be sure."

"Is this why you allowed me to photograph the manuscript, so you could enlist me?"

"Yes," Vogel admitted without hesitation. "When you wrote to inform me you were coming to lecture at the INTF, I thought it was providential. While I appreciate and respect the institute, I try to keep a bit of distance from them. There is an unspoken pressure to donate my family collection to the museum there, as if it is somehow improper for an individual to have such manuscripts."

"I have heard similar complaints from other private libraries I have worked in," Graham said.

Vogel continued as if he hadn't heard. "By offering you access to the manuscript, I thought we could have this conversation in confidence. It seemed mutually beneficial."

"I came to scan manuscripts, not ascend a mountain." Graham spread his arms like a magician showing his hands empty. "I don't have any gear."

Vogel repeated the affected waving away of an objection. "In anticipation of your acceptance, I have made the arrangements of securing the services of a guide who will take you up the mountain. I also took the liberty to see that you will be fully outfitted. You will have everything you need. I even have contacts in the Turkish government who will expedite your permit to ascend the mountain. There is a Turkish consulate here in Münster. What I need now is for you to agree to be my eyes and ears."

"I'm almost fifty years old. And I'm not a very experienced mountaineer."

"Nonsense. You appear to be in excellent shape," Vogel said. "I am told the difficulty of the mountain requires more perseverance than expertise. What expertise you lack will be provided to you by your guide."

"Assuming that's true, how will I know the other expedition is legitimate?" As he said the words, Graham realized they gave the impression he was accepting the mission, a decision he had not made consciously. "Unless they have found the ark, what is it that you suppose is there that would exonerate you? As far as I know right now, it's nothing more than a shaft cut into the ice. Couldn't that be interpreted by the Russians in some way that doesn't exonerate you?"

"You will be able to determine from the equipment that was left at that camp if it is a legitimate archaeological expedition or whether that equipment is foreign to you and could possibly be used for some other purpose."

Graham closed his eyes, collecting his thoughts in a long blink. "Surely I'm not your only option."

"There is no one whom I trust more with this situation or is as knowledgeable about what to look for than you." Vogel's voice softened, sounding almost vulnerable. "Even if there were another such a man, I do not have the time to find him. Your coming here is—as I said—providential. The season for excavation is just beginning. I must act now in order to clear my name. Already, the charge is a burden from which I may not be able to recover."

Graham leaned forward and put his elbows on his knees. "Let me be frank. I don't believe there is anything to be found. I'm not doubting that anomalies were detected by the subsurface radar. But whatever it is, I don't believe it's Noah's Ark."

Vogel gave an inconsequential shrug. "What I need in order to be vindicated is proof that the excavation is being done in earnest regardless of whether something is actually found."

This time it was Graham who made the apologetic smile. "I have to admit, despite my skepticism, I am intrigued."

FIVE

GRAHAM FELT AS IF HE WERE LISTENING TO HIMSELF THROUGH A WALL. On this side of the wall, Noah's Ark threatened to crowd out all other thoughts. On the other side of the wall, detached, he lectured to more than a hundred students at the University of Münster. He had given the talk many times, and after explaining the goal of his work and its technical aspects, he lapsed into anecdotes of the situations he had found himself in. As fascinated as people were by his project, the stories were always the highlight of the talk given that adventures, intrigues, and surprises were not the words that came to mind when they imagined a job photographing Bibles. But the quest to scan every extant New Testament manuscript required traveling to exotic locations to reach ancient libraries in remote monasteries around the Mediterranean and Middle East.

At one monastery, the only way to enter was to be hoisted up by rope through a trapdoor more than thirty feet above the ground. He had to talk his way into private libraries throughout Europe in order to sift through family treasures passed down for many generations.

Several times, while working in a private library, he realized that what the family believed to be loose folios that had become detached from a manuscript were actually from a different codex, amounting to a new discovery. He often had to restrain himself in the display rooms of private collectors who cared nothing about the Bible and treated their manuscripts merely as investments, happily willing to exploit scholarly zeal for profit. And on occasion, he navigated the world of black marketeers, enticed by artifacts—some authentic, others probably excellent forgeries—that had mysteriously become available. Listening to his own stories, he couldn't help thinking he came across as equal parts scholar, salesman, con-man, and adventurer.

After the lecture, Graham answered a few stray questions before being shepherded away through the Bible Museum by Heinrich Steinmeyer, director of the INTF. Steinmeyer's wire-framed glasses, untamed mustache, and fleshy frame packed into a wrinkled suit reminded Graham of a balding G.K. Chesterton.

They walked through the exhibits displaying the history of the New Testament—how it was copied, the different forms it took, and how it was translated. The development of the Luther Bible was featured in a display case near a reproduction of the Gutenberg printing press. Graham had seen it before, but he couldn't help marveling at how clever the primitive machine was.

"Think how difficult it would be to create a whole Bible by setting each letter of text by hand, then stamping one page at a time." Graham had spoken his thoughts aloud, as if contributing to a conversation already in progress.

Steinmeyer looked confused for a moment, then followed Graham's eyes. "Yes, quite tedious. Gutenberg must have had the patience of a saint."

"According to Luther's theology, he *was* a saint—like all other true believers."

"And he did it all without the benefit of spell-check and autocorrect." Steinmeyer laughed at his own joke, which sounded like a stock line he used when showing off the press.

As they entered Steinmeyer's office, Graham noticed several images of a smooth square stone spread across the desk. Two of the corners were worn away, and the surface was scarred and weathered. In the center, a block of cuneiform letters formed a square inscription. Steinmeyer acknowledged Graham's interest by handing him the stack of photographs.

"A brick from the Tower of Babel. The university has been analyzing it and they are preparing the findings for publication."

Graham recalled everything he knew about the ziggurat discovered at Babylon in 1913. Subsequent excavations had been undertaken and revealed that the building had several incarnations, the latter iterations being built over the earlier ones, creating layers around a core. The original structure was found to be made of mud bricks. Another layer of mud bricks fortified with wood beams encased it. A baked-brick mantle had formed the layer above it. And a fourth layer created the shell that had become the outer layer of ruins.

Archaeologists believed the baked-brick mantle was the work of Nebuchadnezzar II, building on top of a tower built by Esarhaddon and his son, Ashurbanipal. The kings were able to be identified and associated with different layers because the bricks used in each rebuilding had their names stamped into them when they were formed. The mud brick core was the remnant of a tower destroyed by Sennacherib when he sacked Babylon in 689 BC. The Temple at Jerusalem was not the only temple Sennacherib tried to destroy. Although Sennacherib's own records say he had the debris dumped in the river, the ziggurat was probably not completely destroyed. And the discovery of the bricks was evidence of that.

"I didn't know the INTF had any artifacts like this."

"We do not," Steinmeyer said. "It is on loan to the university. A good friend of mine in the radiology department is doing the work. Although this is not within the sphere of the New Testament, he knew I would be interested in the results, and asked me to look over the preliminary report before he published his findings. The brick belongs to the Schøyen collection."

Graham nodded. "Well, it makes sense that it would be given a fresh look after the discovery of the inscription on Schøyen's stele."

The Schøyen Collection, the largest private collection of manuscripts in the world, had been in the news recently after an inscription had been recovered from one of its steles that had come from the ruins in Babylon. To the naked eye, the text was too faint to be read. It was recovered only after being loaned to a professor from the University of London's School of Oriental and African Studies. The stele depicted Nebuchadnezzar standing next to a ziggurat with seven tiers. The inscription identified the ziggurat as *Etemenanki*, a temple built to the god Marduk in the sixth century BC. The inscription ended:

> *I built their structures with bitumen and baked brick throughout. I completed it raising its top to the heaven, making it gleam bright as the sun.*

The drawing of the step-pyramid corresponded to measurements given in its description in the E-sangil Tablet, another inscription found in the ruins of Babylon in the nineteenth century, now on display in the Louvre.

"The brick has been analyzed using tomography." Steinmeyer indicated a dark smudge that discolored the brick in one of the images. "And a sample taken from the surface determined that the brick had indeed been coated with bitumen, making it consistent with the Genesis 11 description of the Tower of Babel. Of course, a skeptic would dismiss it as evidence since using natural asphalt as mortar was a common Mesopotamian building technique."

"Do you think the story of the tower is real history?" Graham remembered his interview with Vogel the day before and felt as if the roles had been reversed, with him asking the questions that challenged the history documented in the Bible.

"The reality of the ziggurat at Babylon is beyond question. Whether the story in the Bible is factual, I have no firm conviction."

Graham was struck with the relevance the study might have for the quest he was about to undertake. "Would it be possible for me to have a copy of the report, or at least a summary of the composition of the bitumen?"

Steinmeyer stammered, seemingly unsure how to handle the question. "It is not ready for publication. And I'm afraid it is not my research to share."

"I understand," Graham said. "But it could be of use in research that just came up."

"And what research is that?"

"I'm not sure I can share it."

Steinmeyer formed an exaggerated frown of disapproval. "Surely you understand it is not fair to share unpublished research if you are not willing to reciprocate."

Graham felt a sheepish look come across his face as he wondered how his words would sound. "I am going to Ararat tomorrow."

Steinmeyer's frown turned confused. "You are serious?"

Graham raised his brow, as if he couldn't believe his own words. "On the wildly unlikely chance that I find anything that might be from Noah's Ark, then it should be coated in bitumen. It would be helpful to have the analysis to compare it to. We could see if the bitumen was from the same time and place—roughly—and made of the same material. It would give me a baseline set of information to play off."

Steinmeyer's frown fell away, shaken off by his nods as Graham spoke. "It is an unusual request, but this sounds like an unusual situation. I will talk with my colleague, but I do not think it will be a problem. Perhaps if you agree to allow him to examine anything you find, he would be more amenable. At any rate, I will see what I can do."

SIX

Graham self-consciously eased into his first-class seat, unaccustomed to the luxury despite it being the second flight of the day he had enjoyed the privilege. The hour-long hop from Münster Onasbruek to Münich had only been an appetizer, a novelty compared to the flight to Ankara he settled in for now. Working for Vogel had perks Graham thought he could get used to.

The benefits began with the small package on the back seat of the car Vogel sent to take him to the airport. Graham opened the box and thought it was a case for his iPhone—an unattractive one given the thick, stubby knob extending from the shell like a cigarette sliding out from the pack. The advertising on the box explained that the case transformed the cell phone into a satellite phone—a SatShell, according to the embossed logo. Vogel's note explained it was a piece of technology made by one of his companies and that it was necessary since there would be no cell service on the mountain.

Graham clamped the case onto the phone and followed the instructions to set it up. The battery claimed to hold enough power for three hours of talk time, and thirty-six hours in standby. The short talk time explained why Vogel had included several portable chargers in the package. By the time he reached the airport, Graham had tested the SatShell by setting up a hotspot and downloading Isaac Ross's report on his work at Ararat. Graham wondered if it would work as well on the top of Ararat.

He had spent the first flight reading Ross's report, which had been presented at the annual meeting of the Ancient Near East Society. Over the last twenty-five years, Graham had been absent for only two of the meetings. He had missed the first to be with his daughter, Alyson, as cancer slowly stole her from him. The following year he had missed again, this time to grieve the death of his wife, Olivia. And it was during the meetings he had missed that ross had presented his work to his peers.

Graham respected Isaac Ross's research, and though their professional interests caused them to cross paths, Graham had never worked with him or developed a friendship that grew beyond counting him as an acquaintance.

Because the presentations at the ANES meetings were technical papers read aloud by their authors, Graham knew the report he was reading contained the exact words he would have heard had he been at the meeting. He could even hear Ross's friendly Texan accent as he read the paper.

Ross began by explaining that his was the first permit granted to investigate Mount Ararat since the mid-1980s. He then told roughly the same story as Vogel, though with some details omitted for reasons Graham understood. Ross included more technical details, however, which was expected, given the audience. The radar had penetrated the surface using a process called IM diffusion.

Although the indications of a rectilinear object beneath the ice on the peak was interesting, it didn't justify mounting an expedition. The cost, effort, and time commitment were just too great to invest in the project based on the satellite data alone. But the data was compelling enough for him to devote some time to investigating the mountain's history and association with the ark of Noah. Ross mentioned several eyewitnesses of the ark by name, and Graham found a list of other witnesses in the footnotes. The cumulative weight of eyewitness sightings of the ark combined with the satellite findings had persuaded Ross to investigate the site.

Despite his skepticism, Graham found himself becoming interested in the stories of those who had claimed to see the ark, now that he was going to climb the same mountain. He opened a blank document and made notes, starting with the names Ross had cited.

Graham was fascinated by Ross's description of the preparations and logistics of getting his equipment to the peak of Ararat. In addition to having a team with four archaeologists, a geophysicist, and a couple of graduate assistants, the expedition hired a dozen local workers to carry the gear. The equipment included a SUR 3000 Ground Penetrating Radar unit, two serial data loggers, an OhmMapper, three antennae, several chainsaws, and three generators. They also had to transport the tents and enough provisions to sustain the team for a month.

The supplies were packed into watertight, airtight, impact-resistant Pelican cases. The gear was taken by truck from Doğubayazıt—their headquarters, twenty miles southwest of the peak—to the base camp, five miles from the site. From there, small horses were saddled with the gear and hauled it to the high camp, three miles up the mountain. The final two miles were both the steepest part of the ascent, and—once they reached the plateau just below the summit—the flattest.

Their first attempt up the mountain was aborted when Kurdish freedom fighters—the PKK—took several of their team members captive and killed one of the local workers they had hired. They had been rescued by Turkish soldiers, and during the rescue, had seen one of their PKK captors die in the firefight. But returned the next year to try again, this time successfully.

Ross explained the icecap covered sixteen square miles and was up to a hundred meters thick. It was comprised of blue ice—snowfall that collected on a glacier, then compacted to become part of it. According to Ross, blue ice had a high electrical resistivity, making it easy to distinguish from materials encased in the ice that are not as resistant.

After establishing a camp at the site of the satellite data, the team used the OhmMapper to survey the ice's resistivity, hoping to pinpoint the object beneath the surface. Graham knew that Ross had presented the paper with the aid of PowerPoint slides to show photographs taken during the expedition. Even though Graham only had the text of the paper, he had experience with OhmMappers and could envision the work. The antenna looked something like a suitcase that was dragged across the surface by a harness, while a second operator walked behind it with a monitor showing the data being collected.

As the mapper was pulled, an electromagnetic pulse was sent under the surface to detect different dielectric values of the materials it mapped, indicating what kind of material it was. Ross explained that a 400 MHz antennae was used to penetrate up to forty meters, and a 270 MHz antennae was used to look deeper.

The survey revealed two areas where there was material in the ice that did not reflect the electromagnetic pulse. The dielectric indication was that the object was organic, but it was neither ice nor bedrock. Surprisingly, the data showed what was possibly very hard wood. The survey also revealed that the larger of the two objects had itself broken in two. The second object was a thousand feet from the first, and because it was closer to the surface, they chose that as the primary dig site.

Ross staked out an eight-foot-square area, and they used the chainsaws to cut into the ice. On the morning of the second day of digging, they discovered that the hole had completely filled in with snow. They solved the problem by erecting one of the larger tents over the site and thought they could use it to stow some of the equipment between seasons.

Another difficulty they met with was the exhaust from the chainsaws. The carbon monoxide needed to be vented out of the shaft as it grew deeper, a problem they solved by running a pair of duct tubes to the surface.

When the team settled into a pace, they were able to cut away a meter a day. By the end of the second season, they had sunk a shaft thirty-two-feet deep. But they had missed the anomaly. They had gone deep enough but were thirty feet to one side of it. The work had transitioned from sinking a shaft to cutting a tunnel.

During the second season of digging, they brought equipment to core the ice in order to explore below the surface with fiber optic cable. The ice core from fifty feet down contained strange black granules. The geophysicist conducted a fire sample test, placing the granules on foil and holding it over a flame. The material reacted by melting, indicating bituminous material. Ross reiterated that the site was just below an altitude of 17,000 feet, and that it was rare for organic material to be above the tree line, which is at 11,000 feet.

He had no natural explanation for what they had found.

SEVEN

Graham closed his eyes, intending to think through what he had read, but the memory of why he had missed the conferences where the reports had been presented angered the wound that was never far from the surface, even after three years. The pain and grief ballooned, crowding out all thoughts of Ararat despite how engrossed he'd been in the data. Instead, he found himself retracing events comprising the dark detour preventing him from attending the meetings, taking him into a wilderness from which he had barely escaped.

Juvenile Myelomonocytic Leukemia.

Graham could recall the exact moment he had heard the words for the first time, a cruel, unbalanced fulcrum dividing his life into before and after. He remembered how—despite being spoken with apology—the doctor's voice made his daughter's diagnosis sound like a combination between a lament and a curse. The words reverberated across the next two years like a dissonant note growing louder until it overpowered the innocent melody that had been Alyson's life. The inarticulate howl replacing it cast a cold shadow that became too familiar. She was just five years old.

The taking of Alyson took some of Olivia as well, knocking her out of focus, leaving her blurred and indistinct. The burden of Aly's absence fell on her with a strange weight that made her less substantive—the contradiction of depression. Graham felt helpless, as if he were trapped on an invisible shore, waiting for his wife to drift close enough for him to grab her and pull her to safety. The chemical wings of antidepressants did little more than tether her to existence for six months. It lost its grip one night after Olivia combined it with too much wine, drifted into unconsciousness, and sank beneath the surface of a hot bath.

After Olivia's death, Graham inherited her depression, compounding his own. He had always believed in God's goodness, and that God's sovereignty and omnipotence ensured all things had purpose. He used to take great comfort in the doctrine, but the loss of his daughter and wife so close together made the belief untenable. What possible purpose could his daughter's death have? Where was God as Olivia—asleep—slowly slid down the porcelain wall of the tub? He found himself on the horns of Euthyphro's dilemma. Either God wasn't good, or He wasn't sovereign. Neither option left a God worthy of worship. So, he didn't.

He continued going to church, partly out of habit and partly because it was a condition of his employment as a research professor at Calbi University—a private Christian school. But both the church and the school felt more like movie sets, elaborate façades he passed through as he played his part, saying his lines without conviction. As for his convictions, he left them unspoken because the words terrified him too much to give voice to. He no longer believed in God.

Two years ago, while attending the first ANES meeting after his absence, he began a journey that led to the recovery of his faith—almost literally—at the end of a treasure map that had guided him into the labyrinth hidden beneath the Temple Mount in Jerusalem. And a year ago, he had rediscovered his heart, that he still had the capacity to love.

He still thought of Sarah McAdams almost daily. They had quickly formed a bond after her nephew, Alexander—Graham's graduate assistant at the time—disappeared in Saudi Arabia. Graham's research into the true location of Mount Sinai had inadvertently planted the idea for Alexander to investigate a remote site that required him to enter the country illegally. Graham and Sarah had risked their lives to trespass into Saudi Arabia from Jordan and search for him at the mountain that might possibly be the forgotten location of Sinai.

When they returned to Los Angeles—him to Calbi, her to USC where she worked as a philologist—they saw each other for several months. He learned that she had been married briefly years before, to another candidate in her doctoral program after a short time dating.

She confessed that for someone so deliberate, she had uncharacteristically rushed into it. They were married before they had been together long enough for his character to be fully revealed. But his infidelities were too frequent to be kept hidden, and the relationship quickly lost all of its trust. It left a wound more profound than Sarah had admitted to herself, and in the end it proved insurmountable.

Although she didn't project her ex-husband's crimes on Graham, neither could she afford him the trust that was necessary for them to move forward. They had parted but stayed on good terms. Since the break-up, he could sense the cold darkness needle into him like frost spreading across a windshield. There were days he was tempted to feed the depression, and it took all his effort to resist falling back into the debilitating pit. That's what it was to him: a pit. A depression was a low spot in the ground, an indentation. The darkness that had ensnared him was a pit. Except now things were different. His renewed faith fenced the pit, protecting him from its lies.

He kept in contact with Sarah through Alexander, but now that Graham had been promoted to research professor, Alexander had begun to work as an assistant for another professor in the department. A common love of classic rock and its history formed a running conversation that kept them in touch even when there was no work to discuss. There had been many times Graham had wished he could erase the worthless music trivia he remembered in order to make room for more important information.

As much as he worked with the Bible, he still found it hard to give an outline of the structure of each book. And yet, he could remember Alice Cooper's real name and birthday. Alexander had the same curse. In fact, before disappearing into Saudi Arabia, he had left clues to what he was going to do in a playlist of David Bowie songs he shared with Graham, an idea too clever to actually work.

The memory of the playlist made Graham try to think of songs for Noah's Ark, but nothing came to mind except Vacation Bible School songs. He realized it reflected the academic standing of the topic: Noah's Ark was almost entirely reserved for children.

Until Ross decided to take the search for it seriously.

What Ross had found was creating an unexpected excitement about the mission. And now Graham wanted to know what had convinced Ross.

EIGHT

According to a footnote in Isaac Ross's paper, there had been more than three-dozen sightings of the ark on Ararat since the 1850s. He cited six of them in the body of the paper, but only three were described in detail. Graham opened his laptop to the notes he had taken and found the list of witnesses. Normally, he would have prepared for a site visit by doing as much research as he could, creating a project folder containing excavation reports, notes, reference documents, and background information. But lack of lead time forced him to narrow the scope only to material directly relevant to Ross's work.

Vogel, however, had sent a link to a folder of what he considered the most compelling evidence that tantalized him as an ark hunter. Graham was thankful his desire for more information had been anticipated, but he wondered if Vogel thought it would be helpful for understanding Ross or if Vogel was trying to justify an interest in what Graham characterized as pseudo-archaeology and fringe science.

Vogel's PDFs contained interviews of the most important eyewitnesses, a group that—Graham quickly discovered—formed a sort of canon of authority appealed to by almost all ark researchers. Their testimonies had inspired dozens of expeditions, including Ross's. Graham skimmed Vogel's documents, recognized three of the file names, and clicked the first one Ross had mentioned—the account of George Hagopian.

Hagopian was born near Lake Van, sixty miles south of Mount Ararat, which was Russian territory at the time, and was now eastern Turkey. The Hagopians were a family of shepherds, and like much of the population in the area before World War I, he was ethnically Armenian. During the war, Hagopian served in the Turkish Army in the last days of the Ottoman Empire and fought against the Russians before being taken prisoner. After his release, he immigrated to the United States, settling in Maryland. In 1970—near the end of his life—he began telling the story of something that happened to him as a young boy.

Around 1905, when he was eight years old, Hagopian said he had gone with his uncle to take their flock to graze on the plains at the foot of Ararat. While they were there, his uncle took him up the mountain to see the ark. It rested on a ledge, surrounded by snow and ice, but fully exposed as the result of a drought that caused the snow to melt back. Hagopian said that from a distance he thought it was a house carved from the face of the rock cliff. His uncle led him all the way up to the structure so he could see it up close and touch it.

He remembered feeling the grain of the wood and seeing the dowels that were part of the construction. The wood had been coated with something like shellac, and he recalled some of it was peeling. Other parts of the wood had green moss growing on it. One of the surprising things about the ark was that it had a set of stairs that started about ten feet off the ground and reached to the deck. Looking back on it, Hagopian conjectured previous visitors had added the flight, and that they had built it to match the floor of snow that had been there at the time. After piling up some rocks to stand on, his uncle was able to lift him high enough to reach the bottom step and pull himself up.

Warning flags went up in Graham's mind as he pictured it. No eight-year-old he knew of would allow themselves to be lifted onto a narrow set of forty-foot-tall steps without a handrail, let alone climb them to the top. Not to mention the patches of snow and ice that were probably there. Skeptically, he returned to the account.

Hagopian described the roof as having a catwalk that rose five or six feet above the deck, creating windows or ventilation for the boat. It was too dark inside to see anything, and when he yelled into the opening his voice bounced around the hollow space. There was a hole in the roof, but otherwise it was intact and—considering its age—in good shape. Hagopian estimated the ark to be a thousand feet long.

His uncle tried to remove a piece of the ark, but found the wood was too hard to cut. He shot it several times, but the bullets had bounced off without even splintering the side, leaving them with no proof and no souvenirs. Hagopian estimated they spent about two hours at the ark. When they returned to the village and told family what he had seen, he was surprised to learn that many people had also gone up the mountain to see it. Two years later, he went to the ark again, but this time it was only partly visible, half-buried in snow.

Unfortunately, Hagopian claimed he could not read maps—at least of Ararat—and therefore couldn't place the location. But from his description, researchers narrowed it down to an area just above what was known as the Ahora Gorge, on the northeast face of the mountain. The researcher who conducted most of the interviews with Hagopian was a professional artist who used the details to create an image Hagopian said accurately represented what he had seen. George Hagopian died in 1972, two years after first sharing his story.

NINE

As Graham read the account, the image of a boy being lifted up to the stairs and climbing onto the roof of the ark appeared in his mind, a scene from a long-forgotten movie he had seen when he was about the age of Hagopian during his visits. He didn't recall anything else about the documentary except that the narrator had an over-serious voice he and his younger brother tried to imitate afterward.

The memory triggered others, forming a gallery of sensationalism: Bigfoot, the Bermuda Triangle, the Loch Ness monster, UFOs, spontaneous combustion. They had seen movies about all those things. *Mysteries of the Unknown* or *Unexplained* or something like that. They were basically *X-Files* for the kids who grew up to make the *X-Files*. He and his brother had wondered why these amazing discoveries were only being talked about in movies. And one of the urban legends they told was Hagopian's.

Graham opened a window on Google Earth, spun the globe to Turkey, then zoomed in on the northeast corner of the country, a spur of territory bordering Armenia, Azerbaijan, and Iran. He kept zooming until the satellite image of Ararat filled the screen. From directly above, the icecap on the mountain looked like a splat from a colossal snowball impaled on the peak. Vogel had included a diagram of the mountain that identified its parts as well as many of the locations where eyewitnesses claimed to have seen the ark. Graham compared the diagram to Google Earth and dropped pins at each location, naming each after their witness. Hagopian's location was in a long, severe gorge on the northeast side of Ararat. He jumped back to Hagopian's account and used the details to confirm the location on the diagram.

After studying the screen to familiarize himself with the different points on the mountain, he reopened his notes and the questions he had about the story.

Hagopian had said that the ark looked about a thousand feet long—over twice as long as the biblical description. For the sake of argument, Graham explained the discrepancy as the impression of an eight-year-old boy, an age when everything seemed bigger than it actually was. Graham remembered how much smaller his childhood home seemed to him after not seeing it for several years. He thought the same thing might be going on with Hagopian's memory and decided to interpret the measurement as simply a kid's way of saying *really big.*

But what did that mean for the rest of the account? What kind of allowance would he have to make for the location? Could he trust the description? If his whole family knew about the ark, why had Hagopian kept it secret until the end of his life? Questioning one thing threatened to unravel the others.

Another troubling issue was that the interview with Hagopian was a record of a memory more than sixty years old. Graham was only fifty, but he and his brother often disagreed over the details of incidents from their childhood.

He started to think of examples, but the idea of childhood memories turned his thoughts to his daughter instead. What misperceptions had Aly had? He had been the one she had trusted to protect her. Did she think—in her uninformed, five-year-old way—that he had failed her as her pain grew worse and she grew weaker? He tried to ignore the question, but only succeeded in flipping the perspective, inverting the question. Did he remember her as she was, or did his own memory warp the way she had been? The question suddenly threatened to become an attack of self-pity.

Too many times since the deaths of Aly and Olivia he had allowed self-pity, doubt, and depression to act as an unholy trinity against him. For Graham—who valued clear thinking more highly than any of his possessions or his other abilities—the malignant mixture of thoughts was like pouring ink into clear water. He worked to develop the discipline of telling himself the truth when his emotions obscured and distorted it. He had to remind himself that emotional, truthless thinking would lead to a loss of all meaning, pulling him beneath the surface of despair. He clung daily to the truth that God was the only true anchor to cling to, an anchor that paradoxically lifted him while grounding him.

Graham shook the thoughts out of his mind and distracted himself by opening the account of the next alleged eyewitness mentioned by Ross.

TEN

Fernand Navarra was a French industrialist and demolitions expert who became well-known among ark hunters for claiming to discover wood on at least two of the five times he climbed the mountain between the mid-50s and late 60s. After the first discovery, he had guided other teams up the mountain in search of more wood. He lectured on his expeditions and was frequently cited in documentaries and books on the search for the ark. In 1974, he published *Noah's Ark: I Touched It*, and Vogel included excerpts of the most relevant passages. Graham took notes as he read, then reviewed what he had written, fixing the story in his mind.

During his time serving in the French military, Navarra had been stationed in the Middle East. He learned the location of the ark from an Armenian he had befriended, and they began making plans to visit the site together in 1952. Their five-man team ascended the north side of the mountain, using the Ahora trail, passing Lake Kop.

Graham switched to Google Earth and found Lake Kop on the northwest slope of Ararat, west of the gorge. He could see how the route avoided the severe walls of the gorge and led to the plateau above it and wondered if this was the same trail Hagopian had used.

Before reaching the lake, Navarra's team spotted the bow of the ark, two-thirds of the way up the mountain, a black form sitting among lighter rocks. According to Navarra, the monks at the Armenian Cathedral in Etchmiadzin, Armenia—almost thirty miles away—had shown him the location through a telescope. But as they got closer, they discovered that the ship was actually a rock, not the ark.

Despite the disappointment, the team continued up the mountain to the area above the Ahora Gorge. From that vantage point, they saw a second, smaller gorge, separated from the Ahora by glacial ice. Graham referenced the map, then added the names *Abich I* and *Abich II* to the glaciers on Google Earth. At this point, the rest of Navarra's team refused to go any higher, saying there was a spell on the mountain, and that they did not want to break the unwritten law. That left Navarra alone on the day he discovered the ark.

He was on the icecap at a place with no snow when he saw the ark beneath the ice. He estimated it to be 120 yards long and had the general shape of a ship. He recognized that the length was too short for the ark and theorized that part of the vessel had broken off or been destroyed.

At this point in the narrative, Navarra made a strange aside, claiming to have never had hallucinations and that he was considered to have common sense. Graham wondered why Navarra felt the need to defend himself at that point, especially considering that mountain climbing alone *did* defy common sense. As he peered into the ice, Navarra questioned if it really was the ark, or if it could be the ruins of a building or church. Graham thought that was an excellent question. But Navarra rejected the possibility because he had never heard of any tradition of a building this high on the mountain. He plotted the location as best he could, then rejoined the team with the hopes of returning to it with equipment that would enable him to reach it. He descended the mountain without even a photograph of what he had seen.

Graham looked at the Google Earth image of Ararat, dropped a pin where Navarra had seen the ark. Other than being on the same side of the mountain, it wasn't near Hagopian's pin. He went back to his notes and began writing his questions. *How could Hagopian and Navarra see the ark at different locations?* Graham's frown deepened as he typed the next problem. *Why didn't Navarra bring a camera?* The whole point was to document and prove the existence of the ark. Without a camera, how did he expect to do that, given that he couldn't carry the boat down the mountain. Also, he must have considered the possibility that he would find it but not be able to reach it. Photographs would still be able to provide evidence. And given that the discovery was made alone, uncorroborated by his team, could any of the story be trusted?

How can Hagopian's ark be too long and Navarra's too short? Why did Navarra assume part of the ark had been destroyed after he found that the length didn't match the biblical account when the obvious conclusion is that the boat—if that was what he saw—wasn't Noah's?

The explanation that part of the ark had been damaged and lost seemed too convenient, contrived to fit Navarra's presuppositions. Graham tried to keep himself from being too critical as he moved on to Navarra's next attempt, made a year later.

Navarra was able to find his way back to the spot, but as he drew within sight of the ark, boulders began to fall, loosened merely by the sound of his voice. By the time he was a hundred yards away, his companion on the trip—a Turkish photographer—had already stopped, leaving him on his own. He pushed himself forward another twenty yards before starting to feel faint. The pressure in his head made it feel like it was about to explode, and he sensed he was losing coordination, forcing him to turn back down the mountain. He found the photographer coiled among the rocks, suffering the same illness, and together made the descent. Graham noted that once again Navarra had been alone when he saw the wood, then moved on to the account of the third expedition.

Two years later he returned to Turkey with his wife and sons. Because Ararat was in a military zone, it was difficult to be granted a permit to climb. Officials were suspicious of foreign visitors and treated them as spies. Navarra reasoned that if he vacationed in the area with his family, it would make it easier to get permission. The plan worked, and he ascended the mountain with his eleven-year-old-son, Raphael, in 1955.

Navarra guided them up the mountain easily, and after finding a place for their high camp about a hundred yards from where he remembered the ark, he left his son to rest while he went the remainder of the way to make an initial survey. Like the previous visit, when he came within yards of the ark, he stopped. But this time the barrier was psychological rather than physiological, and he became frozen with an inexplicable fear and felt as if he were being choked by an unseen hand. Bizarrely, Navarra had brought some cocaine in case of emergency. Graham didn't know what kind of emergency justified cocaine, but was fairly certain that if there was such a thing, this was not it. Navarra claimed it was the only time in his life he ever took the drug, and that it cleared his head and gave him energy. That was when he saw the ark. The ice had thawed, making it easier to see, but otherwise the massive structure was just as he remembered.

Graham couldn't resist noting that for a third time, Navarra had been alone when he saw the ark. And to make the claim even more dubious, this time he was under the influence of cocaine.

The next day Navarra finally reached the site. It took the entire morning to climb a hundred yards, and two hours to climb the final hundred feet. Navarra tied his son to a rope and had him lean over the edge of a crevasse that opened above the object. After Raphael said he could clearly see the boat, Navarra had him film the site with an 8mm movie camera. Navarra unrolled a ladder into the crevasse and lowered himself onto a rock terrace where the structure sat. Dark veins webbed inside the translucent ice walls, and Navarra assumed the nebulous thicket was part of the ruins of the ark. Raphael joined him, and together they started to hack the ice to reach the wood. But as they worked, a storm trapped them in the crevasse, forcing them to stay the night in the ice cave.

In the morning, they were able to climb out and bring back more tools. For reasons Navarra did not explain, he left Raphael on the surface as he descended into the crevasse alone. He followed the corridor made by the fissure in the ice until he found dark strips beneath his feet, trapped in the glacier. He dug down eight inches until the ice gave way, creating an opening into a space filled with water. And in the water, he saw a piece of black wood. The beam was too long to pull from the hole, and he had to content himself with cutting off the last five feet.

According to Navarra, it was unquestionably hand-cut, not a natural shape. He took several pictures and shot some footage of the discovery before dragging it back to the ladder. After tying it to a rope, he climbed to the surface and used the movie camera to record the wood being pulled up by Raphael. Navarra noted the exact time of the monumental occasion: seven a.m., July 6, 1955. Navarra had to split the beam into three pieces to carry it down the mountain without threatening his balance, and he had Raphael film him as he reluctantly cut the wood.

Graham's skepticism grew as he made a note that Navarra had recovered the wood while Raphael was on the surface. Although Raphael had seen something in the ice, he had not witnessed the actual discovery of what he had pulled to the surface. Also, Graham couldn't reconcile the times Navarra noted. If they had been trapped in the crevasse overnight on July fifth, how could they have climbed back down to the camp and back up to the site, then extracted the wood by seven a.m. on the sixth? Especially if the day before it had taken them all morning to climb from the camp to the site. Graham supposed the times could be misremembered, but given that Navarra made such a point to mention the exact time, it would be odd for him to have gotten it wrong.

It was thirteen years before Navarra made another attempt, but the expedition ended when Navarra injured his foot within sight of the crevasse.

The following year, in 1969, Navarra led a team of several ark hunters and found wood again. However, this time the location was in a glacial pool, not at the bottom of a crevasse. For some reason Navarra and one of the other explorers stirred up the lake until blocks of ice floated to the surface. And among the ice was a dark rectangular piece of wood. They pulled it from the water, and Navarra not only noted the exact time, but declared it was from Noah's Ark. The team spent the rest of the day chopping ice from the edge of the lake and pulled several more pieces of wood from the water.

This time Graham noted that Navarra was not alone when the wood was found. And yet it was strange to have found the wood at a different location. Why hadn't they returned to the crevasse? Graham knew it was possible that glacial movement had altered the landscape, closing the fissure and opening others. But this site sounded so different from the first location of wood that it added to his suspicions. How many people had been searching for ark wood on the mountain and not found anything? What were the chances that Navarra would find wood once, let alone twice at two different locations?

The last item on the PDF was a note from an appendix of Navarra's book containing the results of the dating tests done on the wood he had found. According to Navarra, the radiocarbon tests indicated the wood was 4,484 years old.

ELEVEN

Graham added pins for each location where Navarra found wood or claimed to see the ark and was surprised to see they were scattered in several different places on the northeast side of the mountain. Not only were Navarra's sightings and discoveries difficult to reconcile with Hagopian's, but they were also difficult to reconcile with each other.

He opened the lab report copied from Navarra's book. According to one of the footnotes, radiocarbon dating tests were performed at three labs, though only one was mentioned by name in Vogel's excerpt. Graham made a note to get a copy of the book and find out who did the analysis. If the tests were performed correctly and the dating was accurate, then—like the measurement of the ark given by Navarra—it was an indication that what he had found was *not* the ark.

If the 4,484-year-old wood was from the ark in Genesis 6, then it roughly fit a face-value reading of biblical chronology. There was enough evidence in the Bible to date Abraham to around 2000 BC. By adding the lifespans in the genealogy from Noah to Abraham, the flood could therefore be dated to about 2349 BC. The dating calculation assumed there were no omissions in the genealogy, a literalistic methodology considered misguided by most scholars, especially given the number of examples of skipped ancestors in genealogies found in other parts of the Bible. Graham didn't have a firm opinion on the date of the flood but agreed with the critique of using genealogy to construct a strict chronology.

On a commonsense level, he thought 500 years was a very short time to repopulate the world enough to fit the Bible's description of Abraham's time. But he also couldn't say how much time would be needed, and he didn't know enough about the speed of population growth to make an informed opinion, making him skeptical of his own skepticism. The question didn't really matter to him. He held a high view of Scripture and believed there were no unimportant parts in it, but there were certainly unimportant arguments about some passages, and for him this was one of them. What he was unshakably convinced of was that God intended the passage to reveal something more important than a precise timeline of history.

Graham pulled himself back on track to his notes and added another question. *Was any of Navarra's wood coated with bitumen? If so, was analysis done?* He wasn't even sure who to ask the question to, but if there was a test, he wanted to compare it to the brick from the Tower of Babel. He followed the question with another. *Where was Navarra's wood now?* There was no way the amount of wood he found would have been used up in the tests. There had to be some remaining. But again, he didn't know who he could ask.

Then he was struck by a thought that further eroded the story. Did Navarra ever visit Ararat and not write about it? Graham remembered several occasions when Alexander—who had been heavily into stage magic as a kid—had performed magic tricks in the imaging lab that could only be explained by planting part of the illusion ahead of time. He wondered if Navarra had done the same thing by making secret trips up the mountain to hide wood that he would then pretend to discover on a later trip. There was nothing in the excerpts he read that would make it impossible, yet he didn't want to convict Navarra of a fraud he hadn't committed.

Graham had reviewed only two of the witnesses and already he had made a list of far more points to research than he could do before his own trip up the mountain. A year ago, he would have asked Alexander to look into some of these things, but he was reluctant to bring him into this. The last time Graham had asked him to research a mountain, Alexander had actually gone there and almost lost his life doing it. Graham decided he would have to find another way to get the information as he opened the third eyewitness account.

TWELVE

Ed Davis was an Albuquerque man who served in the Army Corps of Engineers during World War II. In 1943 he was stationed in Iran, tasked with building a supply road to Russia. Davis befriended one of the local men who acted as a driver for the engineers, and he spent his free time designing a way to run fresh water to the man's village. The driver returned the favor by offering to show him the ark of Noah. Vogel's PDF consisted of excerpts from a transcript of an interview with Davis from the 1980s interspersed with photos.

> *The [driver] said that many years there the ark didn't even thaw out from the ice. But some years it was out where you can see it quite easily. So I said, "I sure would like to see that." He said, "Well, sometime when it's out I'll come and get you and take you up there." And shortly after that, one day, low and behold, he appeared on the scene, and told me we could see the ark.*

The text flowed around a picture of a bald, elderly man with a Groucho Marx mustache, thick glasses, western shirt, and a turquoise bolo tie in the form of a turtle. The image gave a kind, modest voice to the quotes as Graham continued to read:

> *We arrived at this village in the evening. . . . He took me out to a shed, and it was padlocked. . . . He had artifacts that he tells me come out of the ark. Now, these articles that he had were petrified. He had some hasps, some door locks. He had one door off a cage and was about forty inches high, about thirty-six inches wide. . . and it was full of blue moss.*

> *He had corbels that come out of the living quarters, pieces that were hand-hewn and hand carved. He has some shepherd's staffs—crooks—that are petrified. The items that they have was when the ark broke in two.... They're preserved and well kept. He said that everyone that goes there wants to break off some, and that is a no-no to them.... They are trying to preserve it.*

Graham switched to notes and started a list of questions about Davis. *Where was this village with a shed full of artifacts from the ark? Iran? Why would the ark need door locks? Did it really have metal hasps?* Hagopian had seen an intact ark in 1908. Navarra reported a truncated ark with wood apparently scattered on the mountain in the 50s and 60s. In between the two sightings, Davis saw an ark broken in two. The split ark fit with the objects detected in Ross's satellite image, except that Davis saw it in a different location. Like the other two witnesses, Davis had seen the ark in the Ahora Gorge. Graham went back to the interview.

> *By morning we could go down to the ledge to the ark. The first piece we saw was the main structure. From where I was standing, it looked like a blue colored rock. Then we come back a little bit and you could see into the end. You could see the beams in there. And then they showed me the other piece of the ark. It looks kind of like the boards had separated, and they look like they fit.*

A full-color illustration followed the quote, showing a rocky valley with half of the ark on one side and half the ark on the other. Between them, sinewy tendrils of white that Graham took to be snow or ice traced the joint of the valley's opposing slopes. Both segments of the ark were rendered with the broken ends generally facing the viewer in a perspective that allowed a glimpse into the dark interior.

A second image showed a skillful pen and ink drawing of the same scene, but added an intact ark, fully exposed and sitting on a ledge above the fragmented section of the ark on the right. An arrow indicated that it was the position of the ark before it rolled off the ledge and broke. A handwritten note to the right of the drawing explained that the image was a composite of Hagopian's account and Davis's. Apparently, the same artist had interviewed both men, and each had endorsed the renderings he made from their descriptions. This composite was signed by Ed Davis as an endorsement.

Although there were no more interview quotes, the PDF summarized the rest of Davis's story. After being released from the service, he tried to tell people about what he had seen but grew discouraged when he wasn't taken seriously. Scholars did not think the story was credible, and even his own pastors dismissed him. Like Navarra on his first visit to the ark, Davis had not taken a camera, despite expecting to see the ark. He had no pictures, no artifacts, no evidence of any kind. Davis felt so rejected that—like Hagopian—he didn't share his story with anyone for decades.

The story did not become known until 1985 when a doctor in Albuquerque—who happened to be an ark enthusiast—somehow heard about Davis and went to visit him. The doctor introduced him to other ark researchers, and Davis became an important resource, remaining involved in the ark-hunting community until his death in 1998.

Shortly after meeting Davis, the doctor arranged for him to take a polygraph test. The examiner asked six questions that required a *yes* or *no* answer. He was asked if he had been taken to Mount Ararat by Abas, if they climbed the mountain on horseback and on foot, if he had seen a large wooden object, if the object was exposed in the snow for between 100 and 200 feet, and if the object he had seen was broken in two.

Davis answered these questions without showing any indication of deceit. However, the examiner detected stress when Davis was asked if anyone had ever told him about the ark other than Abas and the Bible. Davis broke the yes/no requirements and explained that he had talked to some others about the ark, but that none of them had ever seen it or knew exactly where it was.

The last page in Vogel's PDF on Davis was devoted to the doctor, an optometrist named Don Shockey who also had a degree in anthropology. Shockey's quest for the ark had taken him to Turkey nine times, and up Ararat on three of those occasions. There were no details about his first eight visits, and Graham was thankful to be spared the dubious speculations of a true believer who interpreted data to fit a presupposed conclusion. But the reason for the ninth visit startled Graham so much that he looked around first class to see if anyone had noticed his reaction. Shockey had secretly acquired information gathered by a satellite.

Shockey had contacted a man who claimed he had developed new technology for the government that provided infra-red analysis of earth from satellites. According to Shockey, the man volunteered to use the satellite to scan Ararat if Shockey could tell him what area to search. The work had to be done in secret because the satellite was not allowed to be used for private purposes. Two weeks later, the scientist contacted Shockey and said he had analyzed the area on Mount Ararat and found something. But in order not to leave a trail of evidence that could get him in trouble, the scientist wouldn't tell him anything more specific than that two man-made objects had been detected, a thousand feet apart. Shockey did, however, convince the scientist to circle the spots on a map. Both were on the Abich II Glacier.

THIRTEEN

THE REVELATION OF SHOCKEY'S SATELLITE SEARCH MADE GRAHAM lean back in thought, wondering if it had inspired the technologically updated version Vogel shared. He pushed the parallels aside to finish the account.

For his third visit to Ararat, Shockey wasn't able to obtain a permit to explore the north face of the mountain, the area marked on the map by the scientist. But he ascended anyway, climbing as far as was allowed. Although there was no way the military could monitor where he went on the mountain, his Christian conscience bound him from violating the terms. Instead, he stayed behind while he sent his guides to see if there was anything at the spot the satellite indicated. At the end of the day, the guides returned more excited than exhausted because they had seen the ark and taken photographs of it. Shockey claimed he received the pictures, but none were included in the PDF.

Graham switched to his notes and added the question that had first occurred to him. *Did Shockey's search inspire Isaac Ross to repeat the process with updated technology? Was it a coincidence?* The more he thought about it, the more the story sounded like an urban legend used to justify exploring Ararat. All he had seen was rectangles plotted on a topographical map. Shockey himself never saw the ark, so as far as Graham could tell, the sighting was not verified.

How did Shockey know he could trust the guides to tell the truth, that they weren't simply telling him what he wanted so badly to hear? And if he really did receive photographs from the guides, how could he confirm where they had been taken? For all he knew, the guides could have been running a scam, just like the Hong Kong group thirty years later.

After all, the guides *did* have a reason to lie. Ark hunters provided them work in a poor area of the world that offered few opportunities. The recovery of the ark would very possibly destroy their livelihood since it would mean there wouldn't be any reason for people to be guided up the mountain anymore. It was not in their interest for the ark to be found, only searched for.

Shockey was convinced the location in the satellite information was the same spot Ed Davis had visited, though Davis himself could not be precise about the area. Graham opened Google Earth to add the location indicated on Shockey's map but saw Hagopian's pin already there. Although neither Hagopian or Davis gave enough detail to know their locations with certainty, the descriptions and drawings were so similar that Graham treated them as the same place, just as most other ark hunters did. But what made the location interesting to Graham was that it was not where the anomalies were discovered by Vogel's satellite. Two different satellite surveys of the area had discovered man-made objects roughly the size of Noah's Ark at two different places on Ararat.

Graham felt the plane begin its descent to Ankara's Esenboğa Airport and shut his MacBook Pro. He had left Münster without optimism, sent on assignment more out of obligation to repay the privilege of archiving a rare manuscript than from any legitimate archaeological interest. There had been just enough data to pique his interest despite his effort to resist it. He had left Münster picturing the mission as an abandoned warehouse, a search for nothing in an empty place. After reading what were considered by ark hunters to be the most reliable sightings, the warehouse in his mind had evolved to a hall of mirrors.

FOURTEEN

The gritty groove of "Digging in the Dirt" by Peter Gabriel spilled out of Graham's phone as he stepped into his room at the Esenboğa Airport Hotel. He used a loop from the intro as his ringtone, an archaeological joke he'd grown accustomed to. He pressed the *answer* button without looking, and Alexander Pearl's voice leaped from the phone before he could say *hello*.

"Hey, it's Captain Fantastic!"

After Graham started seeing Sarah, Alexander rarely called him Dr. Eliot anymore.

"You've got the wrong number. I'm way more Brown Dirt Cowboy," Graham said, completing the reference to the Elton John album.

Alexander's voice was a welcome break from the research, along with the references to classic rock that frequently permeated their conversation.

"Funny you should mention that record," Graham continued as if weeks of absence had not preceded the call. "I was just at the INTF and saw the brick from the Tower of Babel."

This time Alexander caught Graham's reference to the album and started singing the chorus to "The Tower of Babel."

"That was terrible," Graham deadpanned.

"Not as terrible as Bernie Taupin's Bible history," Alexander said, referring to Elton's lyricist. "Although he does rhyme 'Tower of Babel' with 'Cain and Abel,' which is clever."

"Rhyme aside, let that be a lesson not to learn your theology from rock stars."

"Here's another thing that's funny. Your name came up in class today. I had assigned a reading from Popper on the Demarcation Problem. Sounds like a German prog-rock band—*Demarcation Problem.*" Alexander attempted a German accent as he made the joke.

Part of Alexander's duties included teaching an intro-level class to undergraduates, and following Graham's advice, he included a short section on the philosophy of science. Most scientists—including Graham—had been educated in the arcana of their disciplines without the benefit of how to think about their work in a way that transcended the technical aspect. Those who were interested in the philosophy of science mostly had to seek it out on their own. Graham had been one of those seekers, and now felt obliged as a teacher to share a brief overview of the topic.

The Demarcation Problem was the criteria used to distinguish scientific knowledge from non-scientific knowledge, such as logic or metaphysics. Scientists themselves often demonstrated an intuitive understanding of the difference by dismissing the philosophy of science precisely because it was not scientific knowledge. Sometimes—as was especially the case for archaeology—the distinction was used to tell the difference between science and pseudoscience, or pseudo-archaeology.

"One of the students used the example of chasing a treasure map found inside a mummy mask as a justification for breaking into the tunnels under the Temple Mount. She asked if that would meet the criteria of archaeology or pseudo-archaeology."

Graham groaned. Although he was convinced the work he had undertaken two years earlier in the wake of Andrew Singer's death was a legitimate archaeological enterprise, he knew it had the appearance of fringe science, speculation dressed up in scientific language. Last year's venture in Saudi Arabia in search of Sinai was even more open to the charge, and he was thankful the incident had been kept quiet with the help of the Israel Antiquities Authority. And now he was on a scouting expedition to one of the biggest targets of biblical pseudo-archaeology—Noah's Ark.

"And you said?" Graham asked, ending on a fill-in-the-blank note.

"I told them to use Popper's criteria of falsifiability. If there is no conceivable way a theory or test could be proven false, then it is not scientific. The theory that papyri containing ancient writing could form the structure of mummy cartonnage was falsifiable but proven true. The treasure map guided you to locations where items were actually found. And you were the first person to visit the network of tunnels and cisterns beneath the Temple Mount in a hundred and fifty years. I said I agreed it was sensational, but that doesn't make it unscientific."

Graham hoped his peers saw it the same way, especially now that he was a research professor and relied heavily on his reputation. "Good answer. Thanks."

"I told them pseudoscience happens when people ignore proper scientific inquiry or decide on the outcome of an investigation before they begin it."

"Presuppositions are everything," Graham agreed.

"I came up with a great illustration of what to avoid. I told them about the feud between Harry Houdini and Sir Arthur Conan Doyle."

Graham smiled at the mention of what had been Alexander's obsession as a child and was now his hobby. "Ah, so you finally found a way to slip some magic into the class instead of performing wonders in the lab. I don't think I know this story."

"Houdini and Doyle started out as friends," Alexander said. "But Doyle got heavily into spiritualism—seances and mediums and all that. Houdini knew that mediums were nothing more than magicians who pretended they really did have the powers they appeared to have in order to take advantage of gullible or grieving people. Mediums infuriated many magicians, but Houdini made a crusade against them. He would go to seances in disguise to expose them. And when the spiritualists caught on to him, he would send people who worked for him who wouldn't be recognized."

"Sounds a little obsessive," Graham said. "Why did he care so much?"

"Probably for the same reason you expose pseudo-archaeologists whenever you can. He protected what he was passionate about. Anyway, toward the end of his life, he even testified before congress about spirit mediums. On his last tour, he devoted the final act of his show to revealing their tricks onstage. Ironically, one of the people taken in by spiritualism was the inventor of the world's greatest detective, Arthur Conan Doyle. How could the man who thought logically and systematically enough to create Sherlock Holmes not see the hoax?"

"That's my question exactly," Graham said.

"Houdini argued with him about it many times, and even showed him how different mediums performed what they claimed were supernatural abilities. But Doyle would say, 'That's *one* way to do it,' as if there were other, more supernatural methods that were better explanations. And if a medium was proven to be a fraud, Doyle would dismiss them as the exception to the rule. He became a kind of evangelist for spiritualism, lecturing about it all over the world.

"After Houdini died, Doyle wrote a book describing many of his spiritual experiences, and he included an entire chapter on Houdini. He said that Houdini's feats were so fantastic that the best explanation for how they were performed was that Houdini was himself a medium who used his power for entertainment."

"You're kidding," Graham said.

"Doyle argued that when Houdini escaped from a locked milk can, or from handcuffs and chains inside a box nailed shut and locked, or the Chinese Water Torture cell, or a jail cell, that the only possible way he could do it was that he had dematerialized and rematerialized outside whatever was restraining him. Doyle declared it—and I quote—'an outrage against common sense to think otherwise.'"

"That's absurd." Graham had read all the Holmes stories at least twice and owned the entire BBC series starring Jeremy Brett. He could hear Brett's explosive, contemptuous laugh at the folly of his own creator. "But it is a great example of how people can have a kind of blindness where they see only what they want to see."

"I thought so too. And it made my inner magic geek happy. So, where to after Münster?"

"I'm not in Münster anymore. I'm in Ankara."

"Ankara? More manuscripts to photograph?"

"No. Something else. Long story," Graham said, keeping it light, not wanting to explain himself or instill any interest in Alexander. "So, to what do I owe the honor?"

"Someone left a voice message for you on the phone at the imaging lab. I came in to process the latest images you uploaded and saw the light blinking. I thought it was a robocall at first and almost deleted it. It's really strange."

"Strange how?"

"I emailed the audio file so you could hear it yourself," Alexander said. "But I wanted to call in case there was something I needed to do. Something I'm not understanding."

Graham felt his phone vibrate once as Alexander spoke. He held the phone away from his face and confirmed he had just received an email. "Got it. Hold on." He opened the attachment and hit *play*.

FIFTEEN

A SYNTHESIZED, IMPERSONAL VOICE GRAHAM RECOGNIZED FROM HIS Mac's text-to-speech feature emitted from the phone. The stilted pronunciation and slightly unnatural inflection warped the words mechanically, and it took Graham half the message to recognize that after the first sentence, the message was in Hebrew. He had to replay it to focus on the words, translating them in his head as he listened.

> *"This is a message for Dr. Eliot. One day, while he was worshiping in the temple of his god Nisroch, his sons Adrammelech and Sharezer struck him down with the sword and escaped to the land of Ararat. Then his son Esar-haddon became king in his place."*

Graham checked to see if Alexander was still on the line. "It sounds like someone translated the Hebrew phonetically, then had the Mac read it. Sounds like Stephen Hawking quoting Scripture."

"Or the 'Paranoid Android.'"

"Ha! Yes, Radiohead must be stalking me." Graham felt like he wasn't entirely culturally irrelevant by picking up on the reference to the song on Radiohead's *OK Computer,* one of the few records Alexander had introduced Graham to.

"You're right about one thing," Alexander said. "It is Scripture. I looked it up. It's actually repeated word-for-word in two places. Isaiah 37:38 and 2 Kings 19:37."

Graham remembered the context. "Sennacherib. It's talking about how he was murdered by his sons."

"Right. But Dr. E., it's not like some new revelation. Why would anyone go to all that trouble to leave a message about a king who ruled Assyria 2,700 years ago?"

"And why would they do it anonymously. Anyone who knows that number would also surely know that no one would be there in the middle of the night. Any clue where the call came from?"

"Not on this relic the university calls a phone system," Alexander said. "I just came in this morning and saw the blink. I didn't notice it yesterday, so I guess whoever it was called last night."

"Hmm," Graham noised, ordering his thoughts.

"It's not exactly an inspirational quote of the day. Although, it is a strange tie-in to the Tower of Babel."

Graham scrambled to make the connection. "What do you mean?"

"It mentions Ararat. You know: 'Just Like Noah's Ark.'"

"I still don't get it."

"You're slipping, Dr. Eliot. Elton and Bernie did a sequel to *Captain Fantastic and the Brown Dirt Cowboy*. Remember? *The Captain and the Kid*."

"Totally forgot about that one," Graham admitted.

"And the best song on it was 'Just Like Noah's Ark.'"

"Aah." Graham stretched the sound in unimpressed epiphany. "Well, thanks for passing the message on. I'll let you know if I ever figure out what it means."

Graham tried to end the call on a light note, hoping it hid the rising anxiety he felt. Was the message a cryptic warning or a veiled threat? Was the anonymous caller a friend or an enemy? Was he being protected from something or was something being protected from him? Whatever else the message meant, someone knew he was going to Ararat.

SIXTEEN

Graham opened a database of ancient texts comprised of early church fathers, ancient historians, Jewish tradition, and apocryphal books—anything that could provide context and background to the Bible. He entered *Sennacherib* and *Ararat* into the search field and was surprised to find only two hits.

The first was from Tobit, a book from the second century BC that was historically and culturally important to the Jews but wasn't considered Scripture because it was neither written by a prophet nor during the time of the prophets. Nevertheless, it was included in the Roman Catholic and Eastern Orthodox canons along with a number of other books, forming the Apocrypha. The Protestant tradition followed the Jews in rejecting it from Scripture. Graham read the passage from Tobit and recognized the words as nearly identical to the verses from Isaiah and 2 Kings.

The other hit was from the Babylonian Talmud, which preserved the traditions and oral laws of the rabbis from the second Temple period, as well as their interpretations of the Hebrew Bible. After the destruction of the Temple in AD 70, and their failed attempts to regain control of the Temple Mount, the scattered Jews committed the unwritten laws and traditions to paper. The result was much larger than the Hebrew Bible itself, and to make it manageable, the teaching—*Talmud*—was organized into different sections called tractates. The passage returned by the search came from Tractate Sanhedrin 96a.

> *When Sennacherib went away he found a board from the ark of Noah. And he exclaimed, "This is the great God, who saved Noah from the flood. I vow that if I will succeed*

> *in the future, I will sacrifice my two sons to him." This his sons heard, and therefore they killed him.... And it came to pass, as he was prostrating himself in the house of Nisroch his god, that Adrammelech and Sharezer his sons smite him.*

The Bible didn't give any backstory on what triggered Sennacherib's assassination, leaving the crime without a motive. Graham would have assumed it was selfish ambition, except that neither of the murdering sons took the throne—a third brother did. But the Talmud characterized the assassination as an act of self-defense. The sons were protecting themselves from a talisman Sennacherib had made from wood taken from Noah's Ark on his way home to Nineveh, modern day Mosul, Iraq.

Graham typed *mountain*, *ark*, *flood*, and *Ararat* into the search bar, and changed the parameters to include ancient works up to AD 700. This time almost three dozen hits came back—far more than he expected. He summarized or copied relevant quotes, sourced each one, and put them in chronological order.

Berossus
Third century BC

> *It is said there is still some part of this ship in Armenia, at the mountain of the Cordyaeans; and that some people carry off pieces of the bitumen, which they take away, and use chiefly as amulets for the averting of mischiefs.*

The Book of Jubilees
Second century BC

> *And the ark went and rested on the top of Lubar, one of the mountains of Ararat.*

Nicolaus of Damascus
First century BC

> *There is a great mountain in Armenia, over Minyas,*

> *called Baris, upon which it is reported that many who fled at the time of the Deluge were saved; and that one who was carried in an ark came on shore upon the top of it; and that the remains of the timber were a great while preserved.*

Josephus
Antiquities of the Jews (two places)
First century

> *After this, the ark rested on the top of a certain mountain in Armenia.... The Armenians call this place, The Place of Descent; for the ark being saved in that place, its remains are shown there by the inhabitants to this day. Now, all the writers of barbarian histories make mention of this flood, and of this ark;...Hieronymus the Egyptian...and Mnaseas, and a great many more, make mention of the same.*
>
> *There are also in [the land of Carra] the remains of that ark, wherein it is related that Noah escaped the deluge, and where they are still shown to such as are desirous to see them.*

Graham copied a footnote from the translator below the passage that explained the Greek word *Apobaterion* had been rendered as *Place of Descent.* According to the note, *Apobaterion* was the name of the first city Noah built after the flood. The Armenian name was *Nakhichevan*, a city in what was now Azerbaijan, east of Ararat.

The next hit came from the Jewish Targums, an Aramaic paraphrase of Hebrew Scripture. It documented the landing place of the ark in the Qardu Mountains. Graham noted that *Qardu* was another term for *Kurdish.*

He continued adding quotes, quickly building a list of references to Ararat that also mentioned the ark.

Theophilus of Antioch
Second century

And of the ark, the remains are to this day to be seen in the Arabian Mountains.

Julius Africanus
Third century

And when the water abated, the ark settled on the mountains of Ararat, which we know to be in Parthia; but some say that they are at Celaenae of Phrygia, and I have seen both places.

Eusebius of Caesarea
Chronicles
Fourth century

As for that ship which landed in Armenia, they say that to the present a small portion of it remains in the Qardu Mountains in the land of the Armenians. Some scrape off the naphtha which had been used as a sealant for the ship and make amulets from it to treat pain.

Epiphanius
Fourth century

After the flood, since Noah's Ark had come to rest in the highlands of Ararat between Armenia and Cardyaei on the mountain called Lubar, the first human settlement following the flood was made there. And there the prophet Noah planted a vineyard and became the original settler of the site.

John Chrysostom
On Perfect Charity
Fourth century

Do not the mountains of Armenia testify to it, where the ark rested? And are not the remains of the ark preserved there to this very day for our admonition?

Isidore of Seville
Etymologies
Seventh century

Ararat is a mountain in Armenia where, historians testify, the ark settled after the flood. To this day, traces of its lumber are seen.

Graham copied the most fascinating passage at the end of the references to separate it from the others.

Faustus of Byzantium
Fifth century

In that time the great bishop…named Jacob Nisibis… came to the mountains of Armenia. He came to Sararad Mountain…in the district of Qardu.…He came with the desire of seeing the saving ark built by Noah and with great fervor he beseeched God, for after the flood it had rested on this mountain.…Now while he was ascending over the difficult, waterless and rocky parts of the Sararatean Mountain, he and those who were with him became weary and thirsty. So Jacob kneeled on the ground and prayed to the Lord, and from the spot where he had placed his head a fountain gushed forth, and he and those with him drank. To this day that fountain is called the Fountain of Jacob.… When he reached a difficult place near the summit, he became very tired and slept. And an angel of God came and spoke to him, saying: "Jacob, Jacob." And he replied: "I am here, Lord." The angel said: "The Lord has accepted your entreaties and fulfilled your request. That which is beneath your head is part of the wood from the ark. I brought it for you from there. Do not climb any higher, for this is how the Lord wants it." With great joy he arose and with great thanksgiving he worshipped the Lord. He saw the board which appeared to have been split from a large piece of wood by an axe.…When the man of God arrived bringing

> *the wood from the saving ark of Noah (an eternal symbol of the punishment which was visited upon all species, a symbol of their fathers' deeds) the entire city and the districts surrounding it came out before him with immeasurable incalculable joy and delight.... To this very day that miraculous symbol is preserved by them—wood from the ark of Noah the patriarch.*

Graham was struck by two things in the accounts. The first was that the ark was at a well-known location where people could not only see it with apparent ease, but also climb up to it and take parts of it away with them. That description didn't match the modern sightings that place the ark at locations difficult to reach. The other thing that stood out was that the mountain had different names in the accounts—Ararat, Lubar, Baris, Sararatean—and that the mountain range was referred to as the Qardu or Cordyaean Mountains. Yet they seemed to be referring to the same place. Graham thought the best explanation for the discrepancies was that the accounts were written by people from three different cultures—Jews, Christians, and pagans—in different languages over the period of a thousand years.

Graham sat back from the screen as he continued to stare at strange passages he had culled from works he thought he was familiar with. His head bobbed forward in exhaustion after the data overload. The last thought before he fell asleep was the thread that ran through the texts: The ancient authors believed the ark existed not just historically, but remnants still existed in their own times. Something was there—or, at least, had been.

SEVENTEEN

Graham hadn't realized how quickly he had grown accustomed to the luxury of first class until he took his seat on the commuter plane to Iğdir the next afternoon. After packing himself into a window seat that was also the aisle seat, he used his phone to check his email.

Steinmeyer had sent the results of the analysis of the brick from the Tower of Babel. Graham scanned the PDF and concluded the information wasn't useful without a sample of bitumen allegedly from the ark that he could compare it with.

The other message he read was from Vogel, explaining that Graham would be met at the airport by his guide, Şahin. Base camp would be the Si-Mer Hotel in Doğubayazıt, which had hosted many of the ark expeditions over the years. Everything he would need would be waiting for him at the hotel. Graham had just enough time to send a short reply promising to keep him posted before putting the phone into airplane mode.

He cocooned himself in noise-canceling headphones and spent most of the ninety-minute flight parsing the notes he had made the night before. When the pilot made an announcement fifteen minutes before they were scheduled to land, Graham ignored it, assuming it was the captain's customary thanks and call to prepare for arrival. But something in the air changed, and he turned his head to look around the cabin. Every face wore a mask of anxiety, an expression that became his own as he pulled off his headphones.

Graham caught the eye of the man across the aisle and translated his words into Turkish before speaking. "Excuse me. What's happening? I didn't hear what the pilot said."

It took a moment for words to break through the man's concerned frown. "The plane is being diverted."

"Diverted? Why?"

"Terrorists have hijacked an ammunitions truck and have driven it to Iğdir, to the airport. It is not safe." The man spat the words, disgusted. "The pilot wants to land as quickly as possible. The nearest airport is at Yerevan."

"Armenia?" Graham tried to picture a map of the region and recalled Yerevan northeast of Ararat, though he couldn't remember how far away it was.

Hoping to find some information about what was happening, he took his phone out of airplane mode and searched the news without success. The electric cold of panic constricted his chest and spread outward to the rest of his body. Time slowed as his mind sped into every possibility—rational and irrational—as he simultaneously tried to will the plane down to the ground. Despite being flown to safety, the threat of danger sharpened his senses, and he became aware of every bounce and shift of the plane, every unusual sound. He became so focused on the minute adjustments of the plane that he didn't realize he was sweating until he felt the bump of the landing gear on the tarmac.

The congested jetway tested Graham's patience before depositing him in a throng of stranded passengers from other diverted flights, all waiting to get through passport control. He pulled his phone out and quickly searched for hotels, hoping to avoid a night in the airport. Armenian geography was not his strong suit, and aside from knowing the name of the capital, he had only a vague idea of where he was.

The map app showed the Zvartnots International Airport about ten miles east of Yerevan, where most of the hotels were. A second, smaller cluster of location pins marked places six miles to the west, in a town called Vagharshapat. Graham was surprised to see that one of the sites he had marked with a location pin during his research was in the city center, but he didn't recall a city called Vagharshapat.

He touched the site and read the label: *Cathedral and Monastery of Etchmiadzin*. That's what he had assumed the town was called—*Etchmiadzin*. Graham remembered marking it because it included the museum housing the purported fragment of petrified wood from the ark. Given that he would be stuck here for the next day while he and Vogel made new plans, he thought he might as well try to see the wood. He could even try to talk to someone at the museum about getting a sample to compare to the INTF report. And if the museum was a bust, at least the hotels in Vagharshapat were a few miles closer to the airport.

A room within walking distance of the cathedral was still available, and he booked it as he reached the customs officer. After a cursory questioning during which he learned Armenia required no visa, he joined the stream of refugees flowing toward Ground Transportation. As he stood in line for a taxi, he picked out languages from the aggregate of confused sound of travelers—Armenian, Russian, French, Greek, Assyrian, and a surprising amount of English. *Just like the Tower of Babel.* The Elton John song stuck in his head, playing all the way to the hotel.

EIGHTEEN

GRAHAM SLID TO THE LEFT SIDE OF THE BACK SEAT OF THE TAXI AS IF caught in the gravitational pull of Mount Ararat as he stared out the window. The enormity of the pyramid of rock jutting out of the plain mesmerized him, looking as if it had been misplaced or abandoned by an unknown range. Its sole companion was Little Ararat, a small peak that looked like a geological toddler hovering around the feet of her mother. The flat, twenty-mile expanse between him and Ararat exaggerated the scale of the mountain, making it seem looming despite its distance.

By midday he was ensconced in a hotel room only slightly larger than the two double beds it held. But it was clean, quiet, and a safe distance from the danger that had altered his route. After the terrorist scare, Graham was too thankful to feel disappointed at not being in a five-star hotel again. Rustic farm wood trimmed the halls, and it was decorated throughout with rusted tools and farming implements, transforming the rural artifacts of local culture into a motif. Graham smiled to himself as he imagined Vogel in the room, trying not to be contaminated by the unsophisticated surroundings, then remembered he needed call Vogel to make new arrangements.

Vogel picked up after one ring, as if he had been waiting for the call. "Dr. Eliot. I am very pleased to hear from you. After I received the alert that your plane was diverted, I was concerned. Are you okay?"

"A little rattled, but I'm fine," Graham said. "Can't wait to get home. Sorry it didn't work out like you planned."

"Do not let the inconvenience of a few rebels keep you from your task, Dr. Eliot. These little skirmishes are common in the area. If not for my responsibilities and my knees, I would be there with you myself. You are out of reach of whatever danger the PKK can pose."

After learning from Ross's report that the PKK often camped on the mountain and had even kidnapped an ark hunter, the initials read more as a warning. "The Kurdish freedom fighters you told me about were the ones who took over the airport? There's no way I'm going up that mountain. I'm done."

"I need you there," Vogel said, unsympathetically.

"Have you ever been on a flight that was diverted because of terrorists?" Graham asked, sharpening his tone. "It's different when it's not hypothetical. I don't want to be anywhere near Ararat. I already told you there's nothing up there anyway. You'll have to find someone else or some other way to clear yourself. I'm sorry." Graham added the apology hoping to soften how harsh his words sounded to himself.

"That is unacceptable, Dr. Eliot." Vogel emphasized the consonants more than usual, bristling his factual voice. "The accusations against me must be cleared as quickly as possible. And *you* are going to help me do that."

Something about Vogel's coldness unnerved Graham, making his own tone more forceful. "I already told you, I am done. I'm going home. And I'm leaving whether you buy the ticket or not."

"I am afraid it is not that simple, Dr. Eliot," Vogel said softly, replacing volume with menace. "Just as I had the ability to make things easy for you to enter Turkey, I can make it hard for you to leave Armenia, also."

"Are you actually threatening me?"

"I make promises, not threats, Dr. Eliot. And if you doubt me, then let me give you a reason you may not want to abandon your work so soon. You recall that folio from Luke's Gospel that you were so interested in, yes? It seems it has gone missing. In fact, no one has seen it since *you* handled it." He held the vowels of *you* accusatorily.

"That's a lie," Graham hissed, leaping to his feet.

"But your own actions condemn you, Dr. Eliot. Your hasty exit from Münster after what appears to be a bribe to Turkish officials to rush your papers through? It appears as if you were trying to reach a place where you could find a black marketeer to take an antiquity off your hands, does it not?"

"I don't have your manuscript." Graham compressed a scream into a hoarse rasp, more breath than sound.

"Of course. That is exactly what would be expected from someone who has sold it quickly. You have connections all over the world—even to the black market, I am sure—and so you could have arranged a ready buyer."

"None of that is true!" Graham despised the note of pleading in his voice, a drop of blood to a shark.

"That is irrelevant, Dr. Eliot," Vogel said, his controlled calm asserting dominance. "Do you think an accusation will harm your professional reputation any less than a conviction? Now you understand my own position. By the time the truth is known—if it is ever known—the damage to your career will have been done. No one will trust you again. At least not in the same way they used to. No exoneration or not-guilty verdict will dispel all the suspicions. There will *always* be suspicion. And that will close the access you have to collections such as mine. I will ensure that. Your work will be taken from you. Is that what you want?"

Vogel's reasonable tone turned the world upside down, disguising evil with rationality, and making what was right appear illogical. Graham's silent reply accumulated like fog obscuring a landscape he thought he knew. Or maybe the fog was clearing to reveal where he really was.

"Okay, let's say I agree to go on," Graham hissed, seething. "The border between Armenia and Turkey is closed. I'm twenty miles from Ararat, but I can't get there now. According to the airline, the only way to Doğubayazıt at this point is by taking a bus north into Georgia and crossing into Turkey from there. That wastes two days—assuming all the connections are made, which they tell me is highly unlikely. And I would still need to go through Iğdir. By that point the terrorists might have the highway closed as well."

"You are a resourceful man of many talents," Vogel said. "I have every confidence in you. Otherwise, I would not have asked you to go on this errand."

"Asked?" Graham said indignantly. "You mean coerced."

"Semantics. That is one of your fields of interest, is it not?"

"And if I run this ridiculous *errand* as you call it, what happens to the folio?"

Vogel sighed. "I have such a large collection and only a single assistant to help tend it. Perhaps the folio has merely been misplaced."

"Just like my trust." Graham hung up before Vogel could reply.

NINETEEN

Gregory Luysavorich was the son of an Armenian prince executed for assassinating King Khosrov II. In the aftermath, Gregory was exiled to Caesarea, Cappadocia, in the center of modern Turkey. While there, he converted to Christianity and grew in the faith, eventually rising to the office of bishop. Although he had a rich ministry in his adopted country, his heart was burdened for his homeland. In AD 285, he returned to Armenia as a missionary. But Tiridates III, son of the assassinated king, had other plans for him. He imprisoned Gregory in a pit twenty feet deep and fourteen feet wide in a remote, barren area on the eastern edge of the plains surrounding Mount Ararat.

During the imprisonment, a group of nuns fleeing the persecution of Christians by Roman Emperor Diocletian took refuge in Armenia. Tiridates became smitten by one of the nuns, but after she rebuffed his proposal of marriage, he had the whole group of nuns executed. Shortly afterward, the king fell ill and lost his mind. After he began acting like a wild boar, one of his advisors called for Gregory to be brought before the king in the hope the missionary could cure him.

Gregory had survived more than a decade in the pit, kept alive by the kindness of a woman who threw a loaf of bread down to him each day. When he was taken before the king who had treated him so cruelly, Gregory healed not just his enemy, but the feud between their families. Tiridates recovered his sanity and received the gift of faith. He was baptized in 301 and declared Christianity to be the official religion of Armenia—the first country to adopt the faith as a state religion.

That same year, Gregory began building the Cathedral of Etchmiadzin—the descent of the Only-Begotten. It had been damaged, rebuilt, and expanded a number of times, but the structure still stood, making it the oldest cathedral in the world—see of the Armenian Apostolic Church.

Three hundred years after Gregory's release, a chapel was built over the pit that had held him captive, called *Khor Virap*—deep dungeon. By the time Khor Virap was built, he had become known as Gregory the Illuminator because he had brought the light of God to Armenia.

Graham finished skimming the history in the visitor's brochure, then studied the map as he entered the grounds of the Mother See of the Armenian Church. The complex—a few minutes' walk from the hotel—included the cathedral, the pontifical residence, several museums, chapels, a monastery, a school, and administration buildings. The main entrance gate was an unexpectedly contemporary stone design featuring stylized depictions of Saint Gregory and King Tiridates jointly holding a cross, one on each side. An open-air altar stood next to the gate, a modern reminder that visitors were entering ancient, sacred precincts.

By medieval European standards, the cathedral was modest in size and far less ostentatious. Several different periods of Armenian architecture had been Frankensteined together, each addition's beige stone aged with a slightly different shade. Despite the alterations, the church retained the basic cruciform layout with four altars and four domes—the first of an architectural plan that was repeated throughout the Byzantine world.

He threaded his way across the flagstone courtyard, weaving through visitors taking pictures and exploring the grounds, to the entrance on the other side of the cathedral. The main door was on the far side of the building, sheltered under a domed portico below the belfry. Although the outer shell of the dome was dull and plain, the underside was ornately decorated, as was the doorway itself. Graham wondered if the contrast was a symbol of a spiritual truth about inner beauty. At the very least, it hinted that more treasures were inside the modest façade.

According to the pamphlet he received with his ticket, the blocks of stone forming the threshold of the cathedral came from Mount

Massis—the Armenian name for Ararat. King Tiridates himself, as a show of devotion to his new faith, ascended the mountain, carried back the stones, and set them in place himself.

The cavernous space inside was larger than Graham had expected, judging from the outside, again defying his expectations. Like most churches in the Eastern tradition, it had no pews, giving it an ambience of capacious otherness intended to evoke the transcendence of God. Having grown up during the time in American Christianity when God was treated like a cosmic best friend, Graham appreciated the thoughtful theology of the architecture that guarded against forgetting the mystery and wonder of the nature of God.

Worshippers and tourists reverently milled across the marble tile, most going to or from the small stone railing that fenced the space before the altar. Intricate patterns detailed the sanctuary, continuing the theme from the entryway.

Renovations to the church in 1958 revealed the original altar built by Gregory in 301. Workers also discovered an even older pagan altar, revealing that Gregory had appropriated an already sacred spot.

The door to the right of the altar led Graham into the first of three rooms comprising the museum. The rectangular space was crowned with a domed ceiling twenty feet above the floor. A kaleidoscopic floral pattern festooned the dome, from which a chandelier sprouted from its center. Lighted glass shelves displayed rows of items in tall wooden cases along the three walls before him. A knot of people were examining the cases on the right wall of the room, prompting Graham to start with the exhibits on the left.

A young woman sat at a desk inside the doorway, staring blankly into her phone, oblivious to her surroundings. Graham passed her, unacknowledged, and couldn't decide between ambivalent docent or negligent guard.

One of the cases on the left wall contained a display of processional crosses and liturgical staffs. Another case was filled with chalices and censers. A third held a number of Bibles bound in silver covers. He kept moving as he turned to investigate an island display in the center of the room featuring illuminated Bibles.

A case along the back wall contained nearly a dozen crosses arranged around a large cross of dull, black metal. A label identified the primary cross as the oldest processional cross in existence. On the glass shelf directly below it, a disembodied metal forearm and right hand lay as if amputated from an automaton. The label explained it was a reliquary housing the right hand of Saint Gregory the Illuminator.

By the time Graham turned his attention to the right wall, the other visitors had moved on, leaving him alone before the glass cases. The first display featured a golden cross adorned with jewels. An oval piece of glass had been mounted in its center like a lens, and behind the glass bead was a dark, unfocused line, giving it the appearance of a reptilian eye. According to the museum card, it was the "*Khotekerats Sourp Nishan Reliquary*—Containing a Relic of the True Cross of our Lord Jesus Christ." He wondered if this was what Sennacherib's talisman had looked like. Had he been murdered over an equally questionable splinter?

Graham sidled to the middle display, which held censers and chalices arranged to frame an elaborately decorated silver reliquary with its shuttered doors open to reveal an ornate black spear tip. The tip was diamond-shaped and had been cast with elongated triangular holes missing from each fin, each shape with its long point oriented to the center so that together they formed a cross. The tag claimed it was The Holy Lance—the tip of the spear belonging to Longinus, the traditional name of the Roman guard who pierced the side of Jesus while he was on the cross, and then became a convert. The dubious authenticity of the spear was not helped by the inclusion of another metal right forearm and hand that housed the remains of the apostle Thaddeus.

According to tradition, the spear tip had been brought to Armenia by Thaddeus on a missionary journey as he evangelized the area between the Black and Caspian seas. The relic was made even less believable by the fact that there were several other competing spear tips claiming to be *The Spear of Destiny*, as it was sometimes called. Graham suppressed a smirk and moved to the next case.

The last case in the room highlighted a reliquary chest with a jewel-encrusted cross. At first Graham thought the cross itself was the relic, but then realized it was only an adornment for what lay behind it: a red-brown block about twelve inches tall and nine inches wide that looked more like dark stone than wood. The understated assertion of the label almost made Graham laugh, as if it were daring visitors to believe it. "Reliquary—Containing a Fragment of Noah's Ark."

He opened the camera app on his phone, then zoomed in, using it as a magnifying glass. From what he could see of the texture, it appeared to be petrified wood. He wished he could see the sides, a cross section, but the reliquary bound all sides of the wood except for the bottom left corner, which looked like it might have been chipped away. He took several photos, trying to think critically about what he was seeing, wondering what—if anything—would be different if he were staring at a genuine piece of wood from Noah's Ark.

The display reminded Graham of his visit to the Topkapi Palace in Istanbul a year earlier where he saw an exhibit purporting to show the staff of Moses, the turban of Joseph, a cooking pot that had belonged to Abraham, King David's swords, and a collection of scrolls that had belonged to John the Baptist. It was complete nonsense, but that didn't stop the tourists from visiting. It was like a religious side show, where the unimportant was treated as important, and the fake was treated as authentic. But unlike the spear of Longinus and the piece of the true cross, the wood from the ark was unique among relics; no other church claimed to have such a thing.

Graham extracted himself from his thoughts and crossed the room back to the girl engrossed in her phone. After introducing himself as a professor of archaeology, he asked to speak to the curator of the museum. To his surprise, the words undid the digital spell, transforming the girl into a hospitable doppelgänger. She excused herself to find someone named Father Vardanyan, leaving him alone to examine the ark.

TWENTY

Graham studied the reliquary, wondering how easy it would be to open, when the entire chunk of wood had last been seen, and if it had ever been photographed apart from its case. What objections could there be to having it scientifically analyzed and dated? He crouched down and angled his head up to examine the bottom through the glass shelf supporting it, almost forgetting what he was waiting for as he considered the questions.

"Excuse me, please." The English words were filtered through a Russian accent, and seemed to be paused in a polite, unspoken demand for attention.

A black cassock cloaked the figure of the man and hung just off the floor, making it look almost as if he were floating. A pointed cowl spired from his head, its tails draped over his shoulders like roots. A long, gray beard scribbled down to his breastbone, stopping short of the bejeweled metal cross hanging from his neck. Dark, hooded eyes brimmed with kindness, framed by round John Lennon glasses. They locked on Graham, intermittently eclipsed by slow blinks. Graham thought they looked full of answers, patiently waiting for the right questions to be asked.

"I am Archimandrite Ovannes Vardanyan, director of the museum." The priest didn't offer his hand—an inaction that came across as more proper decorum than rude or germophobic.

Graham bowed his head slightly in a show of respect, triggering a gleam of appreciation in the priest's languid eyes.

"How may I be of help?"

"My name's Dr. Graham Eliot. I'm a research professor of Ancient Near East Studies."

"It is not often we receive such illustrious visitors," Father Vardanyan said, raising his brow.

"You are too gracious, Very Reverend Father," Graham said, repeating the title the woman had used to address the priest when she made the call. "You have many interesting pieces here."

"And yet it seems you have eyes for only one of them." Father Vardanyan gestured toward the fragment from the ark with liturgical grace.

Graham turned back to the case, wondering how long the priest had been watching before introducing himself.

"It is our most cherished relic. What questions may I answer for you?"

Graham appraised the reliquary as he spoke, not trusting himself to keep skepticism off his face. "Well, I know the story about Jacob and how an angel brought him wood from the ark. And that he was told to go no farther up the mountain in search of the rest of the ark."

"That is correct," Father Vardanyan said on a single nod.

"Please understand, Father, that I mean no disrespect," Graham said, turning toward the priest, "but has there ever been any effort to compare this wood with other wood found on the mountain?"

The hint of a smile appeared on Father Vardanyan's lips. "I assume the intention would be to determine if this wood matched other finds and therefore corroborate the existence of the ark on the mountain? No, not to my knowledge."

"Have you even considered such a thing, given that there have been several explorers over the last hundred years who have claimed to find wood from the ark?"

"It never occurred to me." Father Vardanyan looked past Graham to the reliquary. "The authenticity of the wood is not in question as far as the church is concerned."

"You're not curious to see where the evidence might lead?" Graham said, taken aback by the acceptance of tradition as indisputable fact.

"Not in the least. This *is* where the evidence leads. If other wood matched, then that is exactly what one would expect to find. It would simply confirm what is already known. If it did not match, then the wood it is being compared to could not be from the ark. Neither one of those things is particularly interesting, nor would it change the church's view of the holy relic. Consider the reliquary of Gregory the Illuminator." Father Vardanyan motioned to a case on the back wall. "How many bones would it take to prove his existence? One. The whole body need not be reconstructed to have proof. Two or three or a hundred bones does not make his existence any more certain than having one bone. The same is true with the ark. This piece is all that is necessary to know the ship was real."

Graham nodded understanding, contrary to his feelings. "Has there ever been a carbon dating test done on the wood?"

"There has not. As you know, that would require a sample to be cut off, and we could not allow that to happen regardless of how small a piece is required."

"Not even from that bottom left corner?" Graham asked, pointing at the reliquary. "The test only requires a tiny sample. If a small piece was taken from there, it wouldn't even be noticeable."

"The corner was removed as a tribute to Catherine the Great, one of our benefactors. No such tribute will be made for a scientific test."

"As curious as I am to know what an analysis would show, I do understand wanting to preserve it," Graham said. "I've just come from Münster, Germany, from the university. They are doing tests on one of the bricks found at the Tower of Babel. They've run an analysis of the bitumen that was used in place of mortar. And they were able to use a nondestructive method so that no sample had to be taken in a way that damaged the brick."

A spark of interest faintly lit the priest's otherwise unchanged face. "Fascinating."

"I agree. I also think it would be fascinating if the bitumen could be compared to the coating that is on the wood here."

"To what purpose?"

"If the composition of the bitumen was the same, then there would be reason to believe it was from the same part of the world in roughly the same part of history. It could be a way of confirming the history of the fragment, at least in a general way." Graham left unsaid the possibility that the result could show the wood was too young to be from the ark, a test of falsifiability.

"I do understand why someone would be interested in such a comparison," Father Vardanyan said, folding his hands together across his body. "However, you fail to take into account the fallenness of mankind. Let us say we allow your test, and the results reveal the bitumen is in fact similar in age and composition to that found on the brick from the Tower of Babel. To you and me, it would provide a small, general confirmation of something we already believe. However, there is nothing to prevent someone from interpreting those same results as evidence the wood must be from Babylon, and therefore acts as a disconfirmation as being from the ark."

"There are always alternate theories," Graham agreed, "but they rarely have the same explanatory power."

"Nevertheless, it opens the door to them," Father Vardanyan said. "The church faces enough threats. Why arm the enemy? And as you yourself explained, the wood from the ark was delivered to Jacob by an angel. There are no scientific tests that could confirm its miraculous provenance. A miracle, by definition, is beyond such measurement and examination. The test would be futile, and perhaps counterproductive."

Graham struggled to keep a note of frustration from his voice. "But don't you think investigating biblical history—corroborating it, collecting evidence for it—could result in people coming to faith?"

"Such people would be coming to faith for the wrong reason. Faith is not an object to be quantified and measured in the ways you suggest. Although a favorable scientific analysis might strengthen the faith of those who already believe, it is not itself a reason to believe. Then again, such believers do not need that kind of assurance."

"Well, if you are ever interested, I'm sure the university would love to talk to you about a joint project. Thank you for taking the time to talk to me, Very Reverend Father."

"The pleasure was all mine, Dr. Eliot."

Graham retraced his path through the cathedral and was stepping into the plaza as he heard Father Vardanyan call from behind him. He stopped and turned, watching the priest scan the courtyard, before fixing on Graham. When he spoke, it was soft, almost conspiratorial.

"I can tell you are a man who loves truth, who wants to *touch* truth. You say you want a way to test the story of how Jacob received the wood."

Graham squinted, wondering what was happening, anticipating a contradiction to what he had just been told. "Yes, I would. Very much."

Father Vardanyan let a beat of silence drop between them as he made some final deliberation. "Return tomorrow morning for the service. I may have some guidance for you."

TWENTY-ONE

By the time the service started at seven-thirty a.m., Graham was at the rear of a sea of congregants. About half of the women were covered with headscarves, a distinction that identified them as observant Armenians among the tourists. He had never attended an Armenian service before and was interested in seeing how the ancient liturgy differed from his Presbyterian church's—a service considered high church within his denomination.

On the far side of the worshippers, more than a dozen priests crowded the platform in the chancel, frozen in standing prayer, their red tunics distributed on either side of the priest officiating the service. The celebrant wore a white robe adorned with an embroidered gold sash to give him a vertical stripe. A miter added a foot to his height like a reflection of his long beard.

In front of the railing defining the chancel, a collection of priests in black tunics looked on. Some wore pointed cowls just as Vardanyan had the day before. Graham assumed the colors indicated a hierarchy, but he couldn't figure out why some of their heads were covered while others weren't. The question distracted him from the service, which—despite his interest—wasn't difficult since he didn't speak Armenian.

A choir occupied an apse on his right, and as they began to sing, he had to resist turning to look at them, knowing they were placed out of the line of sight of the worshippers precisely so they would not be perceived as performing. Instead, he studied the decorations ornamenting the building.

He had expected the kinds of frescoes that covered the walls of most Eastern Orthodox churches, but except for the occasional floral shape—the paintings were non-figurative, complex geometrical patterns, more like a mosque. The interior of the domes above each point in the cruciform looked like different stages of the kaleidoscopic pattern he had seen in the museum the day before, and the two-hour long service gave him time to become more familiar with the patterns than he wanted.

A curtain was drawn across the sanctuary, shielding the altar and the ceremony being conducted behind it as the celebrant prepared the gifts for communion. It closed again as he received communion, then a final time as he cleaned the chalice following communion. It served the same purpose as the icon-heavy, wooden templons of Eastern Orthodox churches, but without the permanence of a fixed wall. The curtain contained an image of Christ hovering ethereally over the Etchmiadzin Cathedral. In the background, the peaks of Ararat and Little Ararat rose on either side of him. Saint Gregory the Illuminator and King Tiridates flanked the church, and a host of angels encircled the entire scene.

Graham was surprised to find that the ark of Noah was not included in the picture. Instead, it seemed to be replaced—or at least eclipsed—by Christ. The image inspired him to contemplate the parallels between the two, how the ark was a foreshadowing of Jesus's work of salvation. Although Graham couldn't understand the words of the service, he invited the image to preach to him as he meditated on it, joining his brothers and sisters in worship if not in language.

When the service ended, Graham remained where he was, letting the congregation flow around him as they carried their faith out into the world. Five minutes later, Father Vardanyan appeared in his black cassock, having shed his liturgical vestments.

"Please, let us find a more suitable place to speak."

He gestured toward the main entrance with a graceful, fluid motion that looked borrowed from the service, then shepherded Graham into the plaza. As they separated themselves from the crowd, the priest spoke without looking at Graham—in contrast to the penetrating stare the previous day.

"Have you worshipped in an Armenian Church before, Dr. Eliot?"

"No, but I wish more Christians in America could experience a service like that. There is a weightiness to it that is undeniable and profound. The emphasis on God's transcendence is something that is too often lost in most American churches."

The priest held a long blink, as if savoring the service. "I have never visited your country, but I cannot imagine worship any other way."

Father Vardanyan guided them to the north side of the plaza, to a garden of walnut and poplar trees planted in a grid of rectangular beds along the inner wall of the Holy See. A lane divided the garden, providing access to a hexagonal chapel that looked like a modern addition to the complex. The lane also hosted a monument, fashioned in the same contemporary style as the entrance gate. The asymmetrical tower was formed from several rectangular slabs of stone standing on end and precariously balanced on one another. Most of the enormous tablets featured extruded Armenian crosses—the four branches flaring from the center, and floral decorations attached to each corner—while a variety of figures had been carved in the rest. Graham studied the monument as Vardanyan claimed a park bench facing it.

"That is in memory of the Armenian Genocide."

Graham had devoted himself far more to ancient history than recent events. "I'm sorry, but I don't remember anything about it."

"It occurred mainly in 1915," Father Vardanyan said, "but lasted throughout World War I, until the dissolution of the Ottoman Empire in 1922. One and a half million Armenians were murdered—half of all Armenians at the time. It is what scattered many of our people all over the world, including to your country."

Graham wasn't sure which disturbed him more: news of the genocide or his ignorance of it. "I'm not sure what to say."

"You have already said the only thing that could be said. It is how we ended the service. 'May the Lord remember all your sacrifices.' It is fitting that you should be interested. It will help you understand."

"Understand what?"

"What you are about to learn."

Vardanyan punctuated the sentence by nodding at a man walking toward them from the gardens on the other side of the monument, then stood to greet him.

TWENTY-TWO

"*Shat hoviv Frey.*"

Graham had heard the greeting enough at this point to infer that it meant something like *Very Reverend Father.* Father Vardanyan lifted his right hand and offered it, his palm limply facing down. The man bent to kiss it, carefully avoiding the ring signifying the office of Archimandrite.

"Dr. Eliot, this is Khazhak Poghosyan."

Graham mirrored the man's reserved smile as they shook hands. Mid-thirties, he guessed, and with the slender build, permanent stubble, and dewy eyes of a young Alan Arkin in *Catch 22.* The man sat down on the other side of Father Vardanyan as the priest turned slightly toward Graham and dropped his voice.

"As you may know, the Holy See hosts a seminary. Just over there." He tilted his head, indicating the far side of the garden. "Khazhak is gracious enough to mentor the students when he is not in the field."

"What do you mentor the men in?" Graham asked in English, the language the priest had just used, but then wondered if the man understood him.

"I serve as a missionary," Khazhak said with the same brittle Russian accent as Father Vardanyan.

"We support his ministry, but we also have much use for him here whenever he returns."

"Very important work," Graham said, nodding appreciation. "Where do you serve?"

"I minister to people of Armenian heritage still in Turkey, near Mount Massis." Khazhak glanced in the direction of the mountain.

"There are many Armenians in this region who are separated from their people and their past," Father Vardanyan said. "The boundaries of Armenia do not reflect the extent of the land as it used to be. At one point, Armenia extended all the way to the Mediterranean Sea. Try to imagine America being reduced to the size of just one of your states. That is the Armenia of today."

Khazhak leaned forward, looking around the priest at Graham. "And now the Kurds want to lay claim to it as well. Many Armenians are foreigners in the land of their fathers and grandfathers. Their own land is not their country, though it *is* the same location as their ancestors."

Graham was impressed with Khazhak's passion, the sound and conviction of someone who felt a calling. "I had no idea. I am sorry, but I am afraid I am ignorant about much of the recent history of this part of the world."

Father Vardanyan faced him squarely. "That is one of the reasons why I am making this introduction. Like all missionaries, Khazhak's work is dependent on the generosity of others. He is funded by raising support from those who want to participate in the work of the gospel. It occurs to me that you may know such people."

Graham immediately thought of the constant deluge of solicitations he got from missionary groups and ministries. From the little he had just been told, Khazhak's ministry sounded like a worthy cause with genuine need—features not always apparent to him in the solicitations. But at the same time, he couldn't help feeling disappointed that this was the reason Father Vardanyan had asked him to return. He rebuked his selfish impulse and looked into the missionary's eyes. "I would be happy to help in any way I can, Khazhak."

"And as a mutual show of goodwill," the priest said, pivoting the other way, "Khazhak may also be of help to you."

"Really?" Graham glanced between them. "How so?"

Khazhak lowered his voice to just above a whisper. "I can guide you up Massis. What you call Ararat. I can show you the path taken by Saint Jacob when he was given the wood from the ark."

Graham stammered, taken aback at having his expectations so suddenly crash only to be exceeded moments later. "That would be very helpful to me, but it is so far out of your way. The bus to Georgia and then across the border again and then—"

"You cannot go that way," Khazhak interrupted. "Not to get to Massis. Not while the PKK is there. The Turkish Army will have the highway around Iğdir closed to visitors. And if you tried to go around Ağri to get to Doğubayazıt then it would add two hundred kilometers. And the highway at Doğubayazıt may be closed as well. Even if it is open, the road from there to the mountain would be closed because that is where the PKK camps are. It is the wrong side of the mountain."

"What options do we have?" Graham asked.

"I know how to cross the river."

Graham pictured the Aras River that ran along the edge of the plain forming the boundary between Armenia and Turkey. "But the border is closed," Graham said.

"Not if you know where to go," Khazhak said. "Many of the people I minister to are just across the river, and I need to reach them without the inconvenience of respecting illegitimate borders. It also happens to be where you want to go. And many of the soldiers who patrol it are probably responding to what is happening in Iğdir right now. It is a safe time to cross. And it is certainly the quickest way to get there. We can very quickly pass beyond where they patrol. And even if they do see us, they are more concerned with PKK than a couple of missionaries."

Father Vardanyan pivoted his head between the men as he spoke. "It appears to me providence may be at work."

Graham tried to protest without sounding ungrateful. "Forgive me for disagreeing, but how will I explain myself if I am found in Turkey without the proper papers?"

Khazhak spoke haltingly, testing his reply as he formulated it. "Your flight was diverted to a country whose borders are closed to it, correct? It is already unusual."

Graham shook his head. "I can't count on that as a reason not to have a passport stamp. And I wouldn't lie to the authorities about it."

"*Illegitimate* authorities," Khazhak reminded him.

"Perhaps," Graham said, "but my conscience may be bound on this point where yours is not."

Khazhak raised a finger. "But your lack of stamp would certainly get you detained by the military checkpoints even if you do have an authorized climbing permit. Going the way you suggested would guarantee your failure."

Graham looked each man in the face, then looked down at his feet in thought.

"How important is it to you to see the mountain?"

Father Vardanyan's calm voice contrasted with the riot of thoughts erupting in Graham's mind. Khazhak's proposal was a route he didn't want to take, on a journey he did not want to make, in search of something he did not believe was there. He wondered how once again he found himself having to secretly enter a country in order to explore a mountain. And yet, to reject the plan could cost him his career, his passion, and the access to benefactors that supported not only *his* work but could help Khazhak's as well.

A sigh of acceptance escaped Graham. "It seems my choice has been made for me."

Father Vardanyan repeated the words Graham heard during the final blessing of the service. "*Heeshestseh Der zamenayn Badarakus ko.*" He placed a hand on top of Graham's as he translated the blessing from Armenian. "May the Lord remember all your sacrifices."

TWENTY-THREE

GRAHAM TRIED TO IGNORE THE COLLECTION OF RARE MANUSCRIPTS that surrounded him—another sign that his world had been turned upside down. The Vatche and Tamar Manoukian Library not only housed works related to Armenian culture and medieval history, but it was also a depository for biblical manuscripts. As far as Graham was concerned at the present moment, its main virtue was that it was within the campus of the Holy See and had better Wi-Fi than the hotel.

Khazhak pointed out the building just before they passed beneath King Tiridates and Saint Gregory on their way to Graham's hotel. He told Graham to be ready to go at two a.m., then left him to collect the gear they would need for the expedition. Graham had planned on doing more research from his room but moved to the library after becoming frustrated with the slow internet.

Although Vogel was the last person in the world he wanted to talk to, he knew he had to touch base with him and decided to get it out of the way to keep it from nagging at him. He stared into the blank email, not at a loss for words formulating his report, but trying to compose the unwritten words he wanted to incorporate as a subtext. He wanted a message that didn't cede all control over the situation to Vogel, and that registered his resentment without sounding resentful. And he guessed the fewer the details, the more frustrating it would be to Vogel. He winnowed it down until he could share his plan in six words. "Continuing work. Same mountain, different road." He poked *send* with more force than necessary, jamming it into the Web.

Graham opened Google and entered "Armenian Genocide" into the search bar. The number of hits that came back was overwhelming. He skimmed the abstracts of the first fifty links, then clicked on the top one: The Armenian Genocide Museum-Institute in Yerevan. Graham was shocked at the amount of documentation there was for an atrocity he felt he should have known about.

The menu included a section for research, and within it he navigated to a collection of eyewitness accounts. Some were just a few sentences, while others were long enough to be chapters in books. The material included interviews, memoirs, articles, and official reports. They were different stories that told the same larger story of profound tragedy.

Many witnesses described how all the men in the Armenian villages and refugee camps were killed, and how the women and girls were taken by Muslims for wives or were sold into slavery. Some recorded seeing Armenian children beheaded. One incident detailed how 5,000 Armenian captives had been forced to gather dry grass from a field, were tied together, and then burned to death using the collected grass as fuel for the fire. At another site, a mass grave had been discovered that revealed several thousand people had been tied together and drowned in a river. Some of the prisoners in the camps slowly starved, while others were burned alive.

The Turks—along with the Kurds hired as gendarmes—marched Armenians from their traditional homeland in eastern Turkey, south to the Syrian border. They were placed in camps where their only shelter were caves that were not much more than holes in the ground, pocking the floor of the wilderness. Some survived only through cannibalism.

A number of eyewitness reports were from Christian missionaries who came from eastern Europe to minister in the area. The few pictures and films of the genocide were smuggled out by German missionaries who risked their lives to do so since photographing the columns of Armenians being marched south was punishable by death.

The variety and cruelty of tortures evoked Nazi Germany, and according to one scholar, Hitler himself counted on the ignorance of the Armenian Genocide as he planned the extermination of the Jews. The more Graham learned, the more ashamed he was of his ignorance.

Some of the eyewitnesses were dignitaries, and one of the names on the list stood out to Graham: Gertrude Bell. Bell was an explorer, Arabist, archaeologist, and British intelligence officer who helped form modern Iraq after World War I. But her name meant something to Graham because Bell was the founder of the Iraq Museum. The museum had been infamously looted during the US-Iraq War in 2003, and a few of the priceless artifacts that had gone missing had been accidentally discovered by Graham during his trip into Saudi Arabia to rescue Alexander. The eyewitness archive contained quotes from Bell's intelligence reports about the genocide, and Graham felt a kind of camaraderie with her as he read her words.

> *Some 12,000 Armenians were concentrated under the guardianship of some hundred Kurds at Ras al-Ain.... These Kurds were called* gendarmes, *but in reality mere butchers; bands of them were publicly ordered to take parties of Armenians, of both sexes, to various destinations, but had secret instructions to destroy the males, children and old women....One of these gendarmes confessed to killing 100 Armenian men himself...the empty desert cisterns and caves were also filled with corpses....No man can ever think of a woman's body except as a matter of horror, instead of attraction, after Ras al-Ain.*

In another report she wrote:

> *But in the Armenian villages panic was scarcely laid to rest. Tales of Adana were in every mouth....And as I journeyed farther west I came into the skirts of destruction and saw charred heaps of mud and stone which had been busy centres of agricultural life. The population, destitute and homeless, had defended itself and come off with naked existence.*

According to Bell, previous massacres were, "not comparable to the massacres carried out in 1915 and the succeeding years." Graham checked the date and learned that Bell wrote the entry in the early 1920s, two decades before the Holocaust.

Reading about the genocide made him feel dirty, turning his thoughts black. *If any people deserved judgment like the people of Noah's time, it was the Turks at the end of the Ottoman Empire.* All Armenians alive now were descended from a tiny remnant of survivors, just like the eight people on Noah's Ark had repopulated the earth. Father Vardanyan had told him how important the ark was to the identity of the Armenian people, and Graham thought he was beginning to see one of the psychological facets in the association.

He felt his silenced phone vibrate once, the alert that he had received a text. Graham saw it was from Alexander and opened it, thankful for the distraction.

Hey Dr E, figure out what the message meant?

Graham felt self-conscious about texting in the library and held the phone in his lap, below the desk, as he replied.

Not yet. Haven't given it a lot of thought. He hit *send*, then wrote again.

What do you know about the Armenian Genocide? You should look into it. And look up Gertrude Bell while you're at it. Very interesting.

Graham put the phone down and turned back to Bell's reports. As if following his own advice, Graham scanned the biographical sketch the museum included about Bell. He already knew most of the information, but his eyes caught on the details of her death in 1926. Two days before her fifty-seventh birthday, she committed suicide by taking an overdose of barbiturates she used as a sedative.

The information pushed him back in his chair. It was a few seconds before he recovered enough to slump forward, rest his elbows on the table, and bury his face in his hands. Breath escaped from him in loud gusts, as if a hole had been torn open in a storm. Bell's death had done just that—reopen the wound of his wife's death three years earlier. She, too, had succumbed to a sedative.

In Olivia's case, it was the weight that pulled her below the water of the bathtub, causing her to drown. But Graham had a menacing suspicion he refused to entertain—that she welcomed her death, and possibly even intended it. He felt a heaviness blanket him, his own weight descending on him, pulling him into depression. Suddenly he wanted nothing more in the world than sleep.

When the door to the hotel room closed behind him, he realized he couldn't remember walking back. He tried to distract himself by packing only what he would need for the trip, then collapsed on the bed in a fog.

The pain of Olivia's untimely death conflated with Bell's suicide in his thoughts. As often happened, he became aware of music playing in his head. A song by Chris Bell. Graham thought it must be some subconscious free association, not only in the last name, but also because Chris Bell struggled with substance abuse, before meeting an untimely death in a single-car crash.

Despite being an obscure figure now, Gertrude Bell had been famous in her day. The opposite was true of Chris Bell. Although he died an unknown, the music he made in the early 70s heavily influenced many of the most important bands of the 80s.

Graham listened to the words of one of his last songs, "I Am the Cosmos," written after becoming a Christian. The haunting, yearning melody sung with a ragged, weary voice declared he never wants to be alone. Graham made the words his own as he thought of Olivia.

TWENTY-FOUR

*T*HE SOUND OF UNRELENTING RAIN, HARD AND URGENT, PELTED IN A DRUM*roll of anticipation, telegraphing the fury of the storm. Damp air soaked the smell of freshly cut wood, its normally comforting aroma spoiled, now the stench of judgment. The dark space reduced everything it contained to vague shadows. Clouds—black and bloated—absorbed the sun like sponges wringing water from the light, leaving little illumination to leak through the air holes in the wall. Graham heard his name being called by someone outside the opening. A female voice. Olivia's voice.*

He scrambled to look out the slit in the wall and saw her. She was dressed in the same clothes he had seen in a photo of Gertrude Bell, with a plain ankle-length skirt, buttoned-up coat, practical leather shoes, and a wide-brimmed hat wrapped with a scarf. She stood on the last remaining spot of land in the midst of turbulent water.

One hand reached toward him as she cried his name again. Then he realized where he was: inside the ark, separated from her. Except that the water outside the boat wasn't rising. The water was rising inside *the boat. If he didn't escape, he would drown in the ark. Terror overtook him, and he pounded on the wall. He hesitated a moment, then pounded again. And suddenly the ark was gone, replaced by his hotel room.*

The sound of pounding on the door confused him at first, as if it were a remnant from his dream. He looked at his phone and saw it was 2:15 a.m. Graham had overslept.

He forced himself out of bed and opened the door to find the alert, serious face of Khazhak.

"I'm so sorry. I must've slept through my alarm. I'm so embarrassed. I promise you, that never happens to me."

"It is not a problem. We have not lost much time. But we must move quickly now."

Graham could tell Khazhak was trying to hide his annoyance and decided the best way to atone for his mistake was to collect his things as quickly as possible. Less than ten minutes later, they were out the door.

TWENTY-FIVE

The road-worn van waiting outside the lobby looked like an artless knock-off of an old Volkswagen Microbus. Graham guessed from the utilitarian design and age that it was a relic of the Soviet era. As he walked around the front of the van to the passenger side, he noticed the logo of the manufacturer—ErAZ—was a stylized depiction of Ararat, with its two peaks rising from a plane. The day before, he had been surprised to see Mount Massis on one of the banknotes he received as change, given that it wasn't within the borders of the country. The van's logo was more proof of Father Vardanyan's assertion of how ingrained the mountain was in Armenian identity.

As he slid onto the bench and stowed his backpack, the driver—an older man with short gray hair and an untamed beard—craned around to Graham.

"This is Jirair." Khazhak made an introduction as he climbed into the front passenger seat.

Jirair gave a melancholy smile as Graham shook his hand.

"Jirair has lived his whole life in Vagharshapat. He knows all the roads around here." Khazhak turned to make eye contact with Graham, as if to underline his words. "Many of his relatives died in the genocide. You can trust him to help us."

They headed south through the town, and within five minutes had entered the countryside, though it was too dark to see much of it.

"Thank you for outfitting us." Graham made an effort to build rapport with Khazhak given that he was still mostly a stranger to him. "I was supposed to get my gear in Doğubayazıt. That's where the guide I was supposed to meet is based."

"The route up that side of the mountain is easier," Khazhak said, "but it is longer and less direct. You would have had to go up the southwest side, then cross the plateau near the peak all the way to the north face in order to reach where we are going."

Graham envisioned the route he had planned to take and compared it to Khazhak's description as he spoke. The two seemed to match up with one exception: the location of the ark. Ross's site was on the southeast corner of the plateau. Graham wasn't sure if the discrepancy was his misunderstanding or nothing more than the imprecision of casual conversation.

"How many times have you gone up the mountain?"

"Never," Khazhak said. "I have had no reason to."

The admission made Graham a contradiction: body frozen, mind rattled. He worked to sound more cautious than alarmed. "How do you know where we need to go?"

"There is a village on the mountain near the Ahora Gorge that is said to be where Noah made his home after leaving the ark. The people there believe he planted the vineyard that is there to this day. There are many goat paths there. One leads to the place they say the ark can sometimes be seen. We can hire guides in the village to show us the way and help carry our gear."

The existence of ancient tradition counterbalanced Graham's misgivings in an uneasy equilibrium. "Why haven't you ever climbed the mountain before?"

"Because I do not need to see the ark. It is enough to know that it is there," Khazhak said matter-of-factly. "Too many people have seen it. The tradition is too old for there to be any deception about it."

"What do you think when people say they saw the ark on different parts of the mountain from where we're going, on the other side?"

Khazhak shrugged. "They are mistaken. But that is to be expected. People know this is the mountain and so they look for the ark in the shapes they see. Like children finding shapes in the clouds. I am sure sometimes people have thought they have seen it when they have not."

Graham nodded, asking the obvious question to himself: Given that the people of the village claimed to know where it was, why hadn't other ark explorers confirmed it easily? What made the sightings at this place different? Or was it nothing more than their preferred cloud to find the shape in?

Although the Aras River lay less than ten miles outside of Vagharshapat, Jirair drove southeast, paralleling the serpentine river as it curved around Ararat, the boundary between Armenia and Turkey. Khazhak explained that the closest crossing point in the river would put them too close to Iğdir. He wanted to avoid both military and PKK patrols, and chose the next easiest crossing, near Khor Virap.

Thirty minutes after leaving the hotel, they changed highways, facing them toward the mountain. Jirair took them through a village, then navigated a series of switchback turns on the other side of the last row of houses.

"That is Khor Virap," Khazhak said, pointing at the shape of a church on a small hill silhouetted by night.

Graham could see enough of the building to think it looked like it belonged on the set of a Star Wars movie, on Tatooine somewhere. Jabba the Hut's palace, maybe. He had seen a picture of Saint Gregory the Illuminator's pit as they drove past it, a prison cell like a subterranean silo.

Jirair picked his way onto a dirt road, then to a path running along the bank of the Aras. After half a mile, he parked, but left the engine and running lights on.

Graham unloaded his gear and carried it around to the back of the van and found Jirair unfolding an inflatable raft. Khazhak plugged an air compressor into the cigarette lighter and flipped the switch, hissing the raft into shape. Jirair fit the removable seats and floor panels in place as Graham helped Khazhak unload the rest of the gear.

"How far down the river do we have to go?" Graham asked, setting a backpack down.

Khazhak pointed to the nearest part of the far shore. "We are going across it, not down it."

Graham guessed only about 150 feet separated them from the other side.

"It is not very deep," Khazhak said, "but it would be up to our necks. Too deep to cross easily with our gear. I have brought hiking shoes for you. I borrowed several pairs because I did not know your size. Pick some out and put them on."

Graham was thankful to find a pair that fit and put them on as Jirair tied a rope to the bumper of the van, then threw the slack into the raft. They slid the boat across the pebbled shore and into the water. He followed Khazhak's lead and took an oar as he got in the boat. Jirair pushed them off, then climbed into the rear, steering the raft perpendicular to the current as the other two paddled. When they were close enough, Khazhak leaned over the bow and grabbed a bush on the far bank, then hopped out and pulled the boat to the shore. Jirair tossed him the rope, and Khazhak tied it to a large bush.

"What's the rope for?" Graham asked.

"Jirair can't paddle back on his own. This way he can pull himself across."

"You might let him know his raft has a leak," Graham said. "It's lost air crossing to the other side."

"The raft always gets softer in the cold water," Khazhak said. "He'll be fine."

After they unloaded, Jirair left Khazhak with a hug and Graham with a handshake. They waited until Jirair made it back to the other side and untied the rope.

Graham followed Khazhak into the scrub, away from the river. Within a thousand feet, they reached a road that ran along the river and followed it north to a road leading away from the river, toward Ararat.

They remained silent as they passed through a tiny village cloaked in a thick rural darkness illuminated by moonlight in a clear sky. Even after the village was a safe distance behind them, they broke the silence with voices just above whispers.

"How far are we going tonight?"

"Aralik is about five kilometers away. It is mainly Kurdish, but I minister there. There is a hotel on the west side of the town. We can reach it by dawn. In the morning, you will stay there while I ask about a guide for us. We also need a few more supplies. We will start up the mountain tomorrow."

TWENTY-SIX

Graham awoke in the same position in which he had fallen asleep, disoriented by the foreign room he only vaguely remembered entering hours earlier. The cramped space looked smaller than when he had entered, as if shrunken by light. He blindly felt for his phone, squinting back the morning, and reopened his eyes to learn it was almost noon. He pushed himself up in thick movements, scratching against coarse blankets to sit up in the single bed. The linoleum floor and bare walls made the room feel cold despite the mild temperature.

He stared at his feet, marshaling himself to stand, and spotted a piece of paper slipped under the door. A groan of effort escaped as he bent to pick it up.

> *I am in the town collecting the rest of our supplies. Stay in the room to avoid any curiosity about you. Military patrols may be nearby. I will meet you back here as soon as I can. Khazhak.*

At the thought of staying in the cell all day, Graham opened the window shade, hoping to make the room feel less confining. Mount Ararat dominated the landscape, a thorn embedded in the sky. He had been to the top of 14,000-foot peaks in Colorado, but Ararat looked twice as big as anything he'd seen in the Rocky Mountains. The plain around the mountain isolated it, emphasizing its scale. But the plain was also not very high above sea level, which meant the mountain was not only taller than anything in the Rockies but rose from lower ground. Two-and-a-half miles from the plain, over three miles from sea level.

On their walk from the river the night before, Khazhak had said they were going to trace the route not only of Saint Jacob, but also the first man in modern times to reach the top of the mountain; an Estonian professor named Parrot. Graham remembered the name from his research but hadn't investigated further since he had been interested only in the most recent and most ancient accounts of the ark. He had made a mental note to look into the expedition if he had time, and now he had all afternoon.

He opened his laptop and looked through the documents he had saved to his hard drive before leaving Münster. As usual, he erred on the side of being over-prepared for bad internet and had copied anything that might help his understanding of the site. This included many of the travelogues and accounts from the 1800s for background information. He found Parrot's memoir of his 1829 expedition among them.

A PDF of *Journey to Ararat* seemed like a logical place to start, and he scanned the pages for passages that would have the most bearing on his own journey. Parrot's pilgrimage was notable not only for being the first in the scientific age of exploration, but it was the only one undertaken before an earthquake destroyed the small monastery of Saint Jacob and the nearby village of Ahora. Fortunately, Parrot had preserved the landmarks in sketches made with considerable skill.

According to Parrot, Saint Jacob's Monastery—which he called Saint James—sat at the entrance to a chasm, on the edge of a ravine with a stream. The monastery was on a slope, just north of the village. Parrot described it as, "built in the form of a cross, with a cupola like a truncated cone in the middle, and entirely constructed, even to the very roof, with hewn stone of hard lava." The facing page contained Parrot's detailed drawing of the monastery with the gorge behind it and the peak looming over it. Parrot described the village of Ahora—which he called Arghuri—as being comprised of 175 families, mostly Armenian. The villagers bred horses and cattle, and the wealthier people kept vineyards. Parrot claimed it also had a biblical significance, and Graham copied the passage into his notes.

> *In a religious point of view, Arghuri has an especial claim on the veneration of every devout Armenian. This is the place, according to tradition, where Noah, after he came out of the ark, and went down from the mountain with his sons and all the living things that were with him, had "built an altar unto the LORD, and took of every clean beast, and of every clean fowl, and offered burnt-offerings upon the altar"(Genesis 8:20). The exact spot is alleged to be where the church now stands; and it is of the vineyards of Arghuri that the Scriptures speak (Genesis 9:20) when it is said, "And Noah began to be an husbandman, and he planted a vineyard."*

Parrot also recorded that all the Armenians in the region, "are all firmly persuaded that the ark remains to this day on the top of Mount Ararat, and that in order to ensure its preservation, no human being is allowed to approach it." Graham wasn't quite sure how to take the information, given that Parrot himself had tried to approach it. Three times, in fact. He made his base camp at the monastery, and it took three attempts before he found his way to the peak. But Parrot never saw the ark. Eleven years later, an earthquake sent the landslide that buried the monastery and the village, erasing them—at least for a time—from the map.

Graham looked for the next oldest document in his files, a report written five years after the earthquake by German geologist Hermann Abich. He visited the site on a scientific expedition with more interest in the catastrophe than the ark. His study of the mountain was memorialized by the two glaciers that bore his name: Abich I and Abich II. Graham changed his PDF reader to show two pages of Abich's book at once. The left page reprinted Parrot's drawing, while the right was a drawing made by Abich from the same vantage point as Parrot's. The difference in the images showed a dramatic alteration in the face of the mountain.

Graham opened a travelogue called *Transcaucasia and Ararat* by an

Oxford law professor named James Bryce. In 1876, Bryce followed Parrot's route and described the destruction he found.

> *Towards sunset in the evening of the 20th of June 1840, the sudden shock of an earthquake, accompanied by a subterranean roar, and followed by a terrific blast of wind, threw down the houses of Arghuri, and at the same moment detached enormous masses of rock with their superjacent ice from the cliffs that surround the chasm. A shower of falling rocks overwhelmed in an instant the village, the monastery, and a Kurdish encampment on the pastures above. Not a soul survived to tell the tale. Four days afterwards, the masses of snow and ice that had been precipitated into the glen suddenly melted, and, forming an irresistible torrent of water and mud, swept along the channel of the stream and down the outer slopes of the mountain, far away into the Aras Plain, bearing with them huge rocks, and covering the ground for miles with a deep bed of mud and gravel.*

Graham wondered if anyone had tried to photograph the gorge from the same spot where Parrot and Abich had made their drawings. He skimmed the images and discovered an example of exactly what he was looking for. He opened it in a window next to the others and compared them.

A black gouge pitted the mountain in shadow, like a cavity in a colossal tooth, but made from violence rather than decay. The amount missing from the slope was enough to make a small mountain by itself. The contrast reminded Graham of the 1980 eruption of Mount Saint Helens in Washington. Amazingly, the village had been rebuilt and was now called Yenidoğan—the Turkish word for *newborn*.

As far as he could tell, no attempt had ever been made to excavate the monastery. Several people on more recent expeditions had visited the location, but there wasn't much to see other than remnants of an ancient foundation. And one ark hunter—Astronaut Jim Irwin—had to abandon his visit to the site in the mid-80s because of persistent landslides when he was on the mountain.

Graham found he had also included a chronological list of expeditions. He had copied it to his files without opening it, assuming it enumerated only the more recent sightings, but now saw it started with Parrot. The document was a spreadsheet that included columns for the dates, names of the explorers, purposes of the ascents, and what—if anything—was found. He was surprised to learn that many of the entries from the 1800s had scientific aims unconcerned with the ark.

According to the spreadsheet, Bryce was the first explorer to discover wood without finding the ark intact. And he had made the discovery high above the tree line. Graham switched back to Bryce's account.

> *Mounting steadily along the same ridge, I saw at a height of over 13,000 feet, lying on the loose blocks, a piece of wood about four feet long and five inches thick, evidently cut by some tool, and so far above the limit of trees that it could by no possibility be a natural fragment of one.... Whether it was really gopher wood, of which material the ark was built, I will not undertake to say, but am willing to submit to the inspection of the curious the bit which I cut off with my ice-axe and brought away. Anyhow, it will be hard to prove that it is not gopher wood. And if there be any remains of the ark on Ararat at all—a point as to which the natives are perfectly clear—here rather than the top is the place where one might expect to find them, since in the course of ages they would get carried down by the onward movement of the snow-beds along the declivities. This wood, therefore, suits all the requirements of the case. I am, however, bound to admit that another explanation of the presence of this piece of timber on the rocks at this vast height did occur to me. But as no man is bound to discredit*

> *his own relic…I will not disturb my readers' minds, or yield to the rationalizing tendencies of the age by suggesting it.*

The spreadsheet named three explorers who ascended Ararat prior to Bryce who had carried wooden crosses up the mountain and planted them near the peak. Graham was surprised that an Oxford law professor rejected the obvious explanation for the wood—that what he had found was part of a cross left by one of the previous ascents.

Graham's phone burst to life like a timer going off, making him jump. He stared at it, so deep in thought that he didn't recognize his own phone as it charged in Vogel's satellite case.

TWENTY-SEVEN

"ALEXANDER THE GREAT," GRAHAM SAID, USING THE STAGE NAME HIS former grad student had performed under as a child magician.

"*The Brown Dirt Cowboy*," Alexander replied in a movie-trailer announcer voice.

"Doesn't sound quite right, does it," Graham said, moving to the window to stare at Ararat, dividing his attention. "Maybe I'm somewhere in between Captain Fantastic and the Brown Dirt Cowboy."

"That would put you in the *Garden of Earthly Delights*."

Graham tried to catch Alexander's reference, but the pause grew too long and became a confession that he missed it.

"You know, that painting by Hieronymus Bosch? That's what the cover of the record was inspired by."

Graham pictured the sixteenth-century triptych and compared it to his memory of Elton John's album art. "That's funny. Somehow, I never made the connection. It's obvious now that you said it. And you know what's even more funny is that I'm where the left panel of the painting takes place—in the Garden of Eden."

"The Garden of Eden?" Alexander sounded unsure if this was a continuation of the joke. "I thought you were looking for Mount Ararat."

"I am," Graham said. "But Ararat is fairly close to the headwaters of the Euphrates, and not too far from the Tigris. Where they start is where Eden is located in Genesis."

"Who would have thought the Garden of Eden would be in such a rough neighborhood?"

"What do you mean?" Graham asked.

"Not only is it the first murder scene, but I looked into the Armenian Genocide. I am completely shocked. Why doesn't everyone know about this? Like the Holocaust?"

"I have no idea," Graham said on a sigh. "Did you look into Gertrude Bell while you were at it?"

"Not yet. I got distracted reading the reports of people who claimed to see Noah's Ark on the mountain. Pretty crazy stuff."

"Agreed. I was just reading about some of the early expeditions. What'd you find?"

"Know about Haji Yearam?"

Graham skimmed the spreadsheet and found the row with his name on it. "He was the first person to claim to actually go up to the ark. In 1856."

"That's all you got? Check this out," Alexander said, brimming with one-upmanship. "Haji Yearam was a kid at that time. The story goes that three English scientists who were skeptics of the Bible traveled all the way to Ararat because they were upset that there may be evidence that the story of Noah could be true. Yearam's dad said he knew where the ark was, and little Haji tagged along as his dad guided the men up the mountain. Haji said the ark had several floors and that he saw a number of animal cages with bars.

"The scientists got so upset that they tried to destroy the ark by smashing it, but the wood was too hard. Then they tried to burn it, but it wouldn't catch fire. In the end the best they could do was threaten the lives of Haji and his dad if they ever told anyone else about the ark. Haji didn't tell anyone about what he'd seen until 1918. That's when he saw the obituary of one of the English scientists in the paper. He told the story to one of his caregivers. By then, he was in his late 70s and dying, so I guess he figured the threat had lost its force."

"You win," Graham said. "That's pretty strange."

"Wait. It gets stranger. The caregiver didn't tell anyone the story until the 1950s—thirty years after Haji died. Ark investigators—some of them call themselves *arkeaologists*, get it?— have never been able to find an obituary that matched Haji's story. But that doesn't stop the ark hunters from adding him to the witness list."

Graham snickered. "Isn't it obvious that there's a problem with the timeline? If Haji was a boy when they climbed the mountain, that would make the English scientists at least twenty years older. The obituary would have been of a 100-year-old man. It shouldn't be that hard to find an obituary for someone like that if the story were true."

"I know, right?" Alexander said. "So instead of a witness, it's just a sixty-five-year-old secret told to someone who kept the secret for thirty more years before anyone could look into it."

"Doesn't sound like an eyewitness account at all," Graham said. "More like an urban legend. Except there's nothing urban about eastern Turkey."

Alexander laughed. "All right, all right. Here's another good one. This one's from the 1970s. A television engineer from Saint Louis, Missouri, named Arthur Chuchian. His family immigrated from Armenia. His dad said there's a goat trail that goes up the north side of the mountain. He gave a really detailed picture of how the ark is sitting on a cliff on the right side of a canyon, and how it sticks out of the ice for like forty or fifty feet. He said the cliff has a little pool of water made from the melting ice, and that part of the ark was in it, that the water drains off the edge in a waterfall. He also said that part of the top and one of the sides of the ark are open or have holes."

"Okay, aside from not being an actual eyewitness, what's the problem?"

"I've read several interviews that he did," Alexander said. "A couple in the 80s, one in the 90s. And he sounds like he's sharing his own memory more than his dad's. And sometimes the details are different."

"But don't you think that might happen since he's remembering someone else's memory decades later?"

"Maybe. But sometimes the details seem to be borrowed from a legend about a monk who went up the mountain to find the ark."

"Saint Jacob," Graham interjected.

"Right. Pretty good for an old guy, Dr. E."

"Yeah, well at least I had—"

"All the best music, I know," Alexander cut in, finishing one of Graham's favorite comebacks for him. "Speaking of old guys, do you know about Jim Irwin, the astronaut?"

Graham recalled Ross's mention of Irwin in his paper. "Yeah, he walked on the moon. He went up Ararat quite a few times. Almost died once when he was knocked out by a falling rock. Slid into a canyon and had to spend the night with just a sleeping bag. When he was found the next day, they had to carry him down the mountain."

"I was just reading about that," Alexander said. "One of the times Irwin was on the mountain he tried to follow this guy Chuchian's directions. Turns out, there really *is* a goat path. Unfortunately, it leads to a dead end. It was on the part of the mountain he indicated, but the landmarks he gave—like where the cities were in relation to the peak once you were at the spot—were way off."

"Again, understandable if he'd never been there," Graham said.

"Maybe. But here's where this one gets weird. It turns out this guy was into pyramid power and remote viewing—you know, like ESP. And he believed there was a civilization of people who lived below the surface of the earth."

"Ha!" Graham laughed, as if the credibility of the story had audibly burst. "How ironic: a television engineer who did remote viewing."

"Hadn't thought of that."

"And I guess he never heard of the Demarcation Problem or Popper's criteria of falsifiability."

Alexander chuckled. "Careful. If he really does remote viewing, then he could be listening in. So, speaking of the Demarcation Problem, have you come across the Ron Wyatt quote about why he thought Durupinar was the ark even though it's been proven that the shape is a geological formation?"

"I can't wait."

"He said it to one of the ark hunters. He said—and I quote—'God told me this was Noah's Ark. I don't need university PhDs to tell me otherwise.'"

Graham cleared his throat theatrically. "That's the justification by the man whose work you followed into Saudi Arabia."

"Yeah, but he got that one right. That has to be Sinai."

"And I would've never believed it if I hadn't had to go there and save your life."

Alexander broke into pitchy falsetto. "*Someone saved my life tonight...*"

"Your Elton John is just not getting any better."

"So here's the next guy, and from what I can tell, he thought he *was* Captain Fantastic. A guy named John Joseph Nouri. Most of the time he was called Prince Nouri because he claimed to be the Episcopal head of the Nestorian Church of Malabar South India, and the Grand Archdeacon of Babylon."

"Try to fit that on a business card."

Alexander allowed the quip to pass without comment. "Nouri claimed to have climbed Ararat three times, and that he had found Noah's Ark sticking out from the snow and ice. He said he was able to get inside, and the measurements matched the Bible's description exactly.

"He traveled all over Europe and America trying to raise funds to excavate it so it could be exhibited at the Chicago World's Fair in 1893. I'm not sure how he was going to get the thing down the mountain, but the point is moot because he wasn't able to raise the money. He was, however, invited to speak at the World Parliament of Religions in Chicago and gave several lectures on his discovery. One interesting detail he gave was that the ark had long nails."

"Hmm," Graham noised. "Nails, huh? The other witnesses said they saw wooden dowels. And how did he measure the ark if it was sticking out of the ice? I assume if he got inside the ark, it had a hole in it. But to be able to measure the inside would mean no snow and ice had accumulated inside of it. Doesn't sound quite right, does it?"

"Exactly," Alexander said. "But that may be because he had a few issues with the truth. There is some question about whether he actually held the offices he said he did. As he traveled around the world, he told people that he was on his way to his ordination. But he told that story for over ten years! Wait, it gets better. Nouri spent part of that time in an insane asylum in Napa, California. He said he had been robbed of all his jewels and that the thieves had him committed. He wrote to some of his wealthier contacts—people who had become his patrons after hearing his stories—and one of them bought his freedom."

Graham chuckled. "Sounds like one of those Nigerian email scams asking people to send money."

"For real," Alexander said. "Okay, this next one is one of the more famous sightings, so stop me if you've heard it. This one says the ark was discovered by a Russian test pilot in 1916. As he flew past Ararat, he saw the ship submerged in a half-frozen lake on the mountain. The report reached Czar Nicholas II, who sent two teams of engineers to investigate. The Russian Army found it, measured it, and documented it with photographs and film. But they sent their findings back to Saint Petersburg just as the czar was overthrown in the February Revolution of 1917, and all the documents were lost."

"That *is* a good one." Graham was genuinely impressed by the story, despite not believing it. "Like an *X-Files* episode."

"Turns out the story wasn't published until the 1940s in a little magazine. When the author was questioned about it, he admitted he made up *almost* the whole thing."

"Almost?" Graham asked.

"Apparently, relatives of the Russian pilot said he really had seen *something* under the surface of a lake on the mountain, but soldiers couldn't reach it."

"So the journalist filled in little, unimportant details about it being Noah's Ark. Makes perfect sense. Just imagine what the internet would've done with that."

"No doubt." Alexander gave a weary sigh. "Okay, last one. There was a guy who claimed he worked at the Smithsonian in 1968 in the vertebrate paleontology section under someone named Dr. Robert Geist. They received a bunch of crates from an expedition to Ararat. One of the boxes had human remains, but most of them had fragments of blackened wood. The guy said the wood was from Noah's Ark. There were also photographs taken from a balloon that showed an oblong boat-shape underneath the ice. When the guy asked Dr. Geist about it, he was told to keep quiet because they didn't want religious fanatics to find out about it and cause trouble. The ark researcher looking into this guy's story says he found evidence of possible CIA involvement, but he doesn't say what it was."

"Of course not," Graham said in mock sincerity.

"Here's the kicker: No one named Robert Geist ever worked at the Smithsonian. And when the guy who told the story was given a polygraph, he failed every question."

"Shocker," Graham deadpanned. "Well, story time is over, and the big boys have to go back to work."

Alexander laughed. "Come on, you have to admit this stuff is entertaining at least."

"I can think of better things to do than sifting through the garbage of modern myth."

"You may not like my little gift then," Alexander said. "I just sent a link to a bunch of supposed images of the ark taken on the mountain. Enjoy!"

TWENTY-EIGHT

Graham opened the email he had received during the call. Several PDFs documenting the stories Alexander had summarized were attached. He added the files to the others, then clicked on the link. A new browser window automatically opened to a Google photo album with several dozen images arranged in a grid. The folder included a spreadsheet containing a thumbnail of each image, a description, and the name of the photographer, arranged chronologically by year. Almost half the entries had no thumbnail, indicating missing photographs, or claims of photographs that had been supposedly lost.

Most of the absent images were near the top of the list. The 1916 Russian expedition proved to be the oldest, and for a moment Graham pictured himself discovering a stack of black-and-white prints in a forgotten box in the corner of a basement in some government building in Saint Petersburg.

The second entry was from 1943 and credited aerial pictures of the ark to an army photographer who was flown near the ark after it was spotted by pilots. One of the pictures was featured on the front page of the Mediterranean edition of *Stars and Stripes,* the newspaper for US servicemen. Although many witnesses remembered seeing the issue, the issue itself had never been found, and the photograph disappeared.

Another empty image was dated 1946. Two servicemen showed pictures of the ark at a party in Birmingham, Alabama, taken while they had been stationed in eastern Turkey. When ark researchers looked into the claim, the men were reassigned to Burma and disappeared.

Other entries recorded that photos taken by servicemen from Russia and Australia during World War II were lost. In 1952, an American oil engineer claimed to have taken a whole roll of film of the ark from a helicopter while surveying the mountain. The pilot had been able to get close enough for the man to take images showing details of the planking. More than thirty people claimed to see the pictures over the next ten years before the man was murdered and the photos disappeared. At least half a dozen similar stories of lost pictures filled the rows of the list.

Graham moved the spreadsheet to a new window and started looking at the images that weren't missing, referring back to the comments Alexander had provided. The majority of them showed some kind of dark, barge-like shape emerging from snow and ice. Some pictures only showed a bump in the snow. Very few showed a long rectangular shape completely exposed. But although the uniformity of the shape in the images seemed to corroborate each other, the locations were contradictory. Sometimes the alleged ark was high on the mountain. Some pictures showed it in a valley. And still others pictured it on the side of a precipice, perched on a ledge.

The oldest extant photograph was taken in 1949 by a U2 spy plane but had not released to the public until 1995. The image showed an enormous rectangular block embedded in the snow just below the peak, on the edge of a cliff. Graham thought it looked like a natural rock formation and would have never thought it was the ark had he been the pilot.

His eyes settled on an image of a dramatic canyon blackened by shadow and torn from jagged bluffs, as if the ark sat in the jaws of the mountain. Except that he didn't see the ark at first. He had to look at the next image—a detail of the photograph—to see it.

Although it was fuzzy from being zoomed in, it showed the ark nestled into the narrow groove of the gorge floor, protruding from around the corner of a rock wall. There were no stairs built onto the side, and he couldn't see any holes or damage, nor was it broken apart. But the general description was consistent with almost all the sightings, including the raised catwalk running down the center of the top deck.

Graham felt a crack in his skepticism until he read Alexander's note. "Taken in 1966. Interestingly, the photographer didn't see the ark shape until a couple of years later. Ark hunters were able to make it to the site in the 80s, but discovered it was a block of basalt." Graham looked at the picture again, amazed at how man-made the shape appeared.

The next image showed a similarly shaped object sticking out of the side of a cliff, sitting on a ledge just below the peak of the mountain. It took him a moment to make it out, but once he saw the ark, he thought it looked like it had impaled the mountain. The position on the ledge matched the descriptions of Ed Davis and George Hagopian. Graham opened Google Earth and navigated to the locator pins he had placed to mark their sightings.

He adjusted the view until it roughly matched the picture, then noted it was on the upper right part of the Ahora Gorge, on the Parrot Glacier. He also noted it was near the site of Navarra's first discovery of wood. Despite the ballpark match of the image to the Google Earth pins, Graham thought the image he was trying to match wasn't very compelling in the first place.

The next image made his breath catch again. This time the image featured a strikingly perfect rectangular object with what was apparently a catwalk that left openings—like ventilation holes—along the short walls that supported it. Again, the object was almost identical to the descriptions of Davis and Hagopian and looked like a photograph of what Elfred Lee had drawn. According to Alexander's note, the picture was taken in 1986 from the top of the Ahora Gorge. A year later, other ark hunters went to the site based on the photo and found nothing. Graham wasn't sure what to do with that information, whether it disconfirmed the image or left it unknown.

The most recent item in the grid was a video clip showing several beams jutting from a cliff of ice. The camera was zoomed in to the point that every slight movement was exaggerated and shook the view violently. Graham conceded to himself that it was interesting, but without recovery and analysis, nothing could really be said about it as evidence either way. It might be part of one of the crosses carried up by early explorers. Or it could be a remnant of planted wood from a fraud that wasn't recovered for some reason. Graham wondered if it could be the ruins of a shelter, which made the most sense to him. But there were too many unknowns to give any of the explanations weight.

He scrolled through dozens of pictures, and although a couple of them gave him pause, the great majority were unconvincing at best.

Below the images, Alexander had included a subfolder named *Basalt*. Graham opened the directory and discovered half a dozen pictures of large rectangular blocks of basalt that looked too regular to be natural, as if cast in a mold. And yet—according to Alexander's notes—all of them were shaped by nature, not human hands.

Graham looked away from the screen and thought about everything he had learned in the last few days—Ross's report, ancient histories, early expeditions, local traditions, the stories Alexander had shared, and the photographs he'd just weeded through.

Eyewitnesses not only couldn't agree on a location but described it with different details. And wood had been found—assuming it wasn't planted—at several different sites on the mountain. It was a flood of information, and right now the ark that would save him was his skepticism. The one thing that seemed clear to Graham was that nothing was clear. The whole thing was like a Rorschach Test—people saw what they wanted, or at least saw what was there in different ways. And what they saw said more about their beliefs than what they were looking at.

Believers in the ark on Ararat said the 1840 catastrophe demonstrated that the changing face of the mountain could both reveal and hide the ark if it was still there. That explanation made Graham think that no matter what someone believed about the ark, they could always find an excuse to justify searching for it. Graham could never prove the mountain had nothing to discover, nor did he have any interest in doing so. He believed the biblical account of the flood, but not that there was anything left of the ark to find.

And once again he wondered what he was really doing here. He had undertaken the commission from Vogel out of a sense of obligation he could discharge by doing an interesting errand with the noble goal of exonerating an innocent man. Betrayal and extortion had transformed the trip into a resentful burden. It eroded his trust in his fellow human beings, but even more, it eroded his trust in himself. What did it say about himself that he could be taken in and used like this?

A different flood started to rise within him, one he was too familiar with. It had come as Aly withered away and rose higher when Olivia slipped beneath her own flood. Like the flood of Noah, Graham's had surrounded him for more than a year. But while Noah had floated on the surface, Graham was entombed at the bottom. Now he felt the flood of depression rise again, pulling him deeper as he got closer to the top of the mountain.

TWENTY-NINE

Graham shook himself free of the morass of emotion, walling it up to address the immediate problem. He could understand why people would want to find the ark of Noah, and why amateur archaeologists would be attracted to Ararat. What he couldn't fully get his head around was why a legitimate scholar with an excellent reputation would take any of the sightings seriously or think there might be some remnant to be found.

His instinct was to go to the source and call Isaac Ross, but from what Vogel said, Ross couldn't be trusted. On the other hand, Vogel's actions revealed that *he* couldn't be trusted. As Graham considered who—if anyone—to trust, he found himself scrolling to Ross's contact information on his phone. He decided talking to Ross would give him more data to work with, and he could determine what to trust afterward.

He tapped the number, and as it started to ring, he remembered Ross lived in Virginia, a time-zone eight or nine hours earlier. He was about to hang up when Ross answered, fully awake and energetic.

"Isaac, it's Graham Eliot."

"Graham? What in the world are you doing up at—what time is it in L.A.? Two in the morning?"

"Actually, I'm in Turkey. I thought *I* was the one waking *you* up."

"No kidding? I'm actually in Istanbul. Looking at Hagia Sophia outside my window as we speak. What brings you to this neck of the woods?"

"I have to speak to you about something important."

"Okay, shoot," Ross said, instantly serious.

Graham wasn't sure how to approach the subject, and though he didn't know Ross well, he knew the man to be a straight talker. He decided that speaking frankly would not only appeal to Ross but have the best chance of provoking a genuine reaction.

"I was in Münster a few days ago at Burkhard Vogel's library, photographing manuscripts. He pulled me aside and told me about your expedition."

"Yes, I've presented on it a couple of times at the ANES meetings," Ross said, unfazed.

"I know. But I've only just read the papers. I missed ANES a couple of years."

"Forgive me. It slipped my mind," Ross said compassionately. "I'm so sorry, Graham. How are you doing?"

"I won't lie. It's been hard. It still *is* hard. But I'm doing okay. Thank you for asking."

"I'm glad to hear it. So why was Vogel telling you about the anomaly?" The softer, counseling tone carried over into his question.

The pastoral tone in Ross's voice sent a pang of guilt through Graham that changed the words he was going to say as he said them. "I'm not quite sure how to ask this."

"It's okay," Ross said. "Just say it."

Graham released a heavy sigh. "Please understand, I'm not accusing you of anything. And I'll tell you why I'm asking in a minute. But Vogel told me he was in serious trouble because of how you used the satellite to get your data about the site. He said that you didn't have permission."

"What? That is absolutely false," Ross said indignantly. "*He* was the one who approached *me* and offered the use of the satellite as long as I never revealed my source."

"Really? Didn't that seem strange to you?"

"Yes, that's why I told him no. First of all, every time someone claims to find the ark using a satellite, it turns out it's complete speculation or highly exaggerated. Probably just a rock."

"Like Don Shockey's story?" Graham asked.

"Exactly." Ross sounded impressed at how informed Graham was. "The satellite image Shockey used was taken in the mid-80s. Given the technology at that time, even if the ark had been totally exposed on the top of the mountain, it would have been nothing more than a pinpoint in the picture of the mountain. The resolution back then wasn't good enough to identify anything the size of the ark."

Graham heard his suspicions being confirmed, eroding his trust in Vogel further the more Ross talked.

"I have to say I'm shocked that Vogel told you about the satellite and what I was doing up there. Why didn't you call me sooner?"

"The way Vogel told it, you couldn't be trusted because you had secretly gotten access to the satellite, which he said is illegal. Quite honestly, he made it sound so unethical that I thought I needed to talk to you myself and get a straight answer."

"Then why are you calling me now?" Ross asked, a note of defensiveness sounding for the first time.

"Because I am in Aralik, and I'm about to climb Ararat," Graham said. "Vogel's extorting me and put me in a position where I have no other option. And the way he did it has made me more and more skeptical of his whole story. Everything you have said—even the *way* you've said it—tells me I am right not to trust him."

"That is very disturbing," Ross said, restrained anger still in his voice, but now aimed at Vogel. "I was supposed to make an ascent next week. That's why I'm here. But our climbing permits were revoked because of the terrorist attack. We haven't been allowed on the mountain for two years. And when it finally opened back up, the PKK struck, and the Turks closed it again. We're stuck in Istanbul unless we can clear this up and steer clear of the terrorists. How did you manage it?"

"I had to sneak across the border. Like I said, I have no other choice. I'm calling because I need to know what I will find at the dig site."

Ross answered without any sign he was selecting what to share or was concerned about Graham going there without him. "We had to haul quite a bit of gear up there, leaving anything we could with the expectation that we'd be back the next year. We even built a prefab shed that we could easily carry up the mountain and construct onsite.

It survived for the three seasons we were there. I hope it's still there now. There's a sixteen-man tent stored inside. We needed a place the whole crew could all fit into while we made plans and analyzed the data. But we sleep in the smaller tents that we each used on the way up and back. We left three generators up there, and six or seven Pelican cases of gear and supplies. They have tools, dehydrated food, and fuel. Some first aid as well. Is that what you need to know?"

"Yes, very helpful," Graham said. "It's about what I expected. What about the shaft?"

"It's about a hundred yards east of the shed. We left a domed tent over it to try to keep it from filling with snow. Without it, each day's work would be erased by the snowfall at night. We cut an eight-foot square. Currently, it's a little over thirty-five feet deep. There's an air pump to deal with the exhaust from the chainsaws. When we left at the end of the season, we had started a tunnel at the bottom. The shaft missed the anomaly, and we thought it would be easier to dig across to it than make another thirty-five-foot shaft thirty or forty feet away. So far the tunnel is about fifteen feet long."

"But you haven't actually found anything, right?" Graham asked.

"Right. We are close to whatever the satellite is detecting, but we haven't reached it yet. Actually, we did find one interesting thing. Our geophysicist took a fifty-foot core sample at the site and pulled up some dark granules. We did a quick-fire test on them—you know, put them in some tin and held it over a flame. The granules melted. They were petroleum-based."

"You mean tar or bitumen?" Again, Graham felt a vague challenge to his doubts about the site.

"Yes. It's hard to explain what that kind of organic material is doing that high up the mountain, but we can't draw any conclusions from it. Anyway, please use anything you need when you are there. It is all at your disposal. All I ask is that you let me know what condition the site is in. We're never sure what to expect."

"Absolutely. Thank you for being so gracious, Isaac. And thank you for the backstory on Vogel."

"I'm thankful for the warning," Ross said. "Doesn't sound like either of us should trust him."

"Agreed."

As Graham tapped the button that ended the call, a sharp knock stabbed the room, urgently punctuating the end of the conversation, leaving him no time to think about what he'd learned.

THIRTY

Khazhak pushed into the room and started talking before he had finished closing the door behind him.

"Graham, I am sorry, but I must take you back. It is more dangerous here than I thought it would be."

The optimistic glow from the unexpectedly friendly conversation with Ross instantly dissipated. "I don't understand. Do the Turks have patrols here?"

"The soldiers were here, but they are gone," Khazhak said, fidgeting and anxious. "It is the PKK that we must worry about. It is very tense here. There are many of them in the area. And they have many sympathizers here. If they discover an American in the city, you could become a hostage." He pointed at Graham, underlining the threat. "I need to take you home."

"But…I can't go back." Graham heard himself contradict the conviction he held only twenty-four hours earlier, but instead of sounding principled, he sounded trapped, unable to determine his own fate.

"You must. It is for your own safety."

"No, you don't understand. If I go back now, then I will have nothing to go back to." Graham's resentment grew as he argued Vogel's point. "My reputation—my career—will be ruined. It's hard to explain, but I don't have a choice. I must reach the top of the mountain."

"But you could be killed." Khazhak frowned. "*Both* of us could be killed. And I cannot risk my life for your career when so many people depend on me."

"Then you should stay," Graham said, putting a hand on Khazhak's shoulder. "I understand. I will find someone else to guide me. You have been a great help already. But if I return now, I can be of no use to you when I get home. I have to try to go up."

Khazhak studied Graham silently, trying to weigh what was being hidden from him, and whether it was the secret of a good man or someone he should distance himself from.

Graham had no desire to force Khazhak to help, but he used the pause to improvise a plan, trying to soften it with a logical chain. "If we leave now to go up the mountain, we will be gone before we can be discovered. We're already on the edge of town. We don't even have to go past any buildings to get on the road up the mountain. Yenidoğan is only eleven miles away." Graham gestured out the window at the base of the mountain's slope. "If we can get there, maybe we'll be safe. And after we climb the mountain, we can return home a different way."

"And if you are discovered?"

Khazhak's use of *you* instead of *we* was not lost on Graham, and he shared his options bluntly.

"If I'm found by the Turks, I'll be arrested. If the PKK finds me, I'll be kidnapped. If I go home without the answer I was sent for, then I have no career. And if we go back the way we came, I'll be headed toward all three of those things. I don't have a choice except to climb. Discovery is not an option."

Khazhak continued to stare at Graham, assessing the man as well as the plan. He nodded grudgingly, indicating his conclusion before he spoke. "I pray you are right. Gather your belongings. We must leave quickly."

THIRTY-ONE

Five minutes later, Graham was packed and quietly following Khazhak down the stairs. They passed by the unmanned desk in an alcove that served as the lobby and slipped out the door unseen. Khazhak opened the tailgate of a battered white Toyota Hilux with a hardtop mounted onto the bed of the truck.

Khazhak climbed behind the wheel as Graham slid into the passenger seat and rummaged through his bag. He pulled out a bottle of Tums and popped a couple of tablets into his mouth, chomping them as he turned to Khazhak, wondering why they weren't moving.

"Are you feeling okay?"

"I get altitude sickness." Graham tapped the space between his eyebrows. "Really bad headaches right between the eyes. Someone told me to eat antacid tablets starting a week before going into the mountains. I got these in the airport in Germany."

Khazhak looked confused. "I don't understand how it works."

"Not sure I do either."

"Perhaps your friend was playing a joke on you."

"If he was, then I'm glad he didn't suggest laxative." Graham laughed, glad the tension seemed to be behind them. He poked a thumb over his shoulder at the cargo area. "Where did you get all that gear?"

"There is much goodwill for me here," Khazhak said. "Even from the Kurds. They gave me what we need. The people here do not have much, but they are very generous."

They turned south out of the parking lot, on the edge of the barren plain surrounding the north and east sides of the mountain. Khazhak held a scrap of paper in his right hand as he grasped the steering wheel, positioning it so he could refer to it as he navigated. After using it to take three unmarked turns, he tossed the directions distractedly toward the console to concentrate on the road leading them directly at Ararat. The asphalt was rough with age and wear, but Graham hadn't expected the way to Yenidoğan to be paved at all and was thankful despite the bumpy ride. Khazhak drove cautiously, slowing as the road became steeper.

Seven miles later, a patch of green scrub smeared the brown landscape. Graham could see the ruins of stone houses and wondered if the village was a victim of the catastrophic 1840 earthquake.

On the other side of the village, the engine groaned against the increasing grade of the slope, as if warning them the jagged maw of the Ahora Gorge was preparing to swallow them. A couple of miles later, the road made a hard right turn onto a bridge spanning the dry bed of the stream running down the gorge, ushering them into Yenidoğan.

A knot of irregular dirt roads webbed together rectangular houses built among the ruins of stone buildings. The afternoon had grown long enough to fill the gorge with shadows and spill across the village.

"This used to be an Armenian village." Khazhak's voice sounded loud after what had been a mostly silent ride. "But when people moved back after the earthquake, it became mostly Kurdish. I was given a name of someone to ask for who might help us."

He studied the houses as he spoke, searching—Graham assumed—for a landmark. Recognition lit Khazhak's face, and he pulled up to a small, tin-roofed house.

"It might be best if you stay in the truck until I speak to him."

Before Khazhak could get close enough to knock on the door, it opened, as if he had been expected. The weathered face of a small-framed man appeared in the threshold; cigarette held between the fingertips of a hand paused halfway to his mouth. He looked at least fifty, but moved like a younger man, aged beyond his years.

A fringe of rebellious strands of long black hair escaped from under a turban. His white, blue-striped dress shirt was buttoned all the way up, giving the man a strange layer of formality beneath a brown sweater vest and thermal fleece. Baggy brown pants and worn leather shoes completed an outfit that—like the town—looked cobbled together from leftovers.

As the man stepped out of the doorway, two children—both less than ten and dressed in mismatched layers like their father—pushed past him. The girl stared at the men inscrutably, while the boy smiled as he proudly stabbed a tall stick into the ground like a makeshift staff that Graham realized must be a crude shepherd's crook.

"*Slav.*" Khazhak offered his hand to the man as he said hello in Kurdish, which was all the Kurdish Graham knew. According to Khazhak, the Kurds had to speak Turkish, but preferred their own language.

Graham listened without understanding the words, following the conversation by interpreting the accompanying gestures. The exchange began with traded motions toward the peak of the mountain as they spoke, then transitioned into a choreography of negotiation like bartering at a bazaar, with numbers enumerated on splayed fingers and shaking heads, as if each were trying to guess the number the other was thinking of. The dialogue finally resolved in a signal from Khazhak for Graham to join them.

"Dr. Eliot, this is Sivan."

Graham shook the man's hand as Khazhak completed the introduction to Sivan in Kurdish.

"Sivan has agreed to take us to the place where many have seen the ark. He has also offered to let us sleep here tonight."

"Please thank him for me," Graham said, smiling.

Khazhak repeated the message, and the man returned the smile.

Passing messages through Khazhak would quickly grow tiresome, but Graham fought the impulse to speak directly to Sivan in Turkish, thinking it might insult him. "Please ask him if we are near the place where Saint Jacob was given the wood?"

Sivan broke into a smile and began nodding before Khazhak could finish. Sivan pointed into the Ahora Gorge, then hooked his arm in an invitation to follow him to their truck. Graham mirrored Khazhak's expression, one that wondered what they were getting into, and at the same time admitted they had nothing to lose.

"He says it is very near. Up the hill."

Cigarette smoke filled the cab as Khazhak retraced their route through the town, then forked toward the mountain onto a dirt road just before they got to the bridge. They bumped up the rocky slope to a place where the terrain allowed the truck to cross the dry stream bed, then followed the bank farther up. Graham rolled down his window to escape the smoke and looked up into the gorge. From what he could see, they were on a moraine—a berm of sediment that had flowed down the glacier—and guessed it was another scar left from the 1840 catastrophe.

Sivan interrupted his thoughts as he pointed with his cigarette to a spot above and to their left, to the top of the bluff made by the moraine. Just over a mile from the village, Khazhak made a hairpin turn to the left, doubling them back while taking them to the top of the hill. Sivan pointed again, this time to some rocks scattered on the ground, and motioned for them to stop.

Although it was hard to make out, Graham thought he could trace an irregular rectangular shape the stones made. As he studied the site, Sivan waved his hand over the area as he talked.

Khazhak provided a running translation at a lower volume. "He says this is the monastery where Saint Jacob lived."

Graham pictured Parrot's drawings and description of the monastery, and how the expedition had camped in the small courtyard. He tried to reconstruct the building in his mind among the rocks strewn across the ground but couldn't make it fit. Instead, he looked up the gorge and tried to imagine what the people who were buried by the earthquake and mudslide would have seen as the mountain was falling toward them. He rebuked himself for being morbid and changed his focus from *who* to *what* was buried beneath him.

If tradition was correct, then artifacts going back to the Middle Ages were very probably beneath his feet. But some accounts claimed the monastery also housed a number of relics from the ark, and those would have been buried as well. He wondered what Ground Penetrating Radar would reveal.

Graham took out his phone and documented the site with photographs, then dropped a locator pin in the Google Earth folder he was using for research. He looked north, across the plain to Aralik and was surprised at how high they had come already. The locator pin reported that the altitude was 6,365 feet. He clicked on the pin he'd dropped on Aralik and saw it was 4,000 feet below them, with most of the ascent made in the last three miles of the trip.

He glanced back, comparing the height he'd completed to what remained. Ararat towered above him, clawing the last of the day. He reminded himself the top of the mountain was not what it appeared to be; it was not the peak, but merely the highest point that could be seen from his perspective. The peak was hidden from his point of view, somewhere almost two miles above him.

Once again, he looked across the plain, this time envisioning it flooding, making an island of the mountain. How many people had taken shelter here as the waters rose? Could anyone have doubted this was the safest place they could go? And yet, no one could save themselves from the flood. Graham thought it would make an excellent illustration in a sermon, then realized he had already seen the lesson depicted on the curtain veiling the altar during the Armenian service the day before.

THIRTY-TWO

GRAHAM FELT LIKE A RAG DOLL BEING TOSSED AROUND THE BACK SEAT as the mountain road bucked the truck, refusing to be tamed. The erratic rocking and tilting jostled words out of Sivan between pulls on a perpetual chain of cigarettes. Khazhak focused on the road, leaving most of what Sivan said unanswered, and even less translated.

The road restrained the truck, rarely allowing it to move faster than ten miles an hour. Graham struggled to keep his impatience in check at the maddeningly slow pace, wanting to put this job behind him as soon as possible. He had thought they would be able to reach Ross's site by the end of the day since they were not carrying much with them, but he quickly abandoned the expectation. The meandering road seemed to be leading them *away* from the mountain rather than *toward* it, and their altitude had not increased. He hoped the trail was merely circumventing impassable territory, and that they hadn't taken a wrong turn along the way.

As soon as he began to seriously question the route, the path turned sharply to the left, taking them alongside the north face of Ararat. The trail continued to serpentine and switchback, but the general direction changed, finally orienting their indirect route toward the mountain. The incline of the road pushed Graham back against his seat as their ascent began in earnest.

After a long series of tortuous turns, Graham checked his phone's altimeter and noted they had almost doubled their altitude. As he leaned forward to compensate for the slope, he noticed the trail was degenerating from a single, wide path to a pair of parallel tire tracks. The tyranny of curves finally relented, leaving them in an oasis of relatively even ground. Tension in the truck eased as Khazhak visibly loosened.

Sivan started babbling excitedly, pointing across the field to a group of several tents. Khazhak followed the trail until it faded away as they entered the encampment. Sivan patted the air, signaling Khazhak to stop. Khazhak slipped the truck next to a ramshackle stone wall sheepfold.

Graham had never been so thankful to get out of a car, and he stood absolutely still, savoring the unmoving ground. It took several moments for the cold mountain air to penetrate him, sending him back to the truck for a coat.

"The weather changes quickly on the mountain," Khazhak said, pulling out a jacket for himself from the gear.

Sivan glanced back and forth between them, smiling as he spoke.

Khazhak nodded, then translated. "He says that going from the plain to the peak is like traveling from summer to winter."

"I can see why." Graham's lungs struggled to fill, and he checked the altimeter again: above 10,000 feet. He felt pressure between his eyes and popped a couple of Tums into his mouth.

"Sivan says this is as far as we can go in the truck," Khazhak translated. "He says we must hike the rest of the way. But he says it would be easier if we tried to hire some horses to take gear to a place where we can make a camp. He says the horses can't go all the way up, but we can get farther on the mountain and make a higher camp if we had them. Do you have any Turkish money to offer these shepherds?"

Graham pulled out the passport wallet he wore on a lanyard beneath his shirt and confirmed he still had some Turkish lira. Sivan smiled and nodded, then led them into the camp.

The tent farthest from the truck was made from a canvas stretched across the remnants of the stone walls of a ruined building. A man emerged as they made their way through the small camp, and Graham and Khazhak stood back as Sivan explained who they were. Like Sivan, the man used his cigarette as a prop when he spoke. Graham watched what was almost a repeat of the conversational gestures Khazhak and

Sivan had exchanged the previous day, and just as then, it resolved in a welcome.

Khazhak motioned to the man as he looked at Graham. "Derya is going to help us. He will let us use his horses and take us up to find a place to camp. Tomorrow, he will stay with the horses while we go the rest of the way. He will wait for us and help us back down."

As they unloaded their gear, Derya walked three small horses to the truck. Graham didn't have much experience with horses, and the little he did have made him uncomfortable at best. He hadn't liked not feeling in control of such a large and powerful animal. But these horses looked anything but large and powerful; they resembled something more like dingy unpainted rocking horses that had escaped the shackles of their curved bases. None of them stood taller than Graham, which not only made them unintimidating, but impressive as he realized how much they could carry. Derya and Sivan filled burlap bags with their gear and slung them over the backs of the horses. After filling canteens and water bottles with snowmelt Derya had collected, they were ready to go.

Derya led a horse onto a goat path that continued the trajectory of the road. Sivan followed with the second horse, and Khazhak took a third. Graham chose to stay in the rear to allow bits of conversation to trickle back to him, filtered through Khazhak.

After they fell into the rhythm of their hike, Graham decided to try to learn more about the tradition about the mountain. "Khazhak, ask them what they know about the flood."

Khazhak repeated the question and both shepherds offered Graham knowing smiles.

As Sivan answered, Graham tried to read into the tone of voice, but the inflection revealed nothing. When he was done, Khazhak translated over his shoulder. "He says the flood was made when the male waters above the earth joined the female waters from below the earth."

Graham thought the story sounded more like one of the pagan creation myths than a historical fact left out of the Bible. Before he could ask a follow-up, Derya continued, adding more information.

"The people were evil and mocked Noah when he warned them.

They were arrogant and said that they were too tall for a flood to rise above their heads. And if the water came up from the earth, they would cover the springs."

Derya was still speaking, but Khazhak stalled in concentration. "What did he say?"

Khazhak arched his brow in confusion. "Before the flood, it was different. Mothers gave birth after a pregnancy of only several days. Babies were born with the ability to walk and talk."

Sivan picked up the thread. "When the animals gathered, the sun grew dark, and the earth shook. It began to thunder and lightning. But the people still mocked Noah. Then, when the flood began and the water started to rise, 700,000 people gathered outside the ark and begged for protection. But Noah refused to let any of them in. He asked them, 'Are you not the people who said there was no God?' He told them they had been given 120 years to repent while he had built the ark, but they had rejected God. They only claimed to repent now because they were about to die. The people tried to force their way into the ark, but the animals who were not chosen to be on the ark attacked the people, killing many of them."

Derya added another strange fact to an already strange version of a familiar story. "God made the rain pass through hell first so that it was hot enough to burn the skin of the sinners. They had burned with desire, so God burned them as a fitting punishment."

Graham shared another look with Khazhak. "I think I was absent the day they went over that in seminary."

Khazhak shot a smile over his shoulder, picking up on the sarcasm.

Derya was still talking, and Khazhak refocused. "There was one animal that was too big to fit inside the ark, so it ran behind. Something called a *reem*." Khazhak translated it as a statement, but his face made it a question. "And there was a giant named Og who tried to ride on the roof of the ark."

Graham worked to control his expression, hoping to keep it neutral. He didn't want to appear rude to the men helping them. The flood had left a residue of tradition and myth across the ancient world, and at least these legends were more closely tethered to the biblical account than most.

He decided not to ask any more questions, especially because the thin air had conspired with the exertion of the hike to make breathing more difficult. He waited as long as he could before calling for a rest break. The others obliged, but as he caught his breath, he saw Khazhak didn't seem to need it as much as he did, while Sivan and Derya were totally unaffected by the climb and took the opportunity to smoke. Graham self-consciously tried to control his breathing, for some reason embarrassed he was so winded, and he realized it was cold enough to see his breath.

Derya spoke as they waited, and Khazhak shared what he heard. "He says he knows the path to the ark and has gone up to see it before. But when he has been there, it has always been covered in snow. He has never actually seen it exposed. But he says many people in his family have."

Another non-witness. The only people to see the ark and describe it in detail didn't take photographs of it. The only people to take photographs of the ark lost the photos, and the only people who didn't lose the photos turned out to have taken pictures of basalt blocks. Graham wondered yet again what in the world he was doing. He looked away from the peak, out over the plain, and pictured it as a sea carrying the ark with a giant riding on the roof, clinging to what was literally the last safe place on earth. It was an excellent illustration of the nature of myths, legends, and lies—they couldn't survive without piggy backing on the truth.

THIRTY-THREE

The trail crossed an open area pimpled with scrub and stray rocks, level enough that Graham thought they could've continued farther in the truck. The logic became clear as Derya guided them onto a dry stream bed, against the absent current, directly toward the mountain. Graham stared up the valley and guessed the wash from the snowmelt made this a hazardous area most of the year. The top of the valley was capped with a jagged cliff Graham estimated was at least a thousand feet tall.

As Graham wondered how they were going to get to the top of the cliff, Derya answered by changing course again, stepping out of the dry bed and onto the far side. Whatever gain in altitude Graham had expected by this point was more than made up by the pitch of the valley. The disquieting angle reminded Graham of the times he had been on the roof of his house—a place he avoided unless it was absolutely necessary.

The horses were more sure-footed, and Graham was thankful they hadn't tried to carry the gear on their own. Small rocks pelted him from above, inadvertently loosened by the other climbers, forcing him to keep his head down as he moved forward, adding his own pebbles to the wake of dirt.

The effort required even Derya and Sivan to take frequent breaks, but Graham didn't know which was worse: climbing the scarp or stopping in the middle of it. If he fell from here, it looked like he would roll for miles. As they neared the top of the valley, the incline grew so steep that Graham leaned forward until he felt he was crawling almost vertically up the surface.

After clambering up the last few yards, he joined the others sitting at the top of the hill. A hostile wind steadily pushed against them in a torrent of air as if the mountain had pierced the sky, springing a leak. Their clothes whipped and billowed in the squall, giving them a motion that contradicted the unmoving bodies that anchored them. Graham's sense of accomplishment drained as he looked toward the peak and saw that most of the mountain remained to be conquered, and that it wouldn't be any easier.

All four men rested facing downhill, away from the wind, like spectators waiting for an event to begin. Graham searched for Yenidoğan, but it lay hidden by the ridge they had circumvented in the truck, inside the Ahora Gorge. He scanned the landscape and focused his attention on a moraine, tracing the sediment flow to a hill topped with a crater instead of a peak, like a bowl. As he studied the massive divot, Derya's voice cut through the wind.

Khazhak pointed to the bowl and translated. "That crater is from the volcano."

Graham had forgotten Ararat was volcanic. The detail wasn't important to him except as an interesting device for answering an obvious problem with Ararat as the landing place of the ark. There was not enough water on the earth to submerge Ararat, and there was no less water on the earth now than there was then. So how could it have been covered?

Believers in the mountain argued that the earth as it is now is not necessarily the same as it was before the flood, that geological features had been altered by the catastrophe. Part of that explanation included the possibility that Ararat was much lower at the time of the flood, and that the mountain grew taller after the flood due to volcanic activity, lifting the ark to higher elevations. Graham considered the idea more clever than convincing, and a little too convenient.

Khazhak interrupted his thoughts as he moved his finger to point to the left of the caldera. "And on the other side of that hill—between here and there—is Lake Kop."

Graham recognized the name of the small glacial lake as one of the landmarks mentioned by both Chuchian and Navarra. He tilted his head back, looked down his nose, and elongated his neck in a useless attempt to see over the hill that blocked its view.

Sivan and Derya stood up, signaling it was time to continue. Graham weaved as he balanced himself and leaned into the wind. The top of the hill they had scaled was the ridge of a canyon, and Derya led them up the spine, directly toward the peak. The slope sustained its severe angle, and instead of watching the top of the mountain grow closer, Graham stared at the ground, watching his steps on the loose rock as he trudged ahead. The effort of moving forward was measured by more frequent rest stops. After the second stop in shadow rather than sun, they could feel the temperature begin to drop. Derya announced they needed to start looking for a place to camp. After another stop, Derya found a small outcrop of rock on the other side of the ridge. They could camp below it, giving them some measure of shelter.

Khazhak unpacked a pair of two-man tents as Derya and Sivan took care of the horses. Graham followed Khazhak's instructions as they assembled segments of tubing into flexible poles. They threaded them through sleeves in the fabric of the tent and bent them into crossing arcs to create the domed frame that shaped the water-resistant nylon shell. Once it was anchored to the ground, Khazhak fastened a canopy over the tent, adding a layer of insulation and protection against wind, rain, and snow. They repeated the process for the second tent, then loaded all the gear inside. Khazhak had brought two mummy-shaped sleeping bags, and Graham hoped the tag claiming they were rated for 0-15 degrees was true as he oriented them with the feet on the downhill side of the slope.

He emerged from the tent to find that Khazhak and Sivan had fired up two small propane backpack stoves and were smoking as they waited for water to boil. Derya emptied packets of dehydrated beef stew into four metal bowls, and they took turns adding the water. Graham stirred his dinner to life as Derya shared a loaf of bread and some cheese. He was so famished that the taste of the food was almost irrelevant.

As the food started to restore his energy, Graham spoke through Khazhak to ask the guides what their families said the ark looked like.

The answer came jointly, each adding to what the other said, corroborating and expanding it.

"It is a very long rectangular shape, a little taller than it is wide. The wood has become very hard, like rock, but it still has the grain. They said it was built according to the book."

"Genesis?" Graham asked.

Both men shook their heads.

A squint of confusion contracted Khazhak's face as he conveyed the answer. "It was built according to the book given to Adam by the angel Raziel. It contained all the knowledge in it, both earthly and heavenly knowledge. Raziel gave it to Noah and told him it would explain how to build the ark and how to gather the animals."

Derya nodded as if endorsing Khazhak's unintelligible words, then spoke again.

"The book was made of sapphires and was kept in a golden case. The stones gave off light, which lit up the inside of the ark. It glowed more at night so Noah could tell the day from the night."

"What happened to the book?" Graham asked, looking at Sivan and Derya.

"Noah gave it to Shem, and it was handed down until it became Abraham's. Jacob, Levi, Moses, Joshua, and Solomon also possessed it."

As Khazhak translated, Sivan motioned to the top of the mountain and continued speaking.

"He says Noah came down from the ark and planted a vine where his village is. It was the same vine that was taken from Eden by Adam. The village was the first settlement after the flood."

Graham turned to Sivan. "Where Noah made the first sacrifice?"

Sivan rocked left and right, equivocally, like a scale weighing how to answer. "Noah offered it, but Shem performed it. Noah was not allowed."

"Why not?"

"One day Noah forgot to feed the lions. One of them struck Noah with its paw and injured him so badly that he was lame after that. The injury was a defect that made him ceremonially unclean, and therefore unfit to carry out the priestly duties."

Before Graham could respond, Sivan started speaking again, gesturing expansively over the plain and to the sides of the mountain.

"The sons of Noah started other towns, each named after their wives. Ham built a city called Neelatamauk. Japheth built Adataneses. And Shem built Zedeketelbab. Shem was the only son to stay near Noah. After a time, the sons cast lots to divide the earth. Shem received the middle section here. The south fell to Ham, and the north to Japheth."

The two shepherds waited until Khazhak stopped talking, then closed the topic by collecting themselves for the night. Sivan announced they should start up the mountain by sunrise, then said good night.

Khazhak followed Graham into the other tent. After Graham had squirmed into the least uncomfortable position on the rocky slope, Khazhak added a postscript to the conversation at dinner.

"What do you think of our new friends?"

"For a story I thought I knew everything about, they sure added a lot of new information."

Khazhak chuckled. "Yes, there are many traditions here surrounding the ark and Noah."

"The question is: Did any truth survive the deluge?" Graham stared into the dark and thought it was a good metaphor for his whole mission.

THIRTY-FOUR

GRAHAM COULDN'T MOVE, PINNED ON HIS BACK UNDER THE WEIGHT OF THE thick, empty darkness. Indistinct sounds seeded the air with just enough acoustic clues to define his surroundings as enclosed, yet cavernous. He stared into the void, looking for shadows in the shadows, but quickly gave up, realizing he might as well be looking for a particular drop of water in the ocean. He closed his eyes, crimping them tightly, and found no change in his vision. Air the smell of damp fur, like a wet dog, mingled with animal breathing, as if the blackness were alive.

He reopened his eyes and found they had become sensitive enough to detect a whisper of light at the edge of his vision. He wasn't sure if the object was real or merely the chemical residue of clamping his eyes shut. But instead of receding, it spread, growing without adding detail. A motor softly—almost imperceptibly—cycled on and off. Not a motor; too organic. More like…a purr.

A figure in a blindingly white robe appeared instantaneously, standing still no more than ten feet away. Graham had the feeling the person had been there the entire time, unnoticed somehow. The robe was a raiment of incandescent material that emitted light rather than reflected it, immune to shadow and almost all detail. His face and hands were just as white, nearly featureless. Graham couldn't decide if the figure's hair was long or if light drifted from his head in streaks, weightless as if submerged in water.

The arrival of the person had startled Graham, but as he took in what his restored sight revealed, what he felt was pure fear. And yet, he didn't detect any evil intent. Just the opposite: he feared the person's goodness. It was clear without having to be told: he was holy—so holy that Graham was profoundly aware of his own unworthiness.

Graham's paralysis held him still as the person stepped toward him purposefully. The figure raised a sword above his head with both hands and held the pose. Graham stared at the sword and wondered how he hadn't seen it. The blade was a shimmering blue and orange flame streaked with white.

The sword of fire arced down quickly, like an axe into wood. Except there was no wood, only his body. The blade divided him, separating his hips from his rib cage.

Graham screamed, but no sound came out. Bizarrely, no pain followed, as if his nerves were as muted as his voice. The horror of the vivisection widened his eyes as if he needed to see more of the wound despite not wanting to see it at all. He couldn't breathe and began gasping. His blood felt strangely cold as it began to soak him. It took him a moment to realize it wasn't blood at all, but water. And he was sinking into it. Somehow during the attack, the floor had become water. As he drifted down below the surface, the water scattered the light of the figure, and the figure became more radiant, as if to accommodate Graham's effort to grasp his surroundings.

A long black rectangle appeared, silhouetted against the source of the light, growing smaller as he sank lower. Graham understood he had awoken on the floor of the hull of the ark but had dropped through it somehow. Above him—between him and the ark—a lion drifted into view, pawing at him, pursuing him rather than fighting for air. Was it the one who had maimed Noah?

A claw swiped close enough for him to feel the displacement of the water. He tried to twist away, but still couldn't move his arms or head. He was no longer in halves, but restored, though just as helpless. An observer to his own predicament, unable to move through it.

Another swipe came, tearing three parallel lines across his chest that began leaking syrupy, red blood. As he stared at the wound, the lion struck a second blow, perpendicular to the first. When the third blow landed, it cloaked him in oblivion.

The surreal darkness was replaced by a tangible one. Graham stared blindly into it as the dream dissipated, carried away in the fierce sound of the wind. Despite the cold, he could feel the sweat from his nightmare, and he determined not to fall back asleep despite his exhaustion. But somewhere in the black night he forgot the resolution, closed his eyes, and fell asleep.

THIRTY-FIVE

Frigid wind reached behind Graham's sunglasses, whipping tears from his eyes, undulating his clothes like flags in a storm. After crossing—at times, crawling—over loose rock on a slope steeper than forty-five degrees in points, they had reached the plateau that sat just beneath the peak, 14,000 feet above sea level.

Although they were only a mile from the camp, it had taken half the morning to travel the distance. The altitude's thin air sat heavily between his eyes in a dull ache, though not as much as he had feared, thanks—he thought—to the Tums, which he continued to chew. The exertion and stress of the expedition would have been enough to exhaust him, but as usually happened when he was in the mountains—along with altitude sickness—he had suffered violent nightmares. He awoke unrested, feeling more beat up than when he went to sleep. And the day's work was just beginning.

He stood on the narrow strip of bare ground between the top of the slope and the edge of the snow cap. The narrow strip formed a lip around the northern edge of the Ahora Gorge, like a path leading to the ark. Graham looked back down the mountain toward the camp with a sense of accomplishment, a task checked off the to-do list. The tents were obscured by the outcrop of rock they had camped below, and they had left Derya behind to tend the horses.

He tried to spot Lake Kop on his left, but it, too, was hidden behind the hills. He scanned the rest of the area as he thought about all the expeditions he had researched. The weight of his phone in his coat pocket reminded him he could still access his notes. As the phone connected with the aid of the satellite sleeve, Graham begrudgingly thanked Vogel for the technology. He opened Google Earth and selected the folder where he had saved locations that corresponded to his notes and watched the globe turn, then zoom in to an aerial view of where he currently stood.

The closest pin marked the spot where Navarra claimed to find wood in 1968. Graham turned and looked up the slope of the plateau and to his right. The snow blanketed glacial ice that had frozen, started to melt, and refrozen so many times that it had become discolored by the gray volcanic dirt. Between the dull color and the buckled, distorted surface, the ice appeared more like the skin of an enormous elephant.

The sound of footsteps drew Graham from his thoughts. Sivan started across the dirt lip at the edge of the Ahora Gorge, circumventing the snow cap rather than crossing it.

"Where're we headed?"

Khazhak repeated the question and Sivan answered as he made a gesture indicating they were not far away.

"We must pass the two canyons; the ark is at the top of the third. He says we are close."

Graham tried to reconcile the information with what he had plotted on his map. They appeared to be heading toward the Chuchian site, between the three pins that marked where Navarra found wood. But Vogel's satellite information had taken Ross to the other side of the plateau.

"Is something wrong?" Khazhak studied Graham's face.

"Where you are taking me—it's not where I need to go. But I would like to see what is there. And it is on the way to the place I came to see."

Both he and Khazhak masked their faces with neck gaiters as a layer of protection from the wind. Clouds of breath formed as they spoke, as though the cloth were straining vapor from their words.

"There is another place that you want to see?" Khazhak asked, raising his brow.

"Yes, the person who sent me told me exactly where I needed to go." Graham pointed across the plateau in the general direction of Ross's site. "It's over there, on the other side of the snow cap."

Khazhak repeated the news to Sivan, who stopped and turned to look at Graham in confusion. Graham listened to their exchange and watched Khazhak shrug apologies that mimed the excuse that he was only the messenger. Sivan eyed Graham with doubt, and it required some additional coaxing from Khazhak before Sivan resumed the hike.

They continued along the margin of exposed earth between the icecap on their right and the bluff on their left. The relatively level terrain of the edge of the plateau was a welcome change after the ascent from the camp, and they made quick progress as they walked east across the north face. Twin canyons fell away below the cliff, like grooves etched by a pair of prodigious talons, and Graham realized they were the obstacles that had necessitated their circuitous route.

On the other side of a short rise, the Ahora Gorge opened before them like a rip in the mountain. Even with the morning sun filling it, deep shadows accentuated its sharp, jagged angles. Whisps of clouds and fog drifted below them like aimless wraiths, blurring details as they added moving shadows to the stationary ones. The canyon trapped a terrible beauty, a mystique that didn't need the tradition of the ark to be captivating. The violent scar of rock fractured into a myriad of crags, making it almost impossible to search well—even if it was for an object the size of the ark.

"This is the place."

Graham followed Khazhak's voice to the top of the plateau, and he saw the two guides stopped ahead of him. He joined them at the edge of a small, horseshoe-shaped drop-off that looked as if a giant had taken a bite from the mountain. A ledge jutted out from the wall a hundred feet below, adding a floor to the horseshoe to make a bowl filled with dirty snow and shadow. The scale of the mountain made it seem small, almost insignificant.

Khazhak translated as Sivan explained, looking pleased with himself. "This is where the ark is."

"What do you mean? I don't see it."

"He says it is below the ice and snow. Some years it appears, but most time it remains hidden underneath. And when it can be seen, most of it is beneath the rock."

"Does he mean there was a landslide or something that covered it?"

Khazhak shrugged. "That is just how he describes it. But that would be the best explanation. If it is really there."

"Big if," Graham said, looking at the pile of snow. "There's nothing even vaguely ark-shaped as far as I can see."

Graham used his phone to document the site with photographs, ignoring the incongruity of his words with the action. Sivan spoke again as Graham shifted to different positions along the lip of the drop to cover all the angles.

"He wants to know if you wish to go down to it. There is a short trail."

Graham shook his head. "It doesn't look like there is anything to go down to."

Although he hadn't expected to find the ark, Graham felt a twinge of disappointment. A surprising empathy with the ark hunters he had dismissed as adventurers not to be taken seriously had taken root like a weed in his orthodoxy. He, too, had been bitten by the allure of the chase, by the possibility of finding the legendary artifact.

He switched his phone back to Google Earth and lifted the screen toward Khazhak, pointing to the pin marking Vogel's site. "I really need to go *here*. Can he take us?"

Khazhak repeated the question. Sivan glanced at Graham in confusion, then back to Khazhak as he spoke rapidly.

Graham didn't wait for the translation and tried to make his case. He looked at the screen, calling Sivan's attention to it as evidence. "It is only two miles away. If we follow this ledge, then the first mile isn't even in the snow."

Khazhak didn't bother to translate the argument. "We have no tent. No protection. It is too dangerous."

"There is a shelter there. And supplies."

A mixture of suspicion and surprise clouded Khazhak's face, accusing Graham of not sharing all the information he had, or the real purpose of the expedition.

"But we won't even have to use it," Graham continued, hoping to overpower the glare with more explanation. "We don't need to stay long. I just need to look at the spot and take a few pictures. Just like here. Then we can return. We can probably make it back to camp before the end of the day." He tried to sound assured without revealing he was trying to convince himself just as much as them.

Khazhak and Sivan traded a volley of words that—despite being unintelligible—made it clear they thought the plan was a waste of time. But whatever Khazhak said persuaded Sivan to give a begrudging nod of assent.

Khazhak fixed Graham with a warning look. "If we are to do this, we must leave. Now."

THIRTY-SIX

THE FRINGE OF DIRT BETWEEN THE SNOW AND CLIFF CONTINUED FOR another mile, warping into an *S*-shape as it bent around the Ahora Gorge. Graham studiously stepped where Sivan and Khazhak had been before him, trusting their experience to choose the safest footing. The route narrowed and the terrain became less reliable, sometimes leaving no more than a sliver of loose rock to negotiate beneath overhanging snow.

When the path left them nowhere to go but onto the icecap, Khazhak motioned for Graham to spin around to access his backpack. As Khazhak picked through the gear, Graham stared directly into the gorge. Smaller canyons fed into larger ones, like tributaries to a river, creating a disordered maze of rock. Again, it would be almost impossible to find anything smaller than the ark in the tangle of gullies.

Khazhak patted the backpack, punctuating the end of his task. Graham turned back and took a pair of crampons from Khazhak, then followed Khazhak's instruction for how to fit the steel spikes onto the bottom of his boots.

The three men crowded around the phone and compared the satellite image to their position as they plotted a course. Despite their agreement, none of them stepped onto the snow with conviction. The fresh, unpacked layer absorbed them up to their ankles before the crampons bit into the ice. The effort of nailing themselves to the mountain with each step slowed their pace just as much as the steeper incline they ascended. The pitch was no greater than the first leg of the morning's climb, but being on snow left them nothing to reach for if they slipped. Graham could sense the Ahora Gorge gaping behind him, like a Venus's-flytrap waiting for food to land in its jaws.

After two hours of climbing—tapping into reserves of energy that could only be generated by necessity—they finally reached the saddle of the peak. They were still a thousand feet below the summit, but from this point they only needed to cross the mountain rather than continue up. As they worked their way to the southeast spur of the peak, low-hanging clouds began to block the sun, cutting their ability to see ahead.

"We need to get to shelter quickly. A storm is coming." Khazhak translated Sivan's warning as he checked their bearings on Graham's phone.

They walked three abreast, Graham in the middle, frequently holding out the phone to gauge where they were heading. Graham was staring at the screen when snow began to fall, melting into beads and distorting the image. Sivan called out as he pointed through the haze to a rectangular shape on the edge of the fog. Segments of dirty white panels held in place by a metal frame formed the walls of the temporary house that had been permanently left. Bricks of ice that looked like paving stones had been stacked in an *L*-shape around one of the corners, shielding it—Graham guessed—from the wind.

Khazhak glanced at Graham. "Is that what we are looking for?"

"I think so. That must be the equipment shed left by the expedition doing work here."

"But there is nothing here. This is not where the ark is. Why would they be looking for something in a place where there is obviously nothing but snow and ice."

"They're not. They are looking beneath it." Before Khazhak could ask, Graham added, "I'll explain when we get there."

As they drew near the hut, Sivan stopped, halting the others as he pointed to the ground outside the entrance. Footprints compacted the snow outside the door, and a trail led away in the opposite direction from them.

"Someone else has been here." Accusation returned to Khazhak's face as he looked at Graham.

Graham widened his eyes, amplifying his own confusion in defense. "I have no idea who it could be. The expedition leader told me they could not come because of the attack. There is no way they could have sneaked their way here this fast. Do you think it could be the terrorists?"

Khazhak seemed only partially satisfied by the response, but he repeated the question and consulted with Sivan. After a short exchange, Khazhak spoke for them both. "We do not think it would be the PKK. They would not come to the top of the mountain to hide. They have many better places for that lower down."

"I swear I have no idea whose footprints they are," Graham said. "Maybe the PKK needed supplies and knew that some had been left up here."

"Unless the supplies here include weapons, then I doubt they left behind anything worth climbing the mountain for."

A sense of foreboding rose like a tide in Graham's thoughts as he looked at the scene, hesitant to enter before finding a plausible explanation for it. Sivan took a step toward the hut, but Graham grabbed his arm, holding him back.

"What is it?" Khazhak asked.

"The footprints." Graham pointed at the trail. "They only lead *away* from the house. There are none coming back to it. Something's not right here."

"Someone could be hurt," Khazhak said. "They might need our help."

Graham reached the door first and found it was slightly open. He paused, gave Khazhak a questioning look as he called out. "Hello?"

The deadening acoustics of the snow absorbed the greeting, and Graham took the silence that followed as his answer. He pushed the door open, saw the shed was empty, and stepped inside.

The thick white plastic panels of the walls and roof diffused the light, giving the space a dream-like, dimensionless quality, as if the metal skeleton of the building floated in a contextless vacuum. The nine-by-twelve interior felt larger than it had looked from outside.

Seven or eight all-weather, waterproof Pelican cases had been left behind, just as Ross had said. Impressions on the ground indicated they had been lined up against the walls, fortifying the shed. But several of them had been opened and were strewn randomly into the middle of the space, ransacked. Two of the open cases stored a variety of tools Graham had expected to see—hammers, chisels, brushes, climbing rope. A third case contained dehydrated fruit and meal packets, as well as small tanks of propane.

"I wonder what it was they were looking for," Graham mumbled as he picked through the cases.

"If it was food, they left a lot behind," Khazhak said. "It must not be the PKK. Is this what you needed to see?"

"Part of it," Graham said, not looking up, "but not the main thing. I need to go to the other tent."

As he spoke, the brittle spatter of icy snow on the walls and roof of the shelter began to pop violently. All eyes scattered to different parts of the translucent shell, as if looking for the sound.

Sivan said something, and Khazhak had to raise his voice to translate it for Graham. "Hail. For now, we stay."

THIRTY-SEVEN

THE STORM PERFORMED AN UNEVEN DRUMROLL ON THE PLASTIC shell, annihilating the silence with a rattle that physically pummeled everyone inside. Although it lasted less than ten minutes, it seemed like an hour before the heavy pelts faded away, replaced by ticks of snow.

Sivan fidgeted impatiently, anxious to leave, and stepped outside as soon as the hail had subsided. Khazhak and Graham followed, but immediately stopped on the other side of the door. The world they had left outside was gone—erased by a cloud sitting on the peak as it snowed. Graham couldn't see any details beyond ten feet. He could feel the grip of gravity, and yet he almost had the sensation of floating. He had experienced it once before, on a spring break ski trip to Vail with Olivia just after they were married. A storm had rolled in while they were on the lift to the top of the mountain, and by the time they reached the top, there was neither sky nor horizon.

"Whiteout." Khazhak said the word as Graham thought it.

The first few footsteps leading away from the building had partially filled, their edges rounded with accumulation as they disappeared in the direction of the shaft. "We need to go that way," Graham said.

Sivan barked a reply softened by Khazhak in translation. "Not in the whiteout. Too dangerous." Back in the tent, Khazhak revealed his own frustration. "Please tell us what we are doing here."

Graham rubbed his temple into a resigned expression of full disclosure. "A satellite that is able to see below the surface scanned this area and detected an object the same size and shape as the ark. But it's thirty or forty feet beneath us. For the last couple of years, a team of archaeologists has come up to try to dig their way to it. Supposedly, they've cut a shaft that gets very close to the object. I need to see the shaft."

Sharp, loud words burst from Sivan, bouncing around inside the hut as violently as the hail had the outside. Khazhak answered in intensity—though not volume—leaving Graham to wonder if he was being defended or attacked.

"It is impossible to dig through that ice with picks," Khazhak said, not bothering to translate the exchange. "Not that deep."

"They aren't using picks. They have chainsaws. That's what some of this equipment is. That's probably where those ice bricks come from." Graham gestured to the cases, sweeping his arm toward the corner protected by the ice wall. "They cut out squares of ice, then use them to protect the tents."

Khazhak's eyes lingered on Graham's, as if testing his truthfulness, then shared the explanation with Sivan.

Sivan pointed to the door. "And whose footprints are those?" Khazhak translated.

"I already told you, I don't know. That's the truth."

After a moment of silence, Sivan stood up, shot Graham an angry look, pulled the door open, and spoke without looking back.

"He says it is clearing up," Khazhak relayed. "Let us go look at this shaft. Then we can start down the mountain. Derya is expecting us back. We can still make it before nightfall if we move quickly."

Graham led the way across the snow beneath a gray sky, as if the storm had left a bruise. Fifty yards from the hut—halfway to the shaft—swatches of orange bled through a coat of snow on a mound ahead of him and made it their target. As they grew closer, Graham recognized the gray and orange pattern of triangles and hexagons of the domed tent in the photos of the expedition. He was shocked it had weathered so well, let alone that it was still standing. The sixteen-foot diameter looked bigger than it had in pictures and resembled an oversized golf ball that had landed in the ultimate hazard. What concerned him now was that the footsteps led directly to the entrance.

At the entrance to the tent, Graham looked back at Khazhak, attempting an expression of reassurance he was certain neither of them believed. Before Khazhak could say anything, he stepped through the opening.

The eight-foot-square shaft Ross had described gaped in the center of the space, making the dome seem like a round peg that wouldn't fit in the square hole. Graham moved to his right, along the perimeter of the tent, making room for the others. A stainless-steel hoist, over six feet tall, spanned the mouth of the shaft. Graham hadn't thought about how the ice had been removed after it had been cut away, but the rig was the obvious answer. A quarter of the way down, the shaft diminished proportionally by a foot on each side, leaving a foot-wide ledge for a reason unclear to Graham.

"What is that for?" Khazhak asked, pointing to a pair of ventilation ducts running under the tent on the other side of the shaft, draping over the edge and hanging to the bottom like metallic veins.

"To get rid of the exhaust from the chainsaws," Graham said. "They run on gas. Without the ducts, they'd asphyxiate."

"And the pink ribbons?"

"Sample collection points," Graham said without looking up from the survey flags embedded every three feet down the opposite wall. "To study the ice."

Khazhak translated a question from Sivan. "How long did it take to cut this out?"

"They were able to cut away about three feet a day at most. You can see where the layers were." Graham pointed to the remnants of grooves and scars that marked the layers of progress. "And that opening at the bottom—that's the tunnel they cut to try to reach whatever it is the satellite detected."

A rope ladder dangled the length of the shaft. Wooden rungs gave it structure, and every seven or eight feet, a support rung—wider than the other rungs—pushed the ladder out from the wall five or six inches, anchored by auger segments repurposed after taking core samples of the ice.

"This what you wanted to see?" Khazhak asked.

Graham took several pictures with his phone as he answered, "Yes, but I need to go to the bottom and see what's in that tunnel." Without waiting for an objection, he pivoted his body and stepped backward onto the ladder. "Stay here. I'll be right back. Then we can leave."

THIRTY-EIGHT

As Graham's head passed below the surface of the ice, the change in acoustics gave him the sense that the mountain had swallowed him. The small, long space bounced every sound off the hard surface—a reverberation that brought an unexpected memory of Aly. Suddenly, he wasn't in the shaft at all, but at the playground near their house, chasing his daughter through the cement tunnel cutting through the hill. Squeals of laughter reflected off the walls, doubling and tripling her voice like Elvis Presley on *Heartbreak Hotel.*

"Is everything all right?"

Khazhak's voice broke the hold of the vision, and Graham realized he had paused.

"Yeah. I'm good."

He looked up as he lowered himself to the next rung and found the top of the ladder farther away than he thought it would be. The orange and gray tent hovered above like a quilted patch on the square hole in the ice. The faces of Khazhak and Sivan hung over the edge with a shared expression that was an alloy of curiosity and impatience. He kept his head tilted up as he descended, not wanting to trigger his fear of heights. The deeper he went, the more the shaft felt constricting, ingesting him.

A subtle alteration in the echo made him glance down, and he saw the next rung lay on the bottom of the shaft. As he stepped onto ice, the surface seemed a mile away.

"Does this pit make me look like Saint Gregory the Illuminator?"

Khazhak smiled. "Please try to come back up more quickly than he did."

Graham opened the carabiner on his belt loop and unhooked the handle of the camping lantern he had taken from one of the cases in the supply hut. He stooped at the edge of the five-foot-tall opening, bracing himself with a hand on his knee, and peered into the tunnel. Ambient light bled into the first few feet, and the lantern extended his visibility a bit more before being blotted out by the darkness. He had hoped he would be able to see the end of the tunnel without having to go all the way into it.

He rose and turned away from the opening, gathering his resolve, and found himself looking at a twin of his lantern on the other side of the shaft. He had been too focused on his task to notice it before, but was happy for the serendipity just at the time when he wished he had more light.

"Find something?" Khazhak asked, sounding closer than he appeared.

"There's already a lantern down here, which is great because I'll need all the light I can get."

"It has probably been there since the last time people were here. I doubt the batteries are—"

Light burst from the lantern as Graham turned the switch, cutting Khazhak off.

"Amazing!" Graham said, crouching for a better angle.

"Is there anything in the tunnel?" Khazhak asked.

"Not sure yet. I'll tell you in a minute."

With both lanterns on, enough light permeated the tunnel for Graham to see the other end, almost twenty feet away. His crouched walk reminded him of trying to find his way through the unexplored tunnels beneath the Temple Mount in Jerusalem two years earlier. Now he was inside another sacred mountain, this time encased in ice rather than stone.

As he made his way into the passage, shadows fell away from a clutter of shapes at the foot of the far wall, revealing two chisels and a pick hammer abandoned next to a small cooking stove with a metal kettle sitting on top of the burner. The stove was designed with a squat propane reservoir that doubled as its base, and a triad of fins formed a grill holding a kettle above the burner. He nudged the tools with his boot, wondering what their purpose was since they wouldn't have been used to cut the tunnel. Even if they had done the work, they would have been stored at the end of the season, not left in the open.

But it was the bucket that seemed most out of place. The expedition clearly had a more efficient way of removing the ice, so what was its purpose? Graham tapped it with his toe and watched ripples shimmer across the surface. It took him a second to realize the problem: the bucket was half full of water—liquid water, not ice.

He kneeled next to the bucket, searching for an explanation for the impossible water. A second later, he had completely forgotten about it.

A spur of black wood angled up through the ice, puncturing the surface of the floor, exposing the last three inches. The remainder—about the length of Graham's forearm—remained encased in the ice, a dark unfocused smear beneath the surface. He gently touched the tip and discovered it was hard, like a rock. He tapped it several times, growing progressively harder with each touch, then leaned close with his lantern to examine the material. Undulating ridges caught the light, revealing the unmistakable fingerprint of wood grain.

"Are you okay?" Khazhak called.

Graham sat up and yelled over his shoulder. "Yes. There's something down here."

"What have you found?"

He hesitated, unwilling to say aloud what his mind was still processing. "Not sure yet."

He leaned in again and wondered why the petrified wood—if that was really what it was—hadn't been removed from the ice for testing. Why had it been left poking out of the end of the tunnel?

He cleared the tools away from the space, then moved the bucket, revealing a pile of chipped ice. A channel had been cut away, extending into the floor as it went beyond the back wall. The shape was too tubular to be part of the progress of the tunnel. He ran his fingers along the edges of the cavity, then took out his phone and documented the scene with pictures. What possible explanation would Ross have for what he was looking at?

Light from the flash struck the ice in an almost subliminal frame that boxed the ice around the wood. Graham felt along the surface and discovered a groove, then traced its path. The ice on the inside of the groove, closer to the wood, felt less solid somehow.

"Sivan says we need to leave soon," Khazhak said impatiently.

"Okay. But something isn't quite right down here."

"In what way?"

"Looks like there is wood here, all right. But it's frozen in fresh ice."

"That does not make sense."

"Gimme one more minute."

Graham reached for the pick hammer with his right hand, then shot video with the phone in his left as he started tapping the ice on the outside of the groove. The hammer bounced off the hard surface with the clack of two unyielding objects colliding. He repeated the tap two more times as he moved the hammer closer to the wood, each time with the same results. On the first tap inside the groove, ice chipped away with the brittle crack of fresh ice. He kept the video rolling as he brought the hammer down hard on the ice next to the wood, hoping to break it up enough to wrest it loose.

After surprisingly little work, he pulled the shard from the ice. The rough surface didn't appear to be either hewn or natural, but more like it had splintered away from a larger beam.

Graham was so absorbed as he studied the wood that he didn't register the angry voices at the top of the shaft until they began to escalate. He stared back down the tunnel in a futile effort to see what was happening just as the voices were silenced by a gunshot.

THIRTY-NINE

"Khazhak! Sivan!" Graham froze, tuning his body to detect the slightest sound. He hadn't seen either of them carrying a gun, and he couldn't imagine Khazhak needing one for his missionary work. And if Sivan had one for protection, what would make him use it? Graham yelled again, louder, but again was answered by a silence almost as alarming as the shot. He suddenly felt vulnerable, trapped underground, unable to help, and scrambled out of the tunnel—crampons flailing ice—and up the ladder, wood still in hand.

No one waited at the top of the ladder. He burst out of the tent, then immediately froze. Sivan lay on his back, groaning in animal pain between quick, sharp breaths, as red snow bloomed beneath him. Khazhak kneeled next to him, pressing bloody hands into Sivan's left side, covering the upper abdomen and lower ribs. He noted Graham's presence with a quick, silent glance that kept his focus on helping Sivan.

On the other side of Sivan, a stranger aimed his pistol at Graham, controlling the scene as if the gun were a wand casting a spell of obedience. He was outfitted in a combination of traditional guide clothes and contemporary mountaineering gear. A prominent, aquiline nose anchored the man's expression as it recomposed, giving Graham the unnerving feeling the stranger had recognized him somehow.

Sivan's breathing became more labored, and Graham looked down at him, unsure whether he would be allowed to move closer.

"How bad is he hurt?"

"It is not good," Khazhak said worriedly as he glanced at Graham again. "The bullet may have hit the spleen. Maybe the liver."

He barked something at the gunman, who responded in a curt monosyllable.

"Take over here," Khazhak said, glancing at Graham. "I am going to look for a first aid kit in the supply tent."

"I don't know what to do." Graham could hear the panic in his own voice.

"I have training as a medic. Come here. Now."

Khazhak's command left no room for inaction, and Graham stuttered forward before looking to the gunman for permission. The man gave a single, shallow nod, releasing Graham to kneel next to Khazhak.

"Press down here, like this."

Khazhak's blood-slick hands guided Graham's palms into place as Sivan growled in pain. Graham had expected the wound to feel soft, but he was surprised to find the abdomen tight with pressure.

"It's so hard."

"The pain makes the muscles contract," Khazhak said, checking Graham's position. "Good. Like that. Hold it."

"How do you know what to do?" Graham kept his eyes on his hands, as if looking away would undo his work.

"Many of the people I serve do not have a doctor," Khazhak said quickly. "So I received training in first aid and some basic medical care. It is why some people come to me even though they are Muslim."

"He's trying to talk," Graham said as Sivan mouthed words.

"He probably doesn't know what he's saying," Khazhak said. "He's bleeding out. Keep holding it like that. I will be back as soon as I can."

Khazhak was already rising as he said the last words and ran toward the supply hut.

Graham's focus shifted from the blood stain spreading across the snow and found Sivan's eyes waiting for him.

"*Shaaaheeeeen.*"

Sivan drew the sound out, making it nearly unrecognizable as a word while being too intentional to be meaningless.

The blurred syllables coalesced, their sound taking on the shape of letters in Graham's mind he suddenly recognized. *Shaheen* wasn't a sound; it was a name. *Şahin. The hawk.* Graham's head snapped toward the gunman as he recalled the description of the guide Vogel had hired. Huge, hooked nose, like a beak. Squinty eyes. Bushy unibrow. Now it was Graham who wore an expression of recognition.

Sivan shivered beneath him, though Graham didn't know if the tremor was from the cold or the pain. He tried to say the name again but trailed off halfway through.

Graham could feel life draining away and started encouraging Sivan in English, forgetting the man didn't know the language. "No, no, no, no! Hang on, Sivan, you can make it."

"Coming!" Khazhak yelled, running across the ice, first aid bag in hand.

"He stopped responding!" Graham yelled back, desperate and helpless.

After an eternity of seconds, Khazhak slid on his knees to a stop, pushed Graham out of the way, and jammed his hands onto the wound. A moment later, Khazhak pulled one hand away and felt for a pulse.

Graham's eyes moved from Khazhak to Sivan's inanimate face, then to the gunman, who seemed strangely both concerned and defiant.

"He's dead! You murdered him!" Graham heard himself scream, and again hoped the passion of his voice carried his meaning across the language barrier.

"No, Mr. Eliot, he attacked me."

The gunman spat the words fiercely, but it was the sound of Graham's name—and the English response—that stunned both men. Graham felt Khazhak's accusing, confused eyes on him before he turned to explain.

"What is going on? How do you know this man?" Betrayal and anger barbed Khazhak's voice, emphasized with stabbing gestures.

"I don't know him. But I think he's the man who was supposed to be my guide. Şahin."

"None of this was supposed to happen." Şahin stared inscrutably at Sivan, refusing to meet the eyes of the others.

"You shot this man!" Khazhak screamed.

"He came at me," Şahin hissed quickly, emphatic and defensive.

"He went to the other side of the tent to relieve himself," Khazhak shouted, "and instead, he found *you* hiding there with a gun."

"He foolishly tried to take it from me, and it fired. I was not trying to kill him."

"Why did he know your name?" Graham asked. "That is what he was saying when he was dying, was it not? He recognized you. Called you the Hawk."

Şahin shrugged with a hint of pride at being recognized.

Khazhak rose to his feet, ignoring his bloody hands. "Why have a gun at all? What are you even doing here without Graham or someone else to guide?"

"He's planting wood," Graham answered before Şahin could speak. "He wanted me to think I found pieces of Noah's Ark. He's part of yet another fraud."

"Very good, Mr. Eliot. I did not think you would be able to make it to the top of the mountain so quickly. I thought after your plane diverted that I had at least one more day before you could find your way here. By then I would have been far away."

"You found wood in the tunnel?" Khazhak's asked.

Graham nodded. "He was still working on burying it in the ice when we arrived. I was supposed to find it and report back to Vogel that the team had reached the anomaly. Or a fragment, at least."

Khazhak frowned. "Why would this man, Vogel—whom you apparently both work for—hire one person to plant wood in order to fool the other person he had hired? I thought all you were supposed to do is make sure this was a legitimate excavation."

"That's what I was told. I am just as surprised as you. I don't know what's going on or why this charade is—"

"Enough talk." Şahin raised the gun in Khazhak's direction. "It is time for you to leave."

Graham exchanged looks with Khazhak. "You're just going to let us go?"

"No, Mr. Eliot. *You* are staying. Your friend is the one who is leaving."

"I am not leaving without—" Khazhak took a step forward, then stopped as Şahin pointed the gun at his head, stealing his movement and his words.

"You can walk back the way you came," Şahin said with mock patience, "or I will shoot you and throw your body into the Ahora Gorge. The choice is yours to make, but either way you are leaving the mountain now."

"What about Sivan? What about his body?"

"You may come back for the body as soon as you reach the bottom and bring help. Tell them the PKK is responsible. And tell them they have taken a hostage." Şahin tilted his head toward Graham without looking at him.

"What are you going to do to him?"

"I wasn't sure at first. But Mr. Eliot himself inspired a solution. He and Saint Gregory."

FORTY

THE LAST RUNGS OF THE ROPE LADDER DISAPPEARED FROM THE SHAFT with a final yank as Graham gaped desperately from below. The two ventilation ducts had already been dragged up, though Graham doubted they would have been able to bear his weight. Without a way to reach the top, the surface seemed farther away, as if he were looking up through the wrong end of a pair of binoculars.

"Khaaaazhaaaak!"

He held the vowels out, elongating the scream, making the name almost unintelligible. After the third cry, he stopped, reasoning that if Khazhak was still within hearing range, then he understood Graham needed help, and if he was too far away, there was no point in continuing.

Graham imagined Khazhak hiding, watching for a propitious moment to help. But the hope splintered away as he accepted the fact that the icecap was entirely exposed. There was no place to hide. The only exception was the supply shack, and if Khazhak headed there, then his tracks would give him away even if the obvious choice of shelters did not. Almost certainly, Khazhak would have been forced to start down the mountain to make it back to camp by nightfall or risk his own death from exposure.

As if in answer to his thoughts, Şahin appeared in the square opening above him. "Your friend cannot hear you, Mr. Eliot. He has left. He is not even within sight now."

"Please, Şahin, don't do this," Graham said, hoarse with emotion as well as from screaming.

"I am sorry, Mr. Eliot. I told you it was not supposed to be this way."

Graham was taken aback by the sincere, plaintive note in Şahin's words, and appealed to it. "You were supposed to help me."

"No, Mr. Eliot, I was supposed to *guide* you." Hardness instantly returned to Şahin's voice, devoid of emotion, as if aware of Graham's insight. "You will be found next to the wood I was guiding you to. But now, instead of announcing your discovery, you will look like you died before you could tell anyone what you had found. It will make you a martyr."

"So, you are just going to let me freeze? Is that what Vogel hired you to do—to kill me?"

A slight beat passed before Şahin replied. "I have been left no choice."

Again, Graham discerned a crack in the façade that hinted Şahin was reluctantly performing his duty.

"I was at his library, in his home, just a few days ago to photograph an ancient copy of the Bible. Are you telling me that was bait in some elaborate trap he set so he could lure me to the top of Mount Ararat and kill me for no apparent reason?"

"I was told," Şahin said, armored again, "to guide you to this dig site and to arrange it so that you would find enough wood for news to spread that the ark had possibly been found."

Graham squinted in confusion. "You're saying Vogel *wants* the news to get out about what's up here? Why? Why would Vogel want to bring attention to the very thing that has gotten him into so much trouble?"

"I do not know what you mean." Şahin's face contracted into a perplexed frown, as if his own words tasted sour. "He hired me to ensure you found wood, and that news about it would spread. It is not my place to know why Mr. Vogel wants that."

Graham worried that the explanation wouldn't help him out of the immediate danger and decided to try to appeal to the emotional crack he thought he glimpsed. "Why are you doing this to *me*, Şahin? I am not your enemy."

"I am a guide." Şahin shrugged. "We are poor here, and there are not many ways to make money. But Vogel has hired me for more money than I have ever had in my life. If it became known that I was planting wood on the mountain, I would have no more work."

"No one has to know," Graham pleaded. "I don't have to tell anyone about the wood."

"Vogel knows. That is what makes this necessary," Şahin said.

"No, it's not necessary," Graham said desperately. "If he wants word to get out, then I'll tell *everyone* about the wood. I'll hold a press conference."

"Unfortunately, that is not an option now. A man has died. A press conference cannot solve that."

"He died because you shot him."

Şahin flinched at the words. "If you had come tomorrow or later, this would not have happened."

"*You* ambushed *us*," Graham said. "How is that *my* fault?"

"I came up to get fuel," Şahin said defensively. "The tank I was melting water with ran out. When I got out of the shaft, I heard voices. That is why I hid on the other side of the tent. I hoped that you would discover the fraud, and that I could escape while you were distracted by it."

"But then I would have reported that there was a fraud taking place."

Şahin shook his head. "You still do not understand. Discovering the fraud would be just as good as thinking it was real. The intention was to create controversy that brought attention on this excavation. Whether it was announced as a fraud or real made no difference. What made a difference was being caught." Şahin paused. "I truly did not intend to hurt that man. The gun really did fire accidentally as he tried to take it from me."

The show of remorse moved Graham unexpectedly before he recognized it was the opportunity he was waiting for.

"Just tell the authorities that," Graham said. "Leaving me still won't explain his death. Don't commit the crime you say you are innocent of."

"Martyr," Şahin said, his voice cold again. "Not murder. You will be a hero for either exposing a fraud or for discovering the ark. When you are discovered, it will be assumed *you* killed him. Maybe because he was going to take credit himself? Let others speculate. No matter what happens, you will be famous."

"I don't care about fame," Graham hissed indignantly. "I don't want to be your pawn in whatever game this is."

"That is the nature of pawns." Şahin let the calm taunt drift into the shaft. "They do not have a choice." He held Graham in an impenetrable stare for several seconds, then slid away from the opening, disappearing.

"No! Şahin! I'll freeze to death! Please, Şahin!"

FORTY-ONE

Obeying an irrational impulse to call Ross, Graham pulled out his phone before realizing there was no point. Ross couldn't reach him before he died of exposure. No one could, except Khazhak, and he wouldn't be able to return for at least a day. He stared at the dial pad on his screen before realizing he didn't have a number for Khazhak.

His hand dropped to his side in despair, then thought of the only other person close enough to help—Şahin. Despite the fact that he had been unmoved by Graham's argument and was responsible for putting Graham in this prison, there had been a remorse in his voice that Graham clung to. Şahin had portrayed himself as being in business with Vogel, but it sounded more like he was a hired puppet. But did Vogel really know what was going on? Graham couldn't convince himself that he would go so far as to sanction murder.

He tapped Vogel's name—a malevolent shape among his contacts— once more resentfully thankful for the satellite sleeve. A pair of electronic tones pulsed several times before the call was answered. The dispassionate, mechanical female voice of an automated message explained in German that the number was no longer in service.

Graham hung up and pressed the number again, but again the number was rejected. He tried to convince himself it was a technical issue, something with the way the satellite relayed the signal, not wanting to confront the more obvious explanation that Vogel had provided more proof that he was not who he appeared to be.

The phone chirped as it vibrated once. Graham hoped to see Vogel's name displayed on the screen, calling back. Instead, an alert informed him the phone's battery had dropped below twenty percent. He had spent the portable chargers as they navigated the ascent, and put the phone back in his pocket, not wanting to squander the little power he had left.

Thirty-five feet of empty space separated him from the surface. A little more than a first down in football, he told himself, trying to make it seem closer. He scrutinized the ice walls for a solution and focused on the three support rungs projecting from the wall to prevent the ladder from lying flat against it. They'd been spaced equally, about eight feet apart. The lowest rung hung just over ten feet from the bottom—too high for Graham to grab even with his best jump. He rummaged through his backpack, but found nothing inside to improvise a lasso, just his laptop, empty battery chargers, and trail bars.

The striations made by the chainsaws left superficial furrows too slick to hold on to. The only feature in the ice he thought he could exploit was a column of indentations formed by the toes of boots that had kicked into the ice as workers moved up and down the ladder. The cavities were too shallow and rounded to act as steps, but they were enough to give Graham an idea.

He hurried into the tunnel, put the two chisels in his pockets, shoved the wood into his backpack, and grabbed the pick hammer. As he reached for the handle of the stove, he was struck with a different idea. Maybe he didn't need to climb out to avoid exposure—he had a stove that would provide heat until Khazhak returned the next day. He kneeled next to the tank, before realizing he had no way to light the gas. Then he remembered they had encountered Şahin as he was going to get more fuel. The flame was irrelevant with nothing to light. He took the handle again and dragged the empty tank to the bottom of the shaft.

The last boot divot was at a waist-high spot in the wall. He drove the claw of the pick hammer into the bottom edge several times, shocked to find how hard the ice was. A dozen chops later, he brushed away the chips of ice. It wasn't enough to give him a foothold, but it was enough to prove the idea might work. Another salvo of blows finished the step. He pivoted to face the other wall of the corner, and chopped another hold, head-high, creating a second step.

The hammer hung from one of the straps on his backpack as he positioned the stove in the corner below the steps and pressed it into the ice, twisting it back and forth to embed it in a groove to prevent it from slipping out from under him. *Twelve yards*, he told himself, gauging the distance again without acknowledging it was vertical. *That's all I need.*

He subdivided the goal to manage his anxiety, telling himself he only needed to go ten feet to reach the first rung. And if he could do that, then he could reach the other two.

Carefully, he stepped onto the center of the burner, the crampons sliding across the edges of the reflector bowl with a metallic scrape before taking hold. The precarious footing made his leg wobble as he lifted himself into an uneasy balance. Despite the instability caused by the crampons, he needed to leave them on if he was to have any chance of scaling the ice wall. Rationalization distorted his perception, minimizing the eighteen-inch height as a tiny distance to fall when he looked down, while maximizing how much closer it brought him to the first rung.

Slowly, checking his balance, he lifted his left foot and ground his boot into the first hold, the curved front prongs of the crampons biting the ice. It felt secure, but before he put his weight on it, he realized there was no way to push up on the hold without also pushing out from the wall. He needed to steady himself to keep from falling backward.

He leaned into the wall below the rung, cocked the pick hammer over his shoulder and drove it as hard as he could into the ice, extending his arm as he swung. He didn't trust it with his full weight, but it was embedded enough to stabilize himself as he stepped into the second hold.

The handle stayed in place as he pulled himself up and kicked his right foot into the second step. The hammer wiggled slightly, and he wasn't sure how much longer he could trust it. In one motion, he pushed up on the second step and reached for the rung with his right hand. The flat of his palm slapped the wood and he locked his fingers around it. A laugh of relief escaped his throat, choked into the sound of a cough by the effort to maintain balance. He was secure, and that gave him confidence to continue.

He twisted the hammer from the ice and pounded out a divot below the strut. After stowing the hammer, he grabbed the rung with both hands and thrust himself upward, clawing the wall with his crampons. He perched on the bar with the side of his hip, panting, twisting to face the corner as much as possible.

The contortion made him question his plan—or rather, the lack of one—as he began to appreciate how difficult it would be to stand and balance himself on the strut while chopping out the next toeholds. The first segment of the subdivided task had been a success, but the thirteen-foot drop it created was enough to make him question whether he was being clever or stupid. He looked up again and felt caught between dangers: falling or freezing. But there really was no choice; he had to keep moving.

A cloud of breath billowed into the shaft as Graham sighed, then craned his neck to sight the next indentation. He reached for the pick hammer, carefully removed it, and pounded, squinting against the ice chips falling onto his face. He brushed away the debris and satisfied himself that it felt the same as the ones below.

As he readied himself to stand, he realized he had nothing to hold on to for leverage and wouldn't have anything to secure him as he made the next hold. What he needed was an ice screw or a piton to use as a handle. What he had was a pick hammer.

And two chisels.

The memory of the chisels seemed to materialize them in his pocket, and he was suddenly aware of their weight. Cautiously, he hooked the pick hammer on the rung, then reached into his pocket and pulled out one of the chisels. The six-inch-long steel spike felt like an answered prayer. His left hand still clasped the rung, and he didn't want to let go to hold the chisel in place to hammer. The spike had to be driven into the ice by hand, embedding it deep enough to hammer.

He wound his arm back and struck the ice above him as hard as he could, to the right of the hold he just cut. Splinters of ice spat from the impact, but the tip glanced off the surface. Graham slammed the spike into the same spot again, this time without bouncing back. He let go slowly, testing to see if it drooped under its own weight, but felt nothing give when he released it. After feeling for the pick hammer, he tapped the chisel several times, strengthening the grip. When it felt secure, he hammered it hard, watching the steel slip into the ice in short increments. He pounded until about half the chisel remained visible, then put the pick hammer away.

The new handle felt solid enough in his right hand for his left to release the rung, and he began to pull himself to a stand. He could feel the crampons slip slightly across the wood as he rose, but he kept moving, hoping he could stand before he lost his footing. As he extended his legs, his shoulders rose above the chisel, and he switched grips to hold it like a crutch. He used the hammer to cut the next foot hold, then realized he needed another chisel to steady himself in the upper hold as he reached for the next rung.

Balancing the hammer on the wrist holding the first chisel, he reached into his pocket for the other chisel. But as he pulled it out, the spike caught the edge of the pocket and flipped out of his hand. Graham helplessly watched it turn in the air as it fell, shrinking with distance before clattering onto the ice floor. Options played in his mind as he stared at what he didn't want to see. He still had one chisel. Now that he had two toeholds cut, maybe he could pull the spike out and reuse it.

After crouching back down on the rung, he sank the pick hammer into the ice to hold while he pulled the chisel out with his other hand. He wrenched the spike free in several jerks, then stood, not trusting himself to balance in a crouch for longer than he had to.

As he held the handle of the pick hammer with his left hand, he used his right to drive the chisel into the ice next to his head. The spike bounced off the ice, reflecting his own force against him, pushing him away from the wall, causing his crampons to shoot in opposite directions as he fell backward. He had the presence of mind to grab for the rung, but it was already out of reach. The sickening butterflies of a free-fall rippled through him, emanating waves of panic. Before he could obey his instinct to twist forward, he violently collided with a sudden black.

FORTY-TWO

REMOTE, DISEMBODIED VOICES TEXTURED THE AIR WITH UNRELATED syllables, as if words had shattered into meaningless sound. Graham thought they seemed to be drifting toward him, each a little louder than the last, slowly gaining definition if not comprehensibility. As the fragments of sound grew closer, pairs began to join, attaching to other shards, assembling itself into language. The process of understanding had the sensation of watching a slow-motion film played backward of a water drop or ceramic cup hitting a hard surface, showing the scattered particles retract from all directions, collecting itself into a recognizable shape. Except the language that gathered was foreign to him, as if the blackness in his eyes obscured the words somehow.

His discernment sharpened and he discerned three timbres—threads that unraveled the opaque conversation into three different voices. He tried to focus on each one, but the effort brought a dull pain of pressure that radiated from the back of his skull.

It took all his effort to open his eyes, then several moments to make sense of what he was seeing. Three heads hung over the edge of the shaft, debating something he couldn't understand. As he made a move to try to sit up, pain shot through his head, made worse as the men started in surprise. The rope ladder fell into the shaft, clattering onto the ice floor, followed by two of the men.

The surreal quality of the scene made Graham wonder if he were dreaming. He had the vague sensation of being moved, and the next image he fixed on was the indistinct translucent panel roof of the storage shed hovering above him, gray from the lack of sunlight.

He tried to lift his head, but it dropped back immediately as if his renewed consciousness weighed too much for his head. The motion was enough to draw the attention of one of the men.

"*Emerîkî hişyar dike.*"

Graham heard the voice without apprehension, unaware that it was talking about him. But he was present enough to wonder how much of his lack of understanding had to do with the fog in his mind. He tried to lift his head again, this time getting far enough to see the men filling backpacks with items from the Pelican cases. As he propped himself up on his elbows, all three men turn to look at him.

"*Ew ê derê nabe.*"

This time he grasped that the words were about him, though they were addressed to each other. Strangely, they turned back to their work, unconcerned, giving Graham the sense that they didn't consider him a threat.

One of the men stiffened in alert and raised his head in the direction of the shaft, despite staring into the wall. His hand snapped up, motioning for silence as if snatching all the other sound out of the air.

They froze in a kind of tableau vivant of bedraggled mountaineers. Then he heard it. Graham could tell from the exchange of looks that they all heard it.

A very faint, muffled voice sounded, punctuated by the pop of a gunshot.

The crack broke the grip of the somnolent haze in Graham's head, making him instantly awake.

Two more shots sounded as the three men abandoned their backpacks and grabbed their rifles. The one who had called for silence looked carefully outside, then motioned the others to follow as he ran through the door.

Graham sat up, wondering if it was safer to try to escape, follow, or stay. The answer was made for him as vertigo spun the room around. Another voice called out, dampened by snow, and followed by silence. After an eternity of listening, a hoarse, authoritative voice spat orders into the menacing quiet. Another minute passed before the stillness was punctured by angry shouts.

The pulse of footsteps crossing the snow grew louder until a figure burst into the tent. Graham stared in confusion, unsure whether he was being rescued or recaptured as he locked eyes with Şahin.

FORTY-THREE

"WE MUST GO! QUICKLY!"

"I'm not going anywhere with you," Graham said, disoriented by the reappearance of Şahin and his offer of help. "You left me here to die!"

"And now I am saving you so you do *not* die," Şahin said, emphatically.

"I'm not doing anything until you tell me what's going on. Who were those men?" Graham pointed in the direction of the shaft, then poked at Şahin. "And why are you still here?"

"They are PKK," Şahin said, hoarse with urgency. "Kurdish terrorists."

"Okay, but why are they here?"

"I followed your guide—"

"He wasn't a guide," Graham cut across him harshly. "He was a missionary."

A shadow of regret darkened Şahin's face before he blinked it away. "I did not harm him, but I had to make sure he left the mountain without trying to rescue you. I fired two shots near him to warn him to keep moving. The sound must have been heard by the PKK fighters hiding on the mountain. I saw them come up the path from Lake Kop. I hid behind a boulder as they went across the snow cap. Then I realized that when they found you, they would take you hostage. Nothing would bring them more publicity than an American hostage. I could not let that happen."

"You suddenly grew a conscience."

Şahin continued, unfazed and impatient. "If you were taken hostage, it would not bring any attention to the dig site. That was the whole point. If you were captured, Vogel would not pay me. No one would get what they wanted. Not you, not me, not Vogel. And the PKK is not good for business. If they kidnap climbers, no one will come to climb. There will be no need for guides."

"Well, I'd hate for my kidnapping to get in the way of your fraud," Graham said in mock apology. "Not to mention my murder."

"I told you, I am not a murderer." Again, Graham saw the memory sting Şahin and heard a note of sorrow in his voice. "That man, that guide—it was an accident. And I trusted that you would find a way to escape."

Graham twisted Şahin's logic back at him. "Actually, if it wasn't for the PKK I would have died at the bottom of the shaft. I should *thank* them, not run from them. *You* are the one who put me in the place they rescued me from."

Anger flashed in Şahin's eyes. "The PKK are *not* your friends. You are a tool, nothing more."

"And how is that any different from the way you treated me?"

"The difference is that I am here to save you now. But if you want saving, we must leave immediately. Otherwise, you will remain a hostage. Or worse."

The fierce ultimatum left Graham conflicted, having to choose between two enemies. He still wasn't sure how much—if any—he should trust a mercurial man who tried to kill him only hours earlier. On the other hand, he had a better chance fighting off or escaping a single guide than three armed soldiers.

Graham fixed his eyes on Şahin's, not trying to hide his suspicion. "Okay. Let's go. But let me make this clear: I don't trust you one bit. But I trust them even less."

"I understand," Şahin said. "Follow me."

The sun reflected off the snow, into Graham's face, making him squint despite his sunglasses. During his recovery from the fall, he had lost track of time. Snippets of memories of the soldiers prodding him or shaking him started to make sense. If they had intended to hurt or intimidate him, they would have done much worse. But given his injury—he assumed he had a concussion—they had probably been trying to keep him awake. The low sun in the sky wasn't setting, it was rising. The entire night was lost in a daze. The PKK may have taken him hostage, but they really had saved his life.

"Wait a second," Graham said, "I thought you said the PKK was camped near here. How are we going to get past them?"

"We're descending the other side of the mountain. The southern route is how I came up. It was how I would have brought you. Longer, but easier. But we must leave now."

Faint, panicked calls came from the direction of the domed tent a hundred yards away.

"Is that them? In the shaft?"

"Keep moving," Şahin said without looking back.

"I can't strand them in the same place they rescued me from." Graham halted in protest, again conflicted. "I'm not going to let them die."

"They have the ladder," Şahin said over his shoulder, unconcerned. "I threw it down. Between the three of them, they will be able to figure out a way for one of them to reach the top and help the others out. I am not killing them. I am distracting them."

Graham stayed silent as he followed Şahin through the fresh powder, stepping in the same tracks as much as he could. Halfway across the snow cap, they veered to the left, splitting off the route Graham had ascended. The vast view of the southern side opened before him. Unlike the flat plain on the north, the southern plain was broken by foothills, like a geological retinue attending the court of the majestic Ararat.

Şahin picked his way to a ridge dividing the snow, a passage of earth that channeled them from the peak as it ran along the side of a canyon. Graham was grateful to be rid of the crampons, but his knees quickly reminded him that hiking down a mountain was harder than hiking up. Despite Şahin's assurance they were taking the easier route, the slope tilted them at forty-five degrees—sometimes more—making the mountain seem like it fell away beneath them.

With the snow and soldiers behind them, Graham thought it was safe to continue the conversation. "So, how did you trap the PKK in the shaft?"

"When I saw the soldiers, I followed them, careful to stay far back since I knew where they were going. It was almost sunset when they reached the camp. They looked inside the shed with the equipment, then went to the tent with the shaft."

He paused, and Graham assumed he was concentrating on choosing the best path through the large, loose stones. But when he continued the narrative, Graham understood it had been a memory that Şahin had been trying to navigate.

"When they found the body outside the tent, they readied their weapons as they looked around. I had to hide behind the shed so they wouldn't see me. When they went into the tent, they were in there for a long time—much longer than I thought it would take to find you and get you out. When they finally came out, they were carrying you. One had your ankles, the other two each had an arm. I thought you were dead."

A small boulder fell away under Şahin's footing, causing him to scramble to remain upright as the rock tumbled down the slope. He steadied himself before continuing.

"They put you in the storage shed, and I could hear them talking to you every once in a while. That's how I knew you were alive. By then the sun had set. I found a bivouac for my tent out of view from the door of the shed, and then thought about what to do. All I had was a pistol. How could I overpower three soldiers armed with machine guns?"

"Exactly what I was wondering," Graham said.

"I had to find a way to get them out of the tent and away from you. I thought that since they came because of gunfire that I could use it again to create a distraction. But I could not just shoot into the air. They would know where I was. I thought about this while I was eating, and I found the answer in the flame from the camping stove.

"I went to the shaft as the sun rose and set up the stove on the far side of the tent where it couldn't be seen. I wrapped three bullets in pieces of foil from my meal last night and put them on a small hotplate on the burner. I lighted the propane, then crawled to the side of the tent and laid flat, like when your guide discovered me. I found the end of the exhaust duct and yelled into it, calling for help. It sounded as if the shout came from the bottom of the shaft. I yelled twice before the first bullet popped."

"You could've shot yourself," Graham said.

"There was no danger," Şahin said nonchalantly. "The bullets do not go anywhere. Without a gun, nothing really happens but the noise. A sound effect. Like in movies."

"What happened when the soldiers heard it?"

Şahin smiled proudly as he stole a look back at Graham. "I yelled once more while they were coming to the tent. It worked just as I planned. They really thought someone was down there. One of the men climbed to the bottom. I crawled to the opening and could see the other two at the top of the shaft looking in. They had set their rifles on the ground. I pulled my pistol out and said I would shoot them if they moved. I ordered them into the shaft, and as the second one started climbing down, I crawled to where the ladder was tied, and I cut the rope. The man started yelling when the first rope cut through, and I could see it jerk and swing. He made it to the bottom before I could cut the second. I threw the ladder into the shaft and ran back for you."

A bright orange tent bubbled from the rocky terrain below.

"Do you know them?" Graham asked.

"That is mine," Şahin said, patting his chest proprietorially. "My high camp."

FORTY-FOUR

GRAHAM HELPED ŞAHIN BREAK CAMP, PACKING THE TENT AND OTHER gear onto the small horse that had remained tethered overnight. The heat of the day rose surprisingly fast, and his skin turned clammy with sweat beneath his layers as they worked. The reflection of the sun off the snow on the peak had already warmed him enough to shed his coat when they had stopped to remove their crampons. By the time they were finished, it was late morning, leaving most of the day ahead of them to descend the mountain.

"Base camp is two miles away." Şahin nodded downhill as he finished securing the equipment to the horse. "It is where many of the guides take hikers to start up the mountain. That is about as high as the trucks can go. When we get there, we can warn the guides the PKK is nearby. We can ride with them back to Doğubayazıt."

The plan made Graham reach for his phone before remembering it was almost dead. Even if it still had enough juice to power it on, the effort of booting would probably leave only a few minutes of screen time. Despite having used all the portable chargers, he still had a way to charge the phone. His laptop had remained unused since leaving Aralik, and hopefully the cold hadn't frozen the battery. He rummaged through a pocket in his backpack for a cable, then connected the phone to the computer. The charging icon appeared, and he slipped the phone into the pack, hoping it would be fully powered by the time they reached the base camp.

Şahin guided the horse down the trail, followed by Graham. The slope continued to make Graham feel like Ararat was pushing him off the mountain, ushering him away as fast as it could. Twenty miles away, Doğubayazıt looked like a blemish of civilization on the landscape, almost close enough to touch. He could feel gravity lie to his body, tempting it to run down the mountain, but his knees reminded him of the truth. Already he could feel soreness in his legs, the curse of the previous two days' work.

After they had hiked almost a mile, the pitch began to ease, quickening their pace. An hour later, a short, boxy bus parked at a turnaround in the dirt road came into view.

"Are there really that many people trying to climb Mount Ararat?" Graham asked. "I thought it was closed. Right now, anyway."

"They are day-hikers," Şahin said, waving a hand dismissively. "Tourists. They are not on expeditions seriously looking for the ark."

From a distance, the gaudy paint job of the bus made it stand out from its surroundings like a lost ice cream truck. But as he grew nearer, Graham decided it looked more like a committee hadn't been able to agree on how it should look, resulting in a compromise where each person was given a different section to decorate. *Ararat Turizm* was stenciled in sun-faded black above a phone number. And an amateurish mural of the mountain was displayed on the back. The doors to the coach were at the rear of the bus, and instead of rows, benches lined the sides of the compartment, padded with cushions. The driver lay across one side of the coach and sat up as Graham peered into the window, then he exited the bus to greet them.

Between his head injury and his altitude sickness, Graham could feel a scowl contract his face and worked to recompose it into a friendly expression. The self-conscious effort felt awkward, and he was sure it looked the same. He listened as Şahin explained in Turkish that they had climbed the mountain in defiance of the ban before running into the PKK. Another man had been with them, but the soldiers shot him before they could escape.

The driver divided sympathetic looks between them and agreed to take them back when the hikers returned. He followed the promise by opening a cooler and handing them each a bottle of water.

Şahin took a pull that left the bottle half empty, then used it to point at the bus. "The group should be back in an hour or so. It is maybe thirty kilometers to Doğubayazıt. The bus will take us to your hotel. It is on the way back."

Graham had almost forgotten about the original itinerary. "Agri Expeditions? I'm sure they canceled the reservation."

"No. You still have a room. Vogel paid for the whole week, hoping he could find a way to get you here. You can use it to decide what to do next."

"I heard what you told the driver," Graham said, with a hard look. "How do you know I won't report what really happened?"

"What I did was an accident," Şahin whispered harshly. "What the PKK would have done to you would be much worse. They would have done it intentionally, and there is a good chance they would have killed you just for the attention. Now, *they* will get the blame for your guide's death. No one will believe they did not do it. I had no murder in my heart. But they *did*. It is only right for them to be blamed."

"I disagree," Graham said. "And even though you saved me from them, you did leave *me* there. Your intentions are not exactly blameless."

Şahin leaned toward Graham, pointing a finger in warning. "You are in this country without the proper papers, are you not? I am sure Vogel can use the same connections that were used to bring you here to make sure you cannot leave. Do you really want to give him a reason to do that?"

The threat lingered in the air as Graham looked back up the mountain to avoid Şahin's glare. When Şahin spoke again, his voice was conversational, carrying no remnant of the argument.

"They take the group of hikers to the southwest side, toward the Bird's Eye." He pointed to the far-left side of the slope.

"What's the Bird's Eye?" Graham asked flatly.

"An ice cave." Şahin pointed with more accuracy to a spot halfway up the part of the mountain, above the foothill before them. "The rock some people have thought was the ark is on the other side of it."

The images he had studied so much the last few days cycled through Graham's mind, and he decided the site must be the anomaly seen in the famous U2 spy plane photographs from the 1940s.

He reached for his phone to take a few pictures, then remembered it was charging in his backpack. After it powered on, he saw it had reached sixty percent over two hours—less than he expected, but enough to get him to the hotel. As he started taking pictures, a series of electronic chimes notified him there were text messages and emails waiting to be read. All were from Alexander, each only a few words long.

Call me.

Hey, gimme a call.

It's important.

Where r u? Important.

Alarm began to vibrate in his chest even before he reached the final message. But the last one was more confounding than anything else, making him feel like Alice falling down the rabbit hole.

You are not on Ararat.

FORTY-FIVE

Graham plugged in his laptop, pressed the power button, and felt a wave of comfort at the familiar, calming startup sound as the bitten apple appeared. The sound always recalled the final chord of "A Day in the Life" by The Beatles, and he smiled as he thought how the last twenty-four hours had been anything but a typical day in his life. The aluminum casing of the MacBook Pro had a slight crease between the trackpad and the left corner, but otherwise showed no sign of damage after the fall into the shaft. He filled all four ports with portable chargers, then plugged his phone into a separate outlet.

It had taken all of his willpower not to call or even text Alexander immediately. But he could tell that Şahin was watching him and sensed something had changed as Graham checked his messages. Graham wondered how much had been revealed in his expression as he read the texts, then turned the phone off, pretending it had died again before Şahin could glimpse the screen.

He got the feeling Şahin didn't believe him, a suspicion corroborated by Şahin's lingering presence while Graham checked in to Agri Expeditions, then walked with him to the room. After Şahin promised to be on call to help with anything he needed, Graham closed the door and locked it without inviting him in. He stood listening, waiting for Şahin to leave, and was disturbed that it took several moments before there was any movement in the hall.

But after he was sure Şahin was gone, he found he didn't trust the silence. Graham needed to talk to Alexander without being overheard. And he needed to call Isaac Ross. Despite all that had taken place on the mountain, the hotel room felt anything but safe. It had been arranged by Vogel, after all, and Vogel had sent him here to be a pawn in a fraud. Not only that, but he was being watched by Şahin, the man who had stranded him at the top of the mountain to be martyred for an illusion. And both men knew exactly where he was. Graham was still their pawn. He pictured Şahin with his ear to the wall in the next room, waiting for him to fall asleep or start a shower in order to search or steal his computer and phone.

Graham chastised himself for being paranoid, then admitted it might be justified given that nothing made any sense. Why would Vogel risk delegitimizing a serious and important archaeological excavation by planting wood? Why did Vogel want to focus attention on the site, but not if it distracted from the fraud? Most collectors and scholars would want to avoid the charge of fraud, but he seemed to be courting it. And what was he to make of Alexander's bizarre warning that Ararat was not at Ararat at all? He needed to talk to people he could trust. And he needed to leave here as soon as possible. But where to go?

Ross would know—Doğubayazıt was home base for his expeditions.

Graham picked up the phone, then decided to text to keep from being overheard, and to ask for a recommendation without wasting time with a report on the last two days.

Where do you stay in Doğubayazıt? Need a place.

An ellipsis icon appeared almost instantly, indicating a response was being typed.

Agri Expeditions. Did you reach the peak?

Graham texted back. *I am at the Agri. Need a different place. Yes, I made it. Can't talk now.*

Sarayı Hotel. Hope all is well…

Graham typed "*Thx,*" then closed the Messages app to end the conversation for now. He opened Google Maps and found Agri Expeditions two miles southeast of town—too far to walk after the descent. He entered *Sarayı Hotel* in the search field and watched the map re-orient itself to place it in the center of the screen, which was also the center of the city. The information tab displayed thumbnail images of a clean, western-style hotel. And the name—*Sarayı*, meaning *palace*—

gave him an idea for how to get there in a way that might confuse Şahin in case he was still keeping an eye on Graham for Vogel.

Graham stowed his computer in the backpack and rallied the energy to move, groaning as he stood up. He didn't know if there was a back exit, and decided not to waste time looking for it, opting instead to walk quickly out the front of the hotel. He crossed the parking lot to a path leading up the hill behind Agri Expeditions. The path guided him along the base of a stone wall before depositing him into another parking lot, this one at the entrance to an actual palace.

The Ishak Pasha Palace was begun in the seventeenth century by the bey of Doğubayazıt Province and took ninety-nine years to build. As one of the few remaining Ottoman castles, it was culturally important to the Turks and had become a popular tourist attraction, though a distant second to Ararat. Normally, Graham would have wanted to walk through the 366-room complex, especially to see the Islamic decorations of geometric patterns intermingled with calligraphy featuring verses from the Qur'an.

Instead, he found what he wanted on the outside of the palace entrance. Tour buses. Two long, white coaches and three minibuses sat among a dozen cars. Graham decided to wait for a group to leave and try to get a ride into town with them.

As he waited, he scanned the area, taking in what looked almost like a movie set. The palace had once stood in the center of Bayazıt, a city that had been built on the hills and cliffs on three sides of the palace. Ruins and remains of the old city were still visible, emerging from the bluffs and boulders, making it look as if the mountain was in the process of trying to transform itself into different structures. Graham focused on the cliffs behind the palace at what looked like the remains of another castle, with walls and towers built among jagged formations of rock. He was so absorbed by the scene that it took him a moment to register a group of tourists starting to reassemble at one of the buses.

Graham found the driver and happily discovered the man was more than willing to take him into town for a modest baksheesh. He collapsed in a seat toward the front and had to remind himself several times not to close his eyes. A pair of British accents emerged from the murmur of visitors comparing notes, and Graham found the owners of the voices across from him, a kindly looking elderly couple.

"I am so glad we made the trip," the wife said, giving her husband's knee a satisfied pat. "When would we ever again have the opportunity to see Mount Ararat?"

"Quite the adventure," the husband chuckled. "And this palace is rather impressive, too. Certainly worth the trip up from Van."

Graham opened his phone's map app and refreshed himself on where Van was. "Excuse me. I don't mean to be rude, but I couldn't help overhearing. Are you staying in Van?"

"Yes." The husband said it more as a question, wondering what the point was.

"Does this bus go there?"

The wife smiled, relieved he seemed to be more interested in the bus than in them. "No, it's a local. It goes back into the city. To reach Van, you must take a *dolmuş*."

Graham tried to repeat the foreign word back. "A *dollmoosh*?"

"It's what they call the shuttle that runs between cities," the husband explained.

"This bus goes to the tourist office by the dolmuş stop," the wife added. "If you are trying to go to Van, you can get one there. Cost you twenty lira."

Graham converted the amount in his head and was certain she had misspoken. Twenty lira was only $3.50—not quite the fare he expected for a hundred-mile trip.

"We will show you," she added, patting her husband's knee again.

FORTY-SIX

A WEEK EARLIER, GRAHAM HAD STARED INTO THE OPULENT COFFERED ceiling of Vogel's private library, allegorizing it as a web collecting knowledge. Now he stared into a web of crisscrossing electrical lines draping from the tops of street lamps, holding small, colorful flags like prayer flags at a Buddhist shrine. Instead of walls of books, tired concrete apartment blocks formed the walls of a drab, utilitarian canyon. Rather than the elegant curves of an Eames chair, he sat on a dirty stone wall next to an empty lot furnished with rusting equipment and construction debris. The junction of cobblestone streets at the center of Doğubayazıt where the bus let him off converged to form a misshapen asterisk—a symbol Graham thought qualified his situation appropriately.

He had gained information but felt like he knew less. He had more experience but had no clue what to do. He had ascended one side of Ararat in good faith, but descended the other side cynical, suspicious, disillusioned, and impotent.

Although he had eluded Şahin and Vogel, Graham did not feel safer or freer. The plan to switch hotels lost its attraction on the ride into town as he realized Şahin could still find him easily if he really was trying to keep an eye on him. Given that there weren't many hotels in Doğubayazıt where a westerner could stay without being completely conspicuous, the shell game wouldn't be very difficult to solve.

Graham guessed Şahin assumed he would try to stick with the original itinerary and find his way to Iğdir to fly home as quickly as possible. It was the obvious answer, except Graham didn't know how he could explain his passport being stamped for Armenia but not Turkey. And that meant he needed to get back to Aralik, on the other side of the mountain, then retrace the route to the crossing point near Khor Virap—a route he had taken only once, in the dark, without noting any landmarks to guide him. He also remembered Khazhak saying how the people there were sympathetic to the PKK, which meant going there alone would be like volunteering to be taken hostage. Van was the next closest city with an airport, but it didn't solve his passport problem.

He opened Google Maps on his phone and zoomed out, hoping to find some inspiration for what to do next. The satellite perspective of Doğubayazıt spidered like a chip in a windshield. A spew of air brakes pulled Graham's attention to a tour bus from the castle, idling half a block away outside a small, tin-roofed shed that served as the tourism office. The sight reminded him of the dolmuş the couple from the bus had pointed out. He looked the opposite direction and saw it still parked at the curb, waiting for more passengers before returning to Van.

The eclectic loop of Peter Gabriel's "Digging in the Dirt" brought his phone to life, and Isaac Ross's name appeared on the screen.

"Graham, are you okay?" Ross asked before Graham could speak.

"Isaac. Yes. Well, not really. Something strange is going on and I can't figure out what it is."

"Tell me what happened," Ross said urgently.

"I don't have much time. I'm about to…" Graham started the sentence without knowing how it would end and abandoned it halfway through. The sudden silence made him feel exposed, as if Şahin were somehow watching him.

"About to *what*? What's happening?"

Graham's gaze flitted mistrustfully at his surroundings as he spoke. "I can't say."

"You don't sound right, Graham. Is there anything I can do for you?"

"I made it to the dig. The shed and the excavation tent were still standing."

"That's good to—"

"But someone was already there," Graham cut across him.

"What?" Ross left the word hanging, indignant and confused.

"Someone was planting wood in the shaft," Graham said. "He was trying to freeze it into the ice so it would be discovered later."

"You are kidding me. Tell me that's a joke."

Graham knew Ross's anger wasn't directed at him. "I wish it were. But I got there before he was finished. One of my guides found the guy hiding behind the tent. The guide tried to confront him, but the man had a gun. Somehow they started wrestling for it, and it went off." Graham paused, rehearsing the words before he said them softly. "My guide died."

Ross answered with his own silence before finding his voice. "What did you do?"

"I couldn't do anything," Graham said. "He had the gun. And then he tried to kill me, too."

"He shot you?"

"Thankfully, no. But he put me in the shaft and pulled up the ladder."

"Why would he do that?"

"Turns out the guy planting the wood, Şahin, works for Vogel." Graham paused to let the news register.

"Vogel," Ross whispered. "You're saying Vogel told him to kill you?"

The shock sounded sincere enough for Graham to trust him with more of the story. "Vogel was the one who hired Şahin as my guide to take me up the mountain. Except I was diverted to Armenia. I didn't know it mattered, of course, so I went without him up the north side instead of from Doğubayazıt. Şahin told me Vogel wanted me to find the wood so that the site would become big news."

"Why would he do that?"

"That's what I'm trying to figure out."

"But you got out," Ross said. "You escaped."

"Not exactly. I tried to climb out and got about fifteen feet before I fell into the shaft and knocked myself out. When I awoke, I was in the equipment shed. Some PKK soldiers had fished me out of the hole. I think they were going to make me a hostage."

"What? Did they say that?" Ross asked. "Seems like they'd do far more for their cause if they got publicity for saving an American rather than capturing one."

Graham thought through the sequence of events. "Şahin rescued me from them. He told me that being kidnapped by the PKK was the wrong kind of publicity. That Vogel wouldn't want it."

"You believed the guy who tried to kill you over the guys who tried to save you?" Graham suddenly felt foolish at the obvious question, and was glad Ross kept talking. "I don't understand why Vogel would want publicity about the site at all at this point."

"I don't either," Graham said. "I get why he'd want publicity for helping find Noah's Ark, but why would he use me to try to pull off a hoax? He had to have known the find would be exposed when the wood was tested."

"It almost sounds like what he really wanted was some kind of distraction," Ross said.

"That's it!" Graham stood at the realization. "That's what it has to be."

"What are you talking about?"

"Do you know about his trouble with the Russians?"

"I heard they accused him of hiring out his satellite to spy on them," Ross said, sounding like he was trying to connect Graham's dots. "And you think the charge might be true?"

"Think about it," Graham said. "Announcing that a satellite had been able to detect Noah's Ark and guide archaeologists to the site would not only be a distraction, but a justification. The spy charge would make the Russians look petty, like they were trying to spoil the find just because it was in their own backyard."

"Hmm," Ross noised. "You might be right. I think we may have been played."

"And what if the Russians were right," Graham continued. "What if he was hiring out the satellite to some intelligence agency. Maybe Vogel found out about your expedition and used its legitimacy as cover to hide what he did. It was an opportunity to search for the ark, yes.

But it was also a business opportunity, a way to make a lot of money very quietly. And I became the pawn in the contingency plan."

Ross let out a contemptuous huff. "Any ideas for what to do now?"

"I think I might. But for now, don't say anything. Gotta go."

Graham hung up as Ross started to protest, then ignored the inevitable callback as he texted Alexander, knowing he would answer a text more quickly than the phone.

Where is Ararat?

He hit *send*, then ironically fixed his eyes on the mountain he—and much of the rest of the world—had been calling Ararat. The top half of the mountain had turned red in the alpenglow as the sun sank below the horizon. But to Graham, it looked like an alarm that had been tripped by the realization of Vogel's deception. When he looked back at his phone, an ellipsis icon turned into a response.

Cudi Dagh.

He sounded it out phonetically in Turkish—*Judi Dog*—as he copied the name, pasted it into the search bar in Google Maps, then hit *return*. The map scrolled south and dropped a pin as it stopped. He zoomed out to see the context. Cudi Dagh lay two hundred miles south, near the borders with Syria and Iraq. And in between was Lake Van.

The location surprised him, then quickly crystalized into an idea, injecting him with enough energy to jog the few yards to where the dolmuş driver was leaning against the wall, smoking.

"When do you leave for Van?"

The words were like a spell that cast a hopeful look on the man's face. "When I have enough passengers."

"How many more do you need."

The driver broke into an infectious smile. "Just one. You, my friend."

FORTY-SEVEN

Graham claimed the last pair of empty seats, sinking into the one by the window, and putting his backpack in the other to discourage company. An idea for how to deal with Vogel left him in a disorienting blend of exhaustion and adrenaline that made him restless.

The more he thought about it, the more convinced he became that Vogel had to be guilty of espionage in some way, just as the Russians had charged. That was the only thing that made sense. And his collection of biblical manuscripts and artifacts made the search for Noah's Ark on Mount Ararat a perfect alibi. He could claim the Russians misinterpreted the satellite activity. And publicizing the dig site would not only corroborate his cover-story, it would bring worldwide attention to the site of an object so fascinating that the Russian charge would be overshadowed, especially if something was actually found.

When the Russians froze Vogel's assets, Vogel needed to act or risk losing his business. Ross wasn't ready to publish anything definitive because the dig was not complete. That meant Vogel needed something to be found faster than Ross could produce a report. Otherwise, Vogel not only risked his liberty, but his fortune. He must have been trying to find a solution to the problem when Graham asked permission to photograph his manuscripts while in Münster.

He replayed the conversation he'd had in Münich a week earlier, the jostling dolmuş providing a physical counterpoint to Vogel's smooth assurances. But it wasn't the words themselves he heard now, but the unspoken text, the veiled meaning supporting his theory. If Graham visited the site and found wood, then Vogel could leak the discovery to the press, forcing Ross to reveal his work before he wanted, but bringing attention to it as the first truly legitimate archaeological dig on the mountain.

And if the wood Graham found was exposed as being planted because it was too young and from a different region, then it would still warrant publicity as an elaborate fraud. The NAMI fraud had proven that. But if the PKK took hostages from the site, the incident would overshadow the work. And they had attacked ark hunters before.

Graham felt used, betrayed, angry, and guilty over Sivan's death. But mostly he felt helpless. The emotions pressed down on him, pushing into depression, tempting him to be passive, to just surrender.

He looked again at Alexander's reply. *Cudi Dagh.* The name was like a spell that revealed the weakness in Vogel's scheme, arming Graham. Vogel's plan to keep his freedom, fortune, and power depended entirely on the premise that Mount Ararat was the mountain where the ark landed. But if it were announced that the *real* Mount Ararat had been found—a different Ararat, more likely to be the one referred to in the Bible—then it would undermine Vogel's protection. The dig site on the peak would be irrelevant, leaving nothing to prevent the Russians from pursuing charges against him. But for that to happen, there had to be some kind of evidence to make the case for Cudi Dagh. It didn't need to be conclusive proof—it didn't even need to be true, ultimately—but there did need to be reasons for it to be taken seriously long enough for Vogel to be exposed.

But what was it about Cudi Dagh that made Alexander think it was the real Ararat? How could Ararat *not* be Ararat, while a mountain *not* called Ararat actually *be* Ararat? On its face it sounded too novel to be credible. And yet, he recognized the scholar in Alexander, he trusted him. Now he needed to know what Alexander had discovered.

He wanted to call him, but not on the dolmuş. Graham hated being overheard on the phone and hated listening to others. It was a major pet peeve. Plus, some of the passengers were trying to sleep.

The sleepers reminded him he needed a place to stay in Van. He pulled out his phone, remembered the couple said they were staying downtown at the Hotel Royal, then booked a room. Not only did it look clean, but it was near the dolmuş stop.

As he confirmed the reservation, he received a text from Alexander. There was no content in the message other than a link to a Google Drive folder called *Cudi Dagh*. Graham clicked it and opened a directory of about two dozen images and a number of PDFs. His eyes were too tired to try to read the documents on the small screen, and he wanted to see the images as large as possible, so he activated the personal hotspot on his phone, pulled his MacBook Pro out of the backpack, and connected to the internet.

He changed the view from List to Grid, making a lightbox of thumbnails in order to quickly refer back to an image he found interesting. The majority of the pictures were black and white, and the ones in color were grouped together at the bottom of the grid. Graham assumed the arrangement indicated they were in chronological order, with the most recent at the end.

He clicked on the top left thumbnail and opened a scene showing a hexagonal structure on the top of a mountain with a range of mountains in the background. The building was in ruins, and yet the condition of its decaying walls was too good to be from the time of Noah. Sticks had been laid haphazardly across the top of the walls in a poor attempt to add a rude roof, but there were too few to provide protection. Its effect was of a more recent layer of ruin collapsed on top of an older one—like the remnant of a giant nest.

The second image showed two men and a boy—locals, judging from their dress—striking stiff, oddly formal poses on a pile of rocks with the structure behind them. Like the first picture, the uneven exposure and the slightly soft quality of the photograph gave the impression that they had been taken a hundred years earlier.

The third picture showed the same boy standing next to an inscription carved into a rock face. A smooth, rectangular hollow about six inches deep had been carved into the uneven surface to accommodate the inscription. Next to the text, the figure of an Assyrian king filled the entire right side of the frame, making it look like it was standing inside a stone doorway. It was followed by another image that showed a different relief, this one with an Assyrian figure facing the opposite direction, standing in the center of a similar hollow.

Graham cycled to the next shot, showing the ragged top of a stone wall in the foreground, and a second ruined building in the background. The image was grainier than the previous ones, and there was a soft, dream-like quality as if the lens had been draped with cheesecloth to diffuse the image.

Another image showed three men looking intently at a spot on the snow-covered ground on a mountain peak. Two of the men looked like locals, one standing while the other kneeled down, digging into the ground with a trowel. Behind the digger, a European man bent over his shoulder, holding something in his hand as if examining something they had uncovered. The crisp details of the photograph suggested that it was more recent than the previous pictures. A second image showed the same two locals kneeling over a clearing in the snow with a shovel and a pick.

The final black and white image documented what looked like about fifty people in local garb standing on top of the ruins, revealing a larger scale to the structure than Graham had attributed to it in the other photos.

He opened the first color image, a shot of the hexagonal ruins taken from a vantage point slightly uphill. The perspective clearly showed the ruins on the edge of a peak, with foothills far below. A portion of remnants from a second ruined building peaked above the bottom of the frame. Between the two locations, several people in contemporary clothing seemed to be milling around. Several additional recent images included disheveled soldiers carrying machine guns among the ruins.

Graham scanned back over the grid of images and wondered what he was supposed to be looking at. After all, Noah did not build the ark from stacked stone, so it couldn't be the ark. And Noah obviously would not have carved Assyrian reliefs.

He moved his cursor over the folder of PDFs, but realized his curiosity was overpowered by exhaustion. He shut his computer, followed by his eyes.

FORTY-EIGHT

Graham opened the front door of his house and felt the warmth of the Southern California sun on his face as he made a comical pantomime of looking for the visitor who had rung the doorbell. But the front steps were empty. He exaggerated a look of confusion as he spoke in a cartoon voice. "I guess I must've been hearing things."

Alyson's giggle bubbled from behind the hedge lining his front steps as the door closed. Seconds later, the bell rang again, and he repeated the scene.

"I wonder who keeps ringing my door?"

More giggles followed him as he went back inside.

When the bell rang a third time, Graham awoke in his hotel room and realized the doorbell was the sound of text notifications from his phone, the dings appropriated by his dream. He felt a pang of longing for his daughter, and he felt her absence as if she had just left the room, like smoke lingering in the air after a candle had been blown out. He sat up, struggling to recognize where he was, as if his waking state was less real than his dream.

Van. The Hotel Royal.

He could barely remember how he got to the room. The memory of being awoken by the abrupt stop of the dolmuş, annoyed and feeling drugged with fatigue. The hundred-mile trip had taken two-and-a-half hours, arriving at nine p.m. But as far as his body was concerned, it had been two or three in the morning. He must have zombie-walked from the dolmuş to the lobby of the hotel, and he had only vague impressions of checking-in. Now the phone said eleven a.m. He had slept fourteen hours and would still be asleep except for the texts. All from Alexander, he discovered, blinking them into focus.

Did you get the link?

Not many pictures of that place.

Did you see what the locals call it? The Place of Descent.

The reminder jumpstarted Graham, and he opened his laptop to look through the pictures again. This time, he realized the images had a naming convention. The main batch of black-and-white photos all contained the suffix *GB*. He looked at the PDFs and found they contained suffixes as well, and several of them included *GB*. The first was a PDF named *Amurath to Amurath,* and Graham recognized the title as one of Gertrude Bell's books. He opened the document and discovered a compilation of excerpts from her 1909 travelogue of the Middle East and Asia Minor. The first line electrified him.

> *The Babylonians, and after them the Nestorians and the Moslems, held that the ark of Noah, when the waters subsided, grounded not upon the mountain of Ararat, but upon Judi Dagh. To that school of thought I also belong, for I have made the pilgrimage and seen what I have seen.*

Bell had used the English phonetic equivalent to the modern Turkish *C*, which sounded as an English *J*, but she was obviously referring to the same mountain. Even more arresting was that she listed several traditions he had not come across in his research. Then it struck him—he *had* come across them, but he had misunderstood them. Like most other modern ark researchers, he had read those sources with the assumption of where Ararat was. But Cudi Dagh was two hundred miles *south* of where everyone in modern times had been looking. He moved to the next excerpt from Bell's account.

> *Our path led us over rising meadows to Geurmuk and Dadar, and so into the mouth of a gorge where Hasanah nestles under rocky peaks. The clouds gathered over the mountains and thunder came booming through the gorge as we pitched our tents by the edge of the stream. Hasanah is a Christian village inhabited partly by Nestorians and partly by the converts of American missionaries.... We walked*

> *up the narrow valley, where flowers and flowering shrubs nodded over the path in an almost incredible luxuriance, and climbed the steep wooded hill-side to a point where the rock had been smoothed to receive the image of an Assyrian king, though none had been carved upon it. Above it rose a precipitous crag clothed on one side with hanging woods through which zigzagged a very ancient path, lost at times among fallen rocks and trees, while at times its embankment of stones was still clearly to be traced. On the summit of the crag were vestiges of a small fortress. The walls were indicated by heaps of unsquared stones, many of which had fallen down the hill, where they lay thickly strewn; the evidence afforded by them, and by the carefully constructed path, made it certain that we were standing upon the site of some watch-tower that had guarded the Hasanah Gorge. On the opposite side rises a second crag whereon are ruins of the same description. That the valley was held by the Assyrians there can be no doubt, for it is signed with their name. Below and to the west of the crag to which we had climbed there is another smoothed niche in the rock. Here the work has been completed, and the niche is carved with the figure of an Assyrian king, wearing a long-fringed robe and carrying a sceptre. At a later age, the mountains had been occupied by Christians. [My guide] showed me at the foot of the crag a few vaulted chambers which he declared to be the ruins of a Nestorian monastery, and walking westward for an hour or more along the wooded ridges, we came to a second and larger monastic ruin...*

Alexander had made a note at the first mention of Hasanah, and Graham clicked it open. *Modern name is Kösreli Köyü.* Graham remembered that many of the Armenian and Kurdish names had been replaced by Turkish names when modern Turkey came into being.

He switched to a different tab in his browser where he had already opened the grid of photographs in case he needed to refer to them. He found one of the images of the Assyrian kings next to an inscription and opened it. Sennacherib had been the king of Assyria. And both the Bible and the Talmud associated him in some way with Ararat. Was Sennacherib the figure in the inscription? Graham studied the image as he thought about the question, then returned to Bell's account.

> *We set out from camp at four o'clock on the following morning.... We returned reluctantly to the path and walked till [my guide] announced that the ark of Noah was immediately above us.... We climbed the steep slopes for another half-hour. And so we came to Noah's Ark, which had run aground in a bed of scarlet tulips. There was once a famous Nestorian monastery, the Cloister of the Ark, upon the summit of Mount Judi, but it was destroyed by lightning in the year of Christ 766. Upon its ruins the Moslems had erected a shrine, and this too has fallen; but Christian, Moslem and Jew still visit the mount upon a certain day in the summer and offer their oblations to the Prophet Noah. That which they actually see is a number of roofless chambers upon the extreme summit of the hill. They are roughly built of unsquared stones, piled together without mortar, and from wall to wall are laid tree trunks and boughs, so disposed that they may support a roofing of cloths, which is thrown over them at the time of the annual festival. To the east of these buildings there is an open court enclosed by a low stone wall. The walls both of the chambers and of the court are all, as I should judge, constructions of a recent date, and they are certainly Mohammadan, since one of the chambers contains a mihrab niche to the south, and in the enclosing wall of the court there is a similar rough niche. Farther to the west lie the ruins of a detached chamber built of very large stones, and perhaps of an earlier date. Beneath the upper rocks upon which these edifices stand, there is a tank fed by the winter snows which had not entirely disappeared*

> *from the mountain-top. Still farther down, upon a small plateau, are scattered fragments of a different architecture, carefully built walls, stone doorposts, and lintels showing above the level of the soil. Here, I make little doubt, was the site of the Nestorian monastery.*
>
> *To the east of [the ark] lay Heshtan, which is in Arabic Thamanin (the Eighty), so called because the eighty persons who were saved from the deluge founded there the first village of the regenerated world when they descended from Jebel Judi.*

Graham wondered if one of the non-biblical flood stories mentioned eighty survivors rather than eight and made a mental note to check into it. Alexander's quotes from Bell's book ended with one last passage.

> *I have seen the ship of the Prophet Noah. So it is that I subscribe in this matter to the wisdom of the Qur'an: "And immediately the water abated and the decree was fulfilled and the ark rested upon the mountain of Judi."*

FORTY-NINE

THE CITY OF VAN SPREAD OUT ALONG THE EAST BANK OF LAKE VAN. From Graham's hotel window, the huge salt lake already looked like a sea, but he tried to imagine it rising, inundating the city and the surrounding hills in a massive flood. He wondered if George Hagopian, one of the most important witnesses of the ark on the traditional Ararat, had ever imagined the same thing since he was from here. In fact, much of what Graham knew about Van came from reading about Hagopian.

The rest of his knowledge was acquired from reports of the Armenian genocide. The city of Van had been destroyed, and more than 50,000 Armenians were slaughtered. Survivors were forcibly marched by Ottoman soldiers to camps in Syria, far from the Russians invading the area since the Armenians might see them as liberators.

As he looked again at the city of over half a million and tried to picture it in ruins, a pang of hunger reminded him he needed to eat. Since waking in the shed on the peak of Ararat, all he had eaten was the remainder of trail bars. Graham walked to the hotel restaurant hoping there was something left on the buffet, and to satisfy a day's old craving for Coke Light. The last remnants of breakfast were still available, and he took several pieces of spicy sheep cheese with garlic and a handful of dates back to his room to continue reading.

Alexander had excerpted relevant passages from another travelogue called *Ex Oriente Lux* by Johannes Lepsius. In 1899, Lepsius was traveling to Şırnak to meet with the Agha, a sheik who governed the region. But before he crossed the mountains, he learned the Agha happened to be in the area, and he met him at his encampment.

> *As we came to speak of the Kurdish people and their history of land and cattle, of the primeval times of the land and of the traditions contained in the Qur'an and the Bible, the Agha stood up and gestured his hand on the long mountain chain rising in the distance to the south, from which a dome stood out, and seemed to support a wall or the like at the top.*
>
> *"Do you see that mountain? The ark landed there. There Noah was saved from the flood with his followers and gave his thanks to God. Every year Muhammedans and Christians gather there to celebrate the salvation of Noah with prayers and festivals."*
>
> *We told him that we intended to climb Cudi—that is the name of the mountain. Even if it was a detour of a day or two, we would like to see the site.*
>
> *"I will give you my people," he replied. "They will lead you to the top of the mountain and show you everything. Also, they will bring you to Jema, where Noah built the ark and settled again after the flood. You should also see Gird, the oldest city in the world, which was built before the flood. The mountain and the villages and the land, as far as you can see, and over the mountains to the plain is mine. But my fathers also had the land from here to the Wansee. But now it is extinct and deserted, the villages are destroyed and the people are driven out. Even the trees are burned—these dogs of Hamidieh."*

Graham wondered if *Jema* was another name for *Cizre*, which was pronounced *Jizrah*, making it sound closer than it looked. *Gird* referred to Göbekli Tepe—indeed one of the world's oldest cities, and site of the oldest known places of worship. Alexander put on note on *Hamidieh*, explaining it was the name of the Kurdish Cavalry.

The PDF jumped ahead in Lepsius's account to where they approach the mountain the next morning.

We came to a narrow romantic valley. The rushing waters of the mountain stream flowed above and below us in several streams, artificially dammed for the irrigation of the gardens of villages down the valley. Bridges and high dams walled the path leading up the rocky slope. Mighty old trees and oak trees shaded the way. The foliage was hanging so low in places that we leaned on the horses' necks to get through it on narrow, but apparently well-maintained, mule tracks up the valley. There seemed to be a village in the depths. The path rose higher at a bend of the valley. Oak trees shaded mountain slopes. The narrow path opened and we stopped.

We had slept only a few hours when we rose before dawn to climb Cudi. We climbed slowly up the rocky ravine behind our campsite, and had to keep our horses on the reins for several hours. On the way we met some Kurds in the mountains, who were knocking down oak trees with long poles. It is the only export article here. One of the men used his robe to hold magnificent grapes he had just picked between the rocks. When we came up higher, it was deserted and lonely again. We bent to the east to be at the height to ascend the western, flat, rounded summit of the long ridge that bounds the mountains of Kurdistan against the Mesopotamian Plains and Khabur, an eastern tributary of the Tigris. One hour later, halfway up, we found in a rocky cave a strong spring with fresh cool water.

It was noon when we reached the top and rode up the last height, rising with a flat, round curvature. In front of us lay a square building of hewn stone, roughly piled up. It could have been considered a primitive lookout tower. Some remnants of vaults suggested that once there was a monastery. Now the open-topped rooms apparently served as a deposit for the Pilgrims at the time of the autumn festival. A rough staircase led to a walled terrace, followed by a ruined tower.

To the west, leaning against an elongated ridge, a second rude building, of the same nature and purpose as the first.

Graham opened the folder of images and saw that one of the pictures—the dreamy, soft image—was named with the suffix *LEPS*.

We were standing on a high mountain wall, which dropped steeply towards the plain at 2,000 meters, and in the depths the Mesopotamian Plain spread in the far-off distance. [The men the Agha gave to accompany us said,] "There, behind the green patch the village, is Jema, where Noah—peace be upon him—built the ship. It clung to the rock up here. Over there"—he pointed to a round terrace, perhaps fifty yards below us, shaded by a lonely tree—"he built the altar and sacrificed and prayed. In the fall, many people come together, often coming from afar. Here, the Christians gather, and over there the Yazidis and the Muslims. There is a sacrifice which is eaten, and songs are sung."

The tradition that this is the mountain of the ark, where it landed, still lives. An old Mullah, whom we met the next day at the foot of the mountain, gave us the best proof. "If you had searched, you could easily have found some of the ship's big nails." He made clear to us his length with two fingers. "And pitch, there is a great deal of pitch there, with which Noah—peace be upon him—his ship had been smeared."

Graham wondered if bitumen coated wood could survive six thousand years or more of exposure. He wished he had a sample of bitumen from Cudi Dagh to send to Steinmeyer so he could compare it with the Tower of Babel brick.

The next section made Graham wonder again how the connection of this mountain to the ark could have become lost.

It has long been known to the learned that the Babylonian tradition was present in Berosus and the Peschitta,

> *when in place of the "mountains of Ararat"—as it is called in the Bible—the "Qardu mountains" as the place of Noah's Landing. Think of Cudi, which is also named in the Qur'an as the mountain of Noah. There is no question that the mountain the Europeans call "Ararat" at the border of Russia, Persia, and Turkey is not at all eligible for the tradition, while all the traits that are relevant to the history of the flood in the Bible and in the Babylonian tradition are most closely related to the Syriac Arab tradition of Cudi as the true Ararat.*
>
> *The flood seems to have been conceived as a flood of the oldest civilized world that had spread in the Mesopotamian Plains. The mere fact that it was a ship on which the survivors were rescued indicates that history takes place in a country where there are navigable streams and where a high degree of technical skill could be assumed for shipbuilding. The Babylonian tradition assumes that after the flood of the Mesopotamian lowlands, the rescuing ship settled on the nearby mountains. The land in the north of the Tigris and the Khabur was inhabited by the Chaldeans (Kaldu) or Urartu, whose kingdom extended at times over the entire Armenian highlands. Thus, the northern ridges were called the Kardu Mountains or Urartu Mountains ("Ararat Mountains," Genesis 8:4) by the inhabitants of the plain. The name Cudi is connected with the people of the Goi (compare Genesis 14:1—King Tidal of Goiim).*

Graham began to see how Alexander had become persuaded. The account was similar to Bell's, and had a sober, academic authority to it. Except for the final passage, when she arrived in Cizre.

> *We settled in the shade of a vine roof, and the friendly proprietor brought us a bowl of frighteningly large grapes—grapes of a size that have never been seen by me or the reader. Grapes half arm-length. The Kurds who squatted*

> *around us and their Mullah asserted that they often had grapes "as long as an arm." The berries were the size of pigeon eggs! What does it take for our imagination—which only has joy in the old stories—to get further proof? It was "the vineyard of Noah," the fruits of which we ate. Here the first vine was planted.*

If Cudi Dagh was indeed the true Ararat, it was no less immune to legend and exaggeration than its northern impersonator.

FIFTY

Graham picked up his phone to call Alexander at the same time Alexander's name appeared on the screen.

"Hey, I was just about to call you."

"Gray-ham!"

The exaggerated pronunciation of his name made Graham chuckle—something he hadn't done in so long it almost felt foreign. "What's that? My medieval name? Instead of something like Edward Longshanks, I'm Eliot Gray Ham?"

"Ha! No, it's your autocorrect name. Like when your phone changes what you meant into something you didn't."

"Okay. Why?"

"Because that's where the error's at."

"Still don't get it."

"Didn't you read your last text to me?"

Graham took the phone away from his ear, looked at the screen, and switched to his text app. He had spoken, *Where's Ararat?* But the speech-to-text function had autocorrected him and rendered it as *Where's the error at?* The mistake triggered a full laugh. "That is hilarious!"

"And also true," Alexander said. "Did you look at what I sent?"

"Yes. The photos are fascinating. And I'm reading the PDFs now. Thanks for putting this together so quickly."

"No problem. I couldn't stop. I'd never heard of this place before. Cudi Dagh."

"I hadn't either," Graham said. "How'd you find out about it?"

"Remember how you told me to look up Gertrude Bell? Her writings are archived at Newcastle University. I was able to get access to them online, and it turns out she also photographed many of the places she visited and wrote about. I got sucked into the photo galleries, and then discovered several photos that were labeled *Noah's Ark*. They didn't look like anything I'd seen taken on Ararat, and the captions called it Cudi Dagh. So, I did a text search and found that chapter about it in her book."

Graham shuttled through the images on his laptop as Alexander spoke. "Wish I would have known about it a week ago. Would've saved me a lot of trouble."

"How? You still haven't told me what all this is about."

"It'll have to wait. But this is incredibly helpful."

"So, I did a search to see if anyone else knew about Cudi Dagh and found Lepsius. Turns out that not only was his father a big-time Egyptologist, but he himself was a German missionary and an activist for the Armenian people. He founded the German-Armenian Society to let Europeans know how poorly the Ottomans were treating the Armenians. That was right before the genocide. He wrote that book about ten or fifteen years earlier. And the way he tells it, everyone in that region at that time thought Cudi Dagh was where the ark landed."

Graham clicked back into the folder of PDFs and read the title of the documents he hadn't yet opened. "What's this *Bender* file?"

"Lepsius wasn't the only German who knew about it. There were quite a few, actually. But the most interesting is this guy, Friedrich Bender. He was a geologist who went there in the fifties."

"Interesting," Graham said. "As I was reading the report, I was thinking how these places don't ever seem to be found by someone with the training to appreciate what they were seeing."

"Bender broke that streak. He worked as a petroleum geologist in eastern Turkey for a few years, and his travels took him to all sorts of rural areas."

"Not too hard to do. Except for Van, this area is nothing but rural." He opened the *Bender* PDF, skimming the document as Alexander summarized it.

"At one point, Bender was at a camp in the middle of nowhere and got into a discussion with a hodja about the Qur'an and the Bible. The hodja told him that the Qur'an says that Noah's Ark landed on Cudi Dagh, which is in a mountain range near the Syrian border. Bender said he had never heard of the place. The hodja told him he had been there himself, and that there were still parts of the ship buried in the sand at the top of the mountain. He said if Bender didn't believe him, he could go check it out himself. He also said that all true believers knew about the location."

"Hmm," Graham noised. "Interesting that the accounts we have of it seem to be from people who are not true believers. They're not even ark hunters."

"What he found made Bender one. At least to some degree. But he may have been just as interested in the legend as the reality. Over the next year, he asked the people he ran into while doing his work about the ark, and they all knew about how the ark landed on Cudi Dagh. It was known as The Place of Descent—just like on Ararat. He finally got a chance to visit it himself in the spring of 1954. Get this: to get to Cizre, he floated down the Tigris River on a raft made of inflated mutton skins and willow branches."

A text message arrived on Graham's computer as Alexander spoke. "Just sent a picture I found of it. Crazy."

Graham studied the improvised float that looked like a pad of tree trimmings carried away on misshapen inner tubes. "Crazy is right."

"Maybe when he went ashore he yelled, 'Lamb ho!'"

"That was terrible," Graham deadpanned.

"Anyway, Bender hiked to the base of the mountain and found a guide in a village. The next day they went up the mountain. Bender noted the range looked like it had been pushed up as a result of tectonic movement, and that there was archaeological evidence of a prehistoric flood in the region. When he got to the top, he found a structure he described as—hold on, let me read it—'a conglomerate which was cemented by limestone sinter.' From the way he described it, it was made of uncut rocks about the size of a fist. He said there was another ruin that looked like a hut or a small mosque made with uncut stones."

The description corroborated what Graham was looking at. "Just like in the photos."

"Yep. Bender said there was an inscription on one of the stones, but he couldn't read it. He said he found it in a large basin about a hundred meters down from the peak on the south side. But the snow was pretty thick there."

"At least it wasn't under thirty-five feet of ice."

"What do you mean?"

"Never mind," Graham said, realizing he hadn't shared all the details of his mission with Alexander. "Tell you later."

"Still, it's amazing Bender found anything under that snow."

"Which was…"

"Bender said that based on how it had been described to him, he pictured finding wood beams under the snow, so he started clearing the spot they showed him. Instead, he found sand, like the hodja said. Bender kept digging, and about a meter below the surface, the sand turned brown. Discolored by a layer of something. He dug a little deeper and found blackened wood."

"Blackened wood?" Graham repeated, wondering if that was Bender's characterization or Alexanders.

"The wood was pretty decomposed. The fragments were between the size of a pea and a couple of inches. At first he thought it was old firewood. Then he figured out it was black because it was coated in bitumen."

"And this is all in the report you sent?"

"It's all there. And being the geologist he was, he had brought chemicals with him that could extract the bitumen so it could be analyzed. He tried to dig deeper, but the ground was frozen solid. And the snow was too deep to explore other parts of the basin. Then a storm started to roll in and the guides made him leave."

"I assume he had the wood tested?"

"Twice. Once in the 50s, and once in the 70s. But he didn't publish the results until 1972. The report is at the end of the PDF. The Carbon-14 test said the wood was 6,500 years old. Pre-Sumeric."

Graham jumped to the end of the file and scanned the findings. "Fascinating. Of course, it doesn't mean it was a boat."

"True," Alexander admitted, "but it is an intriguing find. I also read about a Turkish archaeologist who found wood in the same place in the 70s. When you factor in the inscriptions on the mountain, it makes way more sense as a location for Ararat than Agri Dagh or Massis or whatever."

"Yes, the inscriptions are almost as interesting as whatever's at the peak."

"Oh yeah. That's another part of this location that has been examined by an expert. An archaeologist and Assyriologist from Cambridge named LW King."

Graham clicked open the PDF called *KING* and followed along as Alexander explained what was in it.

"He also worked at the British Museum as the keeper of Egyptian and Assyrian antiquities. He examined the inscriptions in 1904, between the time Lepsius and Bell saw them. King said they were made to commemorate the fifth campaign of Sennacherib in 699 BC. How come Sennacherib keeps coming up?" Alexander asked, without waiting for an answer. "He also noted that Cudi Dagh was about three days' travel from Nineveh, where Sennacherib's palace was. About seventy-five miles."

An astonished sigh escaped Graham over the wealth of evidence that was almost entirely unknown even to people devoting their lives to finding the ark. "When you sent that text telling me I was on the wrong mountain, I thought you were joking. But the more I learn about it, the more this site seems much more plausible. Did you see all the ancient sources about the location of the ark?"

"Yeah. Surprised me how many there were."

"Me too. Remember how many of them said the ark could still be seen and visited?" Graham asked. "This mountain is less than 7,000 feet tall. The traditional Ararat is 17,000 feet, and it's difficult and dangerous to climb. According to what you sent me, Cudi Dagh sounds like a day trip. That makes far more sense of the ancient accounts. Not only that, but the Sennacherib inscriptions give some evidence to support the story that he visited the ark and took away a piece. And it explains why his sons went to the area after assassinating him. They already knew the place. And there is no Sennacherib connection to the traditional Ararat."

"It's a lot to consider." A note of pride rang in Alexander's words at having persuaded his mentor into sharing his position. "Could be a whole other dissertation there…"

"Don't even think about it," Graham warned comically. "Last time you did field research, I almost got killed saving you."

"Whatever. Without me you'd still be handcuffed in a shed in Nowhere, Saudi Arabia."

Again, Graham was thankful for the laugh, and felt it counterbalance the stress of the previous days.

"One last thing you might enjoy," Alexander said. "I found a bit of a coincidence."

"Oh yeah? What's that?" Graham prepared for a punchline.

"I went to the INTF site to look something up and got distracted. I ended up looking at the bio for Heinrich Steinmeyer. Guess where he did his doctorate?"

"You'll have to tell me. My brain is not in the guessing mood."

"Newcastle University, where the Gertrude Bell archives are."

"Small world. That reminds me—I need to call him and compare notes on the Babel brick with Bender's report."

"Have a ball, y'all."

Graham recognized the line from the chorus of Elton John's "Tower of Babel." "At least you didn't try to sing it that time."

Alexander started singing the line as Graham hung up.

"Later, Elton."

FIFTY-ONE

Graham skimmed the lab report at the end of Bender's PDF but didn't learn anything Alexander hadn't already shared. He opened the results of the INTF tests on the brick from the Tower of Babel in another window to compare them, then called Steinmeyer.

"Heinrich, it's Graham Eliot."

"Graham, good to hear from you," Steinmeyer said warmly. "I was worried when I heard the PKK had attacked the airport."

"Thanks. I'm okay. The plane diverted to Yerevan, and I ended up visiting the cathedral with a relic of petrified wood they claim came from Noah's Ark."

"Providential, indeed. Did they allow you to examine it?"

"Not really. I saw it on display. I did speak to the director there, but he was not interested in having it tested for various reasons."

"That is not surprising," Steinmeyer said. "I can imagine what the reasons are."

"I'm sure you can," Graham snickered. "I let him know about your work with the Tower of Babel in case he ever has a change of heart."

"I am grateful. Did you arrive home safely?"

"Actually, I'm in Van."

The news surprised Steinmeyer into German. "*Warum bist du in Van?*"

"Long story," Graham said. "But listen. I have learned that there is another mountain with a much older tradition claiming to be the place where Noah's Ark landed. A place called—"

"Cudi Dagh!" Steinmeyer cut across him. "I see you got my message."

"What messa—" This time Graham interrupted himself with the

memory of the strange robotic voice message mechanically sounding out Hebrew. "That was you?"

"Please forgive the little intrigue," Steinmeyer admitted.

"Why didn't you just tell me what you knew about Ararat instead of being so cryptic?"

"I know of Burkhard Vogel's interest in the ark. I know that he—like so many others—is convinced Agri Dagh is Ararat. But I wanted to leave you a clue that led you in what I believe might be a more profitable direction without creating more tension between the INTF and Vogel. Especially now that he is allowing us to archive his collection through you. I thought insinuating myself into your expedition would not be welcomed by Vogel, given the trust you have developed."

"You don't have to worry about that anymore."

"Did something happen?"

Graham released a sarcastic huff. "You could say that. But I don't have time to go into it. How did you know about Cudi Dagh?"

"I am aware of a few German explorers who have visited there. For reasons unknown to me, their work is not widely known."

"I think I'm reading some of their work right now," Graham said. "I didn't put your clue together with Cudi Dagh until this morning after I already learned of the traditions about the mountain. I assume you know of Friedrich Bender's work?"

"More than that," Steinmeyer said. "He was an acquaintance of sorts. We exchanged some correspondence at one point early in my career."

"Really? I thought he worked mainly in Germany."

"He did. But before that, he was the person responsible for the geological mapping of Jordan in the early 1960s. It related to some of the work I was doing at the time."

"Have you compared his lab report on the wood he found at Cudi Dagh with the Babel brick?"

Steinmeyer hemmed. "I am embarrassed to say I had not thought of that. If I remember correctly, the test was published in the early 1970s. I cannot recall when the actual testing was done. But radio isotope dating technology and procedure has become far more precise since the wood was found in the 1950s. It might shed some light, but not as much as a current test."

"I understand," Graham said. "Just trying to work with what we've got."

"I appreciate the suggestion. What are your plans now? I take it if you are in Van, you will be visiting Cudi Dagh."

"I don't think I have a choice."

FIFTY-TWO

Graham puzzled over the best approach to Cudi Dagh and how to find the easiest way up the mountain as he familiarized himself with the area through Google Earth. Şırnak was the closest city on the north side of the range that was supposedly the *mountains* of Ararat named in Genesis. But the ascents in the travelogues and reports he had read were all approaches from the south. They all mentioned Cizre, southwest of the peak, but the city was only a mile from the Syrian border—too dangerous, especially if he were traveling alone.

He would probably call too much attention to himself just for being an American wherever he went in the area, and he couldn't think of any plausible story to explain what he was doing there. Telling the real reason—that he wanted to see the landing place of the ark—might not be welcomed, let alone elicit help. After all, if Cudi Dagh was the actual landing place of the ark, there seemed to be no effort to advertise that fact.

The travelogues documented that the people in the region all knew the tradition about Cudi Dagh, that it was sacred to them. And yet, they did nothing to call attention to it. There was no tourism centered around the mountain, no publicity. As far as he could tell, there were no guides who made their living taking adventurers to the peak, and no outfitters to accommodate visitors. And there definitely wasn't a Noah's Ark Welcome Center like there was at the Durupinar site near Doğubayazıt—and that was nothing more than a geological oddity exploiting the tradition. About the closest Cudi Dagh got to having some kind of Noah's Ark industry was the traditional site of Noah's tomb in Cizre.

Even if there had been a tourist industry, the political situation was no longer the world Lepsius, Bell, King—and even Bender—had traveled in. The Armenian genocide, the formation of modern Turkey, the PKK, and the refugee crisis created by ISIS took care of that.

Graham knew he needed help. After Sivan's murder, there was no way he could ask Khazhak. The cost of his help had already been too high and left no room to ask him to betray his conviction that Agri Dagh—or Massis—was Ararat. Even if Graham did want to enlist his help, he had no way of contacting him. He wondered if Khazhak knew about Cudi Dagh, and what he would say if Graham told him he was going there.

Obviously, Graham couldn't turn to Şahin. Even if his story of Sivan's accidental death was true, he had left Graham for dead—not exactly a credential of trustworthiness. And if Graham had been willing to ignore the attempt on his life, Şahin was still an opportunist who not only needed people to think Agri Dagh was Ararat, but made it clear he was allied with Vogel—although that loyalty seemed to be measured in money. If Cudi Dagh became known as the real Ararat, Şahin's life would be—well—shipwrecked.

Graham smiled inwardly at his word choice, then realized how apropos it was of his situation, how alone he was. At least Noah had seven other people, though that was the entire population of the earth. Graham thought Noah still must have felt isolated and alone, given how he was the only one God spoke his terrifying instructions to. And what did Noah do after the waters receded? He built an altar and offered a sacrifice. He prayed.

Prayer.

Not for the first time in his life—or even this trip—Graham felt guilty about neglecting prayer. He could hear his pastor's favorite aphorism in his head: *Prayer is not our last resort, it is our first response, our strongest tool.* Graham pivoted his chair away from the laptop, closed his eyes, and prayed in a spot that—regardless of which mountain was the true Ararat—was once underwater, submerged in judgment by the flood of Noah.

After he finished, he reached for his phone to take it off silence and saw he had just missed a call from Isaac Ross. The name made him instantly conflicted. Ross's experience in the area meant he could probably recommend someone who would be able to help him. Yet it didn't seem appropriate to ask Ross to facilitate research on a site that might undermine his own work. On the other hand, as an academic, Ross would probably be curious about what was on Cudi Dagh. Ross presented himself as a man whose faith grounded his interested in archaeology, but his successful career would not have been possible without a great deal of ambition. All things considered, Graham decided if there was a downside, it couldn't put him in a worse position than he was in right now.

He touched the *call back* button and watched the phone as it connected. Ross's voice burst onto the line as if a dam of silence had broken.

"Graham, what's happening? Are you okay?"

"Isaac, I'm sorry, but I need to ask another favor." The words sounded more tentative than he had intended, mismatched to Ross's energetic display.

"Of course. I'll help any way I can."

"It's kind of awkward, and I certainly don't want to offend you since you've been—"

"Graham, it's okay," Ross interrupted. "What do you need?"

"Are you familiar with Cudi Dagh?"

"Yes. They have a local tradition it's where the ark landed."

Graham squinted, suddenly wondering what he was missing if Ross discounted the site. "But you don't think there's any truth behind the tradition?"

"Not really," Ross said. "It is interesting. But there are too many eyewitnesses of the ark on Ararat. And, of course, subsurface satellite imagery shows there is something there that is the right size and looks man-made. Cudi Dagh doesn't have any of that."

"So, the pictures Gertrude Bell and Lepsius and others took don't sway you at all?"

"Clearly, there is *something* there. If the tradition is right about anything, I think it's that there was a Nestorian monastery there.

Monasteries are kinds of arks, in a way, protecting God's people from the world. Maybe that's where the idea came from."

"Huh," Graham noised equivocally. The observation sounded more like a justification to dismiss the tradition rather than a plausible explanation for it. "What about the Talmudic story of Sennacherib visiting the ark and taking wood from it to make an amulet? There are a number of inscriptions from Sennacherib around Cudi Dagh, but not Ararat."

"Sennacherib left behind lots of inscriptions. And as far as I know, none of the ones at Cudi Dagh say anything about the ark." Ross spoke with academic detachment, without a hint of defensiveness. "If Sennacherib did take wood from the ark, I don't think he was at Cudi Dagh. Why the sudden interest?"

"I just learned about it, and it gave me an idea for how to deal with Vogel. Think about what would happen if an announcement were made that Noah's Ark had been found at Cudi Dagh? It would take away his cover, which is your dig. It would expose him. Please don't take this the wrong way, but since your work is incomplete, all he really has to corroborate his claim is a hole in the ice. Looks impressive, but if the ark were discovered 200 miles south, then his story falls apart."

"But I don't think you're going to find anything at Cudi Dagh," Ross said.

"I don't have to. Just to claim it is the location might be enough to draw attention away from Ararat—at least temporarily—and remove Vogel from both of our lives. And like you said, there *is* something there. And your project will still be there for you after this blows over. But until it does, you can't continue your work."

"What exactly do you need from me?"

"I've never been here," Graham said. "I have no contacts in the area. In fact, I'm not even in the country legally. Do you know anyone in Van who can help me get to Cudi?"

"As a matter of fact, I think I might. There was a symposium on the current state of ark research hosted by Şırnak University a few years ago."

Graham switched back to Google Earth. "Şırnak? That's at the foot of Cudi Dagh. And you've been there?"

"No. The symposium happened to be during one of the times when I was on the mountain. I assume the university hosted it there to help bring attention to Cudi Dagh. But the place is so remote, I'm not sure how well attended it was. I have the papers from it, but there wasn't any important advance announced in them. Anyway, I was invited by someone who might be able to help. They work at the museum there in Van."

FIFTY-THREE

A great god is Ahuramazda, the greatest of gods, who created this earth, who created that sky, who created man, who created happiness for man, who made Xerxes king, one king for all, one ruler for all. I am Xerxes, the great king, the king of kings, king of all kinds of peoples with all kinds of origins, king of this earth great and wide, the son of King Darius, the Achaemenid.

The Jews who had not returned from exile in Babylonia as Jerusalem was being rebuilt called him Ahasuerus, including Esther, whom he made queen. To the Persians at the core of his vast empire, he was Xšayaršan. But he was mainly known to history by his Greek name, Xerxes I.

During his rule in the first half of the fifth century BC, he inscribed the lines into a panel carved into the side of a cliff, sixty feet above the ground. The message was repeated in three different languages, but even though the characters were large, Graham couldn't make out any words, just elongated triangular divots that formed the cuneiform text.

He scanned the top of the cliff, taking in the ruins of the castle that had been the seat of the kingdom of Urartu during the time of David and Solomon. Then, it had been called Tushpa. Now the ancient ruins were adjacent to the Van Museum.

Ross had texted back to say he had a contact there who would meet Graham at the inscription at nine a.m. Graham had wondered why he didn't simply meet the contact at the museum where he worked.

But now that he was here, Graham quickly became lost in the history before him, letting the past become more present in his thoughts than his own time.

"Graham."

He realized it was the second time his name sounded, as his historical reverie vanished, leaving him confused by what he was seeing. Isaac Ross was walking toward him.

"Isaac? What are you doing here?"

Ross smiled as he opened his arms expansively, like a welcoming host. "I thought I'd make the introduction in person. You didn't think I could resist seeing what was on Cudi Dagh, did you?"

Graham returned the smile as he offered his hand, thankful for the company and for someone who had more experience in the area. "Did you bring your chainsaw?"

Ross chuckled. "That's half the reason I came. For once, I wanted to search for the ark in a place where I didn't have to cut an elevator shaft into ice." Ross shifted gears, anticipating Graham's question as he looked around the cliffs. "This guy said he would be here at nine."

Graham turned back to the ancient castle, searching for the person they were supposed to meet despite not knowing what he looked like.

Ross pointed to the top of the cliff. "There he is."

A figure appeared on the edge of the bluff, silhouetted against the sky, apparently waiting to be seen. The man motioned down and to his right while he poked the air several times.

"I think the way up must be over there," Ross said, already moving toward the spot.

Graham followed along the base of the cliff to a passageway cut into the rock wall. A path guided them through several switchbacks before depositing them at the top of the formation.

As they ascended, Ross explained what Graham had already learned. "All this used to be a fortress and a castle. Kind of a long strip built on this fin of rock."

A labyrinth of ruins divided the uneven ridge into levels. Graham thought some points of it resembled a battered version of the Great Wall of China. He looked out over the grassy field that was the site of old Van. The foundations of the pre-genocide city remained, a stubble of the past that gave the terrain a leathery texture from this vantage point. The modern city lay beyond a mosque standing like a sentry between the old and new Van. Behind them, Lake Van spread out in a vast plane of water reminiscent of the Great Salt Lake. Beyond the new city, a range of mountains enclosed in the area. On the other side of the plateau, Graham could just see a part of the roof of the museum below them.

Several tourists milled around the hilltop ruins of the castle grounds, but they easily found the contact. Graham was surprised at how young the man was, but was encouraged by his friendly, reserved face.

"Dr. Ross. It is my pleasure to finally meet you in person."

Ross took the man's hand. "Good to meet you face-to-face, Zeki. I'm sorry it couldn't have been at the symposium."

"You were missed. But now, here you are." Zeki made a gesture intended to absolve any sin of omission for being absent from the symposium.

Graham questioned the wisdom of trusting someone Ross apparently knew only through email correspondence. But before he could reconsider their plan, Ross reached to his side as if to pull Graham away from his thoughts and introduced him.

"Graham Eliot, this is Zeki Bozkurtlar. He's the assistant director of the archaeological works section."

Graham shook his hand, trying to mirror the cautious expression.

"Forgive me for asking you to meet me here, but we could not risk being overheard." Zeki bowed his head while keeping eye contact, apparently thanking them for indulging him. "What you are asking about, it could be dangerous. There is much PKK here. You know PKK?" Zeki looked at Graham, arching his brow.

Graham nodded, trying not to reveal the understatement he felt.

Zeki raised an open palm to the mountains in the distance behind them. "They have a base on Cudi Dagh. And the government, they have soldiers who try to keep people from going on the mountain."

Graham and Ross exchanged apprehensive glances that agreed it might be harder to reach the mountain than they thought.

"Why would that make meeting at the museum unsafe?" Ross tilted his head toward the museum building.

"I do not know for certain that it would be unsafe. But if someone learned of your plans to go there and alerted either the government or the PKK, then it could be bad for you. And I know there are many people in Van who have family near Agri Dagh. Many believe the ark is there, and many of them depend on the tourists who go there because of it."

"What do they believe about Cudi Dagh?" Graham asked.

"There is certainly a strong tradition there. The people in that region accept it as fact. I studied at Şırnak University, very close to Cudi. There is a professor there in the theology department who has been on the mountain many times. He has found the inscriptions from Sennacherib there."

Graham glanced at Ross again but saw no surprise. "I have heard about those. Have you been on the mountain yourself?"

"No. There were too many PKK when I was there."

"It's important that we see what is at the peak of Cudi," Ross said. "Can you help us?"

"The best way I can help is to send you to Professor Akyol."

FIFTY-FOUR

ALTHOUGH ŞIRNAK WAS ONLY EIGHTY-FIVE MILES SOUTHWEST OF VAN, traveling there required an indirect route three times that distance. Ross had suggested hiring a taxi rather than waiting for a dolmuş, and Graham agreed, wanting the privacy to make plans. But after collecting their things from the hotel, Ross's ebullience had dampened, leaving gaps of preoccupied silence Graham self-consciously struggled to fill. After using his phone to book rooms at the Nuh Otel near the university, he made a final attempt to kindle conversation.

"Didn't your mother ever tell you not to trust anyone you meet on the internet?"

Ross arched his brow uncomprehendingly.

"Zeki," Graham said. "You know him through a couple of emails? We've got a lot on the line to trust such a tenuous connection."

"A tenuous connection is better than no connection. What choice did we have?"

"I get it. Know anything about this professor—Akyol?"

"I hadn't heard of him until the symposium," Ross said. "I think he's the department head for Islamic History. Something like that."

"You haven't come across his work before?"

"Like I said, I had no interest in Ararat or Noah's Ark at all until Vogel shared the satellite data with me. That's what started this whole thing. The data was so compelling that when I came across anything about Cudi Dagh, I didn't give it much weight. And Akyol's focus is on Cudi. Other than that, I don't know anything about him or his work. The ark might not even be his main interest."

"And now we're all in the same boat, as it were." Graham half-suppressed a laugh at his own joke. "The question is where it will land."

Six hours after leaving Van, the taxi reached Şırnak, which—the driver explained—meant the city of Nuh. Graham and Ross both feigned ignorance, curious to see if the driver offered any information or tradition they hadn't come across so far. The man pointed out the windshield as he explained that the ark of Nuh had come to rest on the mountains on the other side of the city. He nodded, agreeing with himself as he added that pilgrims used to come to the mountain to see what was left of it.

Ross leaned over the seat, as if trying to spy the remains of the ark. "Is there anything still there?"

"No more wood." The driver shook his head, taking a hand from the wheel to make a horizontal slashing motion. "The last wood was taken to Cizre, to the tomb of Nuh—peace be upon him."

"Have you been there?" Graham asked.

"No," the driver said. "But there are many here who have. They can tell you."

"I thought Agri Dagh was Mount Ararat," Ross said, trading glances with Graham. "People say they have seen the ark there."

"That is not the place." The man frowned. "This is where the ark of Nuh came to rest. There can be no doubt." He gave a single, sharp nod, hammering the air with his nose to close the question.

They skirted the west side of the city on a road leading them to the entrance of Şırnak University, set a mile outside of town like an academic enclave. A guard gave a lackadaisical wave from his booth, and a gate raised, ushering them onto the campus.

"Where do you need to go?" The driver took his hands off the steering wheel to point simultaneously to his left and right as the entrance T-boned an intersection.

"There." Ross pointed to the left. "Go to the mosque."

Minarets speared the air, distinguishing it from the blocky cement buildings of the campus.

"I figured since Akyol is the director of Islamic History, someone there might know where his office is," Ross said.

The road encircled the main body of the campus, making a loop around the modular concrete and glass buildings.

"There seems to be a kind of parking garage aesthetic here," Graham said.

Ross smiled. "Well, if you think about it, the landing place of the ark *was* the world's first parking spot." His hand shot out suddenly as he looked back out the windshield. "There! Go to that building."

Graham followed the finger toward one of the few buildings on the outside of the loop. The name of the nondescript structure had been carved above the main entrance: *Islamic History and Arts*.

After paying the fare, they stepped into an empty lobby. "There's nobody here."

"I bet the term hasn't started yet." Ross zeroed in on a directory on the wall, listing the room numbers for classes and offices.

"*Hoş geldiniz.*"

The sound of the voice coming from behind them gave them a start, spinning them around to face a middle-aged man in western, business-casual dress. An arch of dark hair outlined his balding head, encompassing a friendly face behind wire-framed glasses and a goatee. An ID badge hung from a lanyard, displaying his face next to his name. *Akyol.*

Graham and Ross offered the customary response. "*Hoş bulduk.*"

"This is an unexpected pleasure, Dr. Ross," Akyol said in English, pleasantly surprised. "You are rather far from your site, are you not?"

"Thank you, Professor. I take it Zeki was able to contact you. And yes, I admit I am somewhat out of my depth. Or height, I guess I should say."

"And you are Dr. Eliot." Akyol nodded. "Very good to meet you, sir."

Graham noticed the university logo on Akyol's lanyard as they shook hands. A green gestural line formed a stylized mountain. Beneath the triangular form, two wavy blue lines ran at an angle. An orange curve sat on the top of the triangle, and a pair of red *s*-curves seemed to be emitted from the bowl.

"Professor, what exactly is that design?"

"Ah, you come directly to your point." Akyol pronounced the *r*'s with a percussive tap, convoluting an already difficult accent requiring

Graham to work for the words. "Do you not see? It is the ark of Nuh on Cudi." He indicated the different elements as he spoke. "This is the Tigris River down here. And the red is the fire of science."

A smile broke across Graham's face as he turned to Ross appreciatively. "Looks like we've come to the right place."

FIFTY-FIVE

Akyol's utilitarian office was lined with brown, press board bookcases facing each other from the two side walls. Graceful Arabic lettering on the spines of the books stuffing the shelves created a kind of filigree, the only ornamentation in the room. Windows along the back wall offered a view of the campus. Akyol installed himself behind a generic office desk facing into the room.

"What is it you would like to know about Sefinet Nebi Nuh?"

Graham sensed the use of the Arabic phrase for *The Ship of the Prophet Noah* was more than just how the locals referred to it. It was a test to see if they had researched the site enough to understand it, and it was a claim on the story by the Islamic tradition. Ross gave Graham a look that told him to take the lead.

"I have just come from Ararat, and Dr. Ross was preparing to continue his expedition there." He motioned to Ross as he spoke, drastically editing the story to the bare minimum that would justify their visit without lying. "But we met up in Van, and I discovered there was another—apparently older—tradition for Cudi Dagh. Ross had heard of it, too, and suggested we talk to Zeki, who sent us to you. We thought since Ararat was too dangerous right now that it was a perfect opportunity to investigate this other tradition. We thought it would be irresponsible not to try to see the site since we were in the region."

"You would know these things if you had come to the symposium, Dr. Ross," Akyol mock-scolded with a good-natured smile. "Yes, yes. The traditions are very much older. Very many ancient references."

Ross took the teasing with a chuckle. "Have you investigated the site?"

"Yes, I have been there three or four times. Unfortunately, there is very little left to see. The Nestorian sect built a monastery up there in the third or fourth century, but it burned down in the seventh century. Some of the remains are still there, though very little. Very little. Two or three other structures are there as well, but they are also in very poor shape."

Graham smiled inwardly at the overuse of *very*, apparently the only English superlative Akyol knew, and pronounced *veddy*. "Have you ever found any wood?"

"No, no wood." Akyol frowned. "For many centuries very many visitors took small pieces. The last of the large pieces of the wood were used to make the tomb of Nuh in Cizre. And, of course, some wood was taken to Hagia Sophia."

Graham pictured the iconic sixth-century cathedral in Istanbul, constructed when the city was still Constantinople, the seat Eastern Orthodoxy. After the city was conquered by the Muslims, the church was converted to a mosque and remained in use until it was preserved as a museum in 1935, after the founding of modern Turkey. Amidst the chaos of 2020, it was reactivated as a mosque.

"What about Hagia Sophia?"

"The Imperial doors into the sanctuary." Akyol gestured to his office door as if the words required an illustration. "The wood used to make them was taken from what was left of the ark. From Cudi Dagh."

Graham looked at Ross. "I've never heard that."

Akyol smiled apologetically and shrugged, absolving himself of their ignorance.

"Zeki told us you have seen the inscriptions made by Sennacherib," Graham said.

"Oh, yes! I have spent very many hours studying them. There are two sets. One at Sah, and the other at Hasanah. Seven of them. Two additional panels were cut but were never inscribed. I have taken the most recent photographs of them. The inscriptions are not in very good condition, I am afraid. Of course, they are very, very old. Sah is built on top of the first city the prophet Nuh—peace be upon him—built after leaving the ark."

"Is there still a village there?"

"No, no, ruins only. The place of the first city is buried below the ruins."

"Hmm," Ross noised. "Interesting. Have you been able to do any excavations there?"

"Unfortunately, no. There are greater needs here. There is much trouble with Syrian refugees and PKK. But the inscriptions are in danger of wearing away. They need to be preserved."

"Do the inscriptions say anything about the ark or the prophet Nuh?" Ross asked.

"No. They are just what King and Luckenbill said in their translations. They are boasts of one of Sennacherib's successful campaigns. Very much like other Sennacherib inscriptions. 'Sennacherib, the great king, the mighty king, king of the universe, king of Assyria, the exalted prince. I devastated the rebellious people.' Something like that. I am sure you know how it reads."

Graham nodded. "And are they all the same message?"

"There are minor differences, but yes, it is the same general message."

"We would like to see them for ourselves," Graham said. "And Sefinet Nebi Nuh. Could you show us on a map where to go?"

"It is very dangerous. Very dangerous. The soldiers often turn people away. However, they are more worried about Turks and Kurds than visitors from America, so there is a possibility they would let us pass. The problem is PKK is often camped on the mountain. The soldiers do not want them to have any support."

"They camp in the ruins?" Ross asked.

"Sometimes, yes, in the ruins. But there are also times the PKK has allowed people to pass by them and visit the site. It is not a difficult hike. But it is very difficult to make it past the guards. Very difficult."

"Can you tell us how to do it?" Graham asked.

Akyol smiled broadly. "No, I will not tell you. I will take you. I will go with you to the ark."

FIFTY-SIX

"Not nearly as impressive as Ararat, is it?"

Ross's rhetorical question articulated how underwhelmed Graham was by the mountain range as it slowly grew closer. "I must agree with you there. Looks more like the Great Smoky Mountains than where I pictured the ark landing."

Akyol had picked them up at the Nuh Otel, less than a mile from campus, as the first light of day spilled over the foothills surrounding the city. Graham and Ross had wanted to leave earlier, hoping to begin the hike by sunrise, but Akyol refused, claiming it was too dangerous to drive at night with the PKK active in the area. And it would be difficult to explain why they were heading toward an area known to harbor PKK soldiers. It would be hard enough to reach the peak during the day. He explained that it was the reason why he was driving a university vehicle; being academic tourists would lessen suspicion. At least he hoped that would be the case. Graham had noticed the university logo on the doors of the white Dacia SUV when it had pulled up but hadn't realized the official vehicle was a tactic.

Although ten miles separated the hotel from Cudi Dagh, the route—like the road from Van—wove through the hills like a loose thread, doubling the distance they needed to travel to reach the peak. And the last four miles would have to be crossed on foot. Two miles before the range rose out of the basin, they turned off the highway onto a well-worn, unpaved road. After passing through a tiny village, the road degraded into a rough, temperamental trail. Graham wondered if the passage was an ancient road preserved from antiquity.

Akyol confidently turned onto one of the anonymous paths at an intersection of several crisscrossing ways. Graham was just finishing a silent prayer of thanks they had a guide as they rounded a turn to find two Turkish Army soldiers in the track, waving them to a stop.

Graham and Ross traded apprehensive looks as the soldiers walked to each side of the car and stooped to inspect the interior of the SUV while keeping their machine guns readied.

"*What business do you have here?*"

The guard barked at Akyol's window, authoritative and intimidating, slowing Graham's comprehension. He felt himself drift into a detached state, becoming an observer of his own experience rather than a participant.

"*I am a professor of Islamic history at Şırnak University.*" Akyol displayed the ID on his lanyard. "*These men are professors from America. I am taking them to Cudi Dagh to see Sefinet Nebi Nuh.*"

The guard seemed unimpressed by Akyol's academic credentials and focused in on Graham and Ross. He bent to stare deeper into the car and talked past Akyol rather than moving to the back seat window. "*Who are you?*"

"*Isaac Ross. He is Graham Eliot. We are archaeologists.*"

The guard looked at Graham, then turned back to Ross. "*Show me your papers.*"

A bolt of cold panic shot through Graham, as he remembered his passport had never been stamped for Turkey. He hoped his self-conscious movements would appear normal as he handed over the small blue book. He began to compose a response in his defense as the soldier compared the identity pages with the men in the car.

"*Americans,*" the soldier said aloud to himself, as if he hadn't heard the information a few moments earlier.

The soldier unfolded the printout of the visa tucked inside the front cover, skimmed it, then returned it to the passport without turning the page to find an entry stamp. He handed it back to Graham as he made eye contact.

"*You are here to see Sefinet Nebi Nuh?*" The soldier spoke to Graham but seemed to think the words would have to be translated by Akyol or Ross.

"*Yes. We want to see the true place of descent.*"

The soldier glanced at Akyol, making a final appraisal of their threat.

"*They also want to see the inscriptions,*" Akyol added to their bona fides. "*On the other side of the mountain.*"

"*The other side is not safe.*" The soldier glanced at the back seat. "*Americans should not go there. The PKK is in the area. You should have been warned.*"

Akyol looked like he was preparing to plead their case, but the soldier continued, cutting him off before he could start.

"*You can go to the top, but do not go down to see the carvings on the other side. You must leave immediately if you see any PKK.*"

Akyol thanked him, then eased the SUV past their truck. Graham realized he had been holding his breath and had broken out in a sweat. The road twisted them out of sight, taking them into another small valley before Akyol broke the silence.

"That was not uncommon. If I had been alone, I would probably have been sent back. But we must still be careful."

Ross studied Akyol. "You trust what he said?"

"It is hard to know quite what to believe. But that is nothing new. There is a very old story about a man who traveled a month to see the ark. He had almost arrived, very close, just a short walk away, when the Devil appeared. He deceived the man and told him the ark was still a great distance away. The man was so discouraged that he abandoned his journey. He built a house where he was and lived there for the rest of his life. Some say the remains of the house can still be seen."

Graham looked at Ross. "Sounds like the story they tell about Jacob on Ararat."

Ross nodded. "Except instead of an angel, it's a devil."

Akyol raised a finger, making a point. "That is how you know it is a legend."

"What do you mean?" Graham looked at Akyol's eyes in the rearview mirror.

"The flood was foretold by the prophet Nuh—peace be upon him—and the ark is an artifact of that miracle. The flood authenticated the prophet's message of God's judgment, and the ark is the evidence. The ancient writings are clear that hundreds of years later, the ark was seen and touched by many before Jacob visited the mountain. So, why would an angel suddenly stop a holy man trying to visit it? Does that make sense to you?"

"No, it doesn't." Ross glanced at Graham, wondering where Akyol was leading. "I never really thought of it that way."

"Does it not make more sense," Akyol continued, "for the Devil to deceive those who wish to see the evidence? And here is another thing to consider: Where was Jacob from?"

The answer was still fresh in Graham's memory, "Nisibis."

"And where is Nisibis?" Akyol paused to let the implication of the question register. "A little over one hundred kilometers southwest of here. On the Syrian border. Except it is now called Nusaybin. Very far from Ararat. Very far. Tell me, please, why Jacob would ignore the traditions he surely must have known about Cudi Dagh and instead make a pilgrimage to Agri Dagh, many times farther away?"

"I can't think of any reason he would," Graham admitted. "But what about the wood he found that is at the cathedral in Echmiadzin?"

"I have never had the chance to examine it, but if it is authentic, if it truly is a piece of the ark, then it came from Cudi Dagh, not Agri Dagh."

They lapsed into silence again, leaving Graham and Ross to process what they had just heard as Akyol continued up through the harsh hills, barren of everything but scrub brush. Graham thought they were near where they would begin the hike as the truck reached the peak of a ridge, but the trail continued down the other side, into yet another valley. The zigzag through the terrain made Graham think of the hills as giant moguls.

"This is the mountain." Akyol made the announcement as the path began to ascend out of the valley, following a ravine that looked like it drained snow and rain from the peak, though it was currently dry.

The SUV circumvented a small bluff, and Graham saw that again the road was blocked. But this time the men with machine guns were not in uniform.

Akyol stopped the truck as they watched one of the four soldiers approach, one of them waving his machine gun to direct Akyol to step out of the car.

"PKK. Stay calm. I will speak to them."

Akyol stepped out of his door, leaving it open, raising his hands defenselessly. He held the pose during a rapid exchange that left Graham filling in the blanks of the words he couldn't pick out. Akyol was clearly trying to explain who they were, and as he motioned to the truck, the gunmen turned their attention to them.

Graham kept his eyes on the conversation as he whispered to Ross. "Think he's the Devil or the angel?"

"I think we're about to find out."

As if they had overheard, the soldiers accompanied Akyol back to the truck.

FIFTY-SEVEN

Akyol's heavy face weighed on Graham as he and Ross continued up the path on foot. Although they were long out of sight at this point, he could still feel Akyol watching, reminding them of the promise they had made. Graham's thoughts were so loud in his head that it didn't feel he was breaking the silence when he finally spoke.

"I can't believe he did that. I hope he's okay."

Ross's brooding, distracted mood from the day before had returned, even worsened, but Graham ascribed it to the bargain they had made. He was about to repeat himself when Ross replied.

"This expedition has cost more than I... It's not worth putting a life on the line."

"We had to leave him," Graham pleaded, mostly to himself. "If we didn't continue up the mountain, they would have thought we were lying. On some reconnaissance mission or something like that. The only way for all of us to get out of this safely was for him to do what he did."

Ross glared, as if Graham were having trouble understanding. "He offered himself as a hostage."

"It was the only guarantee we could give them." Graham kept his voice level, refusing to challenge Ross's intensity. "All we have to do is follow the trail, see what's there, and come back. Then they'll let him go." He tried to believe his own words, that it would really be that simple, but the situation was so surreal that he again felt the tug of detachment, tempting him to become a spectator to his own life.

He distracted himself with Google Maps, tracking their progress on his phone. The ravine Akyol had told them to follow bent around

Cudi Dagh in a crescent as it channeled them to the peak 3,000 feet above.

Before making the final ascent, they stopped to rest as they got their bearings using GPS. Graham shuttled through the satellite images of this part of the mountain and found one showing it covered in snow, making it look vaguely like a molar. Ross looked over his shoulder and studied the locator pins labeling the specific parts of the site.

"Cistern. Shrine. Domed hut? What's that?"

"I'm not sure. Looked kind of like an igloo. It's not there anymore. The latest picture I have of it shows it in ruins. But I found another from a couple of years ago where it's still standing."

"What happened to it?"

Graham shook his head. "Don't know."

Ross continued reading the waypoints. "SW corner of church. East wall of monastery. Bender. That's where Bender dug?"

"As far as I can tell. And it makes more sense for the monastery to be built next to the ark than on top of it."

Ross looked up from the screen, toward the summit. "Good thing the Crusaders didn't visit this site. They would have paved the peak in marble and built some ridiculous edifice on top of it."

Graham chuckled, picturing how the Crusaders had done that very thing to the likely locations of Jesus's tomb and his birthplace. In the interest of preserving the holy sites, they had destroyed them, transforming them into what they thought places of veneration should look like rather than how they actually appeared. Graham had used the difference as an illustration for his students on how not everyone shared the same philosophy of history. And he was thankful Ross's quip broke the sullen mood that had clouded him.

Ross followed up the sardonic observation with another, delivering it with a raised brow. "Let's hope there's some wood left up there we can take for good luck like Sennacherib. We need all we can get right now."

Graham smiled and stepped past him, beginning the last leg of the ascent. The remainder of the trail turned steep as it guided them onto the southern ridge. The smooth mound of the summit was crowned with an outcrop of rocks, and they clambered to the top, giving them a panorama of barren rolling hills spanning the borders of Turkey, Iraq, and Syria.

"Sure we're in the right place?" Ross voiced the same question Graham was asking himself. "Doesn't look like any of the photos you showed me."

The mysterious hexagonal structure in the Lepsius and Bell photos was gone. And yet there were ruins of stacked stone walls. Graham opened the Bell photos on his phone, compared it to what he was standing on, then walked to the other end of the summit and looked back to where he had been.

Graham tapped the ground at his feet. "This must be the shrine. We were standing on top of it. So much of it has been destroyed in the last hundred years."

Again Ross peered at Graham's phone and compared Bell's black and white image with the site in front of them. "I think you're right. That corner there—" He pointed at a ninety-degree angle of two rows of stone. "I think it's *there*," he said, moving his finger to the screen showing an interior wall of the structure Bell had seen.

"Looks right to me. I wonder what happened to it. Maybe it was the PKK. Akyol said they sometimes used it for a base."

"Doesn't look like it survived them very well."

Graham looked at the waypoints on his GPS again and indicated an area to his right, to the bottom of the mound at a small set of remains forming another right angle. "That must be whatever the little building with the domed roof was."

"Where did Bender find the wood?"

Graham referenced the screen, then pivoted to the left. "On the edge of the bluff over there."

The south side of the peak sloped into a basin at the top of the steep drop of the southern face of the range. Graham followed the GPS across the basin to the pin marked *Bender*.

"How do you know this is the place?"

"I don't," confessed Graham. "Not exactly. But his report says the location was in this basin. A couple of German researchers interviewed

Bender's wife after his death. She also showed them his private papers. This spot is an educated guess. But given that the ark was so big, the exact spot of Bender's dig might not be necessary. We just have to be in the same area." He zoomed out the view and held up the screen for Ross to see, showing the satellite image of the basin. "See how this part of the basin is a depression that doesn't quite follow the line made by the rest of the ridge? See how it kind of jogs out from it? Want to take a guess how long it is?"

"Given the set up to the question, I'd say about 450 cubits."

"You paid attention in Sunday school, Isaac," Graham said, shrugging off his backpack, cuing Ross to do the same.

They found the camping shovels Akyol had loaned them, then studied the ground.

"This is your show," Ross said, waving the blade over the surface. "Where do you want to dig?"

"I guess right here is as good a place as any."

Graham sank the spade into the ground, and again Ross mirrored the action, piling the sandy dirt to the side of the hole.

"How far down did Bender dig?"

"A meter," Graham huffed between shovels. "Maybe a little less."

Despite his exhaustion—part stress and part exertion—the adrenaline of the thrill of the hunt energized him. The soft ground enabled them to cut a trench without much difficulty, creating a small pit of sandy walls. Three feet deep, the sand changed color, the dark gray indicating a layer of a different composition.

Graham stopped as soon as he recognized the change. "Hey! Look at that!"

Ross dug two more spadefuls, reaching deeper into the layer where there was less sand in the mix. He kneeled down, grabbed a handful of the dark clumps—some the size of peas, the rest no larger than sea salt rocks. He stood back up and poured half into Graham's palm.

"Looks like rotted wood," Ross said, pushing the granules with his index finger. "But black, like volcanic sand."

"Just like Bender described," Graham replied without looking up.

He emptied the granules into a pocket of his backpack, then knelt down and reached into the trench for another handful, adding it to the first. He clawed out several more chunks, carefully set them on the shovel's blade, then pulled out a lighter from the backpack. "Akyol loaned it to me," Graham explained.

He flicked the lighter and turned his wrist so the body of the lighter was parallel with the shovel in order to get the flame as close to the substance as possible, trying to make direct contact. He held the lighter steady, rotating the shovel to heat the whole substance. Ross bent down to get a closer look at the reaction as the black pebble began to change shape and turn lighter.

"It's melting! It's bituminous. If we can collect enough to test, then we can—"

Ross jerked to a stand and kicked the shovel from Graham's hand, peppering the air with the dark granules.

Graham moved his mouth in wordless, voiceless shapes as he stared up uncomprehendingly. Ross loomed over him, weaponizing the shovel, holding it like a baseball bat.

"I'm sorry, Graham. I can't let you take that."

FIFTY-EIGHT

GRAHAM'S VOICE RASPED, FINALLY CATCHING TRACTION. "WHY? I don't understa—"

"Vogel's forcing me. He said he would implicate me along with him in the spy charge if I don't stop you. Even if it doesn't stick, my reputation will be ruined. My career will be over."

Graham heard his own words unwittingly said back to him, convicting him. "He did the same thing to me. But you don't have to do this. We can fight him."

"You don't know him. I have worked with him for years. He is vicious when he doesn't get what he wants. The most cutthroat person I've ever seen." Ross's voice paused and grew softer, almost pleading. "I have no choice, Graham. I'm sorry, but I don't."

"Ross, listen to me. You *do* have a choice. You didn't have to call Vogel and tell him what I was planning."

"You're right. I didn't have to call. Because he already knew."

"That's impossible. He couldn't have—"

"Think about it, Graham. Look at your phone."

Graham held it up as if it were a foreign object.

"We used the GPS to navigate to this exact spot. How did you do that without any cell towers around? Satellites. And who gave you the SatSleeve? Who do you know who owns communications satellites? Vogel has tracked your movements the whole time. He knows where you are *right now*. I don't have to tell him."

Graham felt like a fool, the phone growing heavy in his hand as he remembered the prayers of thanks he offered for the very tool that had betrayed him. He had to restrain the impulse to throw it over the bluff, but the possibility that he would still need it constricted his hand in a resentful clench. "But why did he send *you*?"

"He didn't," Ross said. "Vogel sent Şahin to follow you. He followed the dolmuş you took to Van. He even checked into the same hotel. But then you called me. Vogel recognized my number in the call log. When Şahin saw me check in at the hotel, Vogel figured out I was coming here to help you. And I genuinely was, I swear. But when we went back to the hotel to check out and leave for Şırnak, Vogel called. He took advantage of my being here and changed his plans. He forced me into this."

Ross paused, swallowing hard. "I've been struggling with it, trying to think of a way out, but I just don't have a choice. I was hoping we wouldn't find anything. That would make the whole trip worthless, and I wouldn't have to do anything. But now I don't see any other way. Please don't make me do anything to hurt you. Fill the hole, walk away, and keep your mouth shut. Wait a few years and come back or send someone else. But you can't find anything here right now."

Graham could hear the sincerity in Ross's voice and scrambled to take advantage of it. "So now *you're* the hostage."

Ross blinked hard, as if blinding himself would render him deaf to the words.

"Isaac, remember who you are. Look at what we just discovered. We might well be standing on the very spot where Noah's Ark came to rest. We might have solved a mystery thousands of years old. Don't you care about the truth?"

The shovel wavered in Ross's hand as a desperate, trapped expression revealed he knew the truth but couldn't act on it. Graham recognized he had connected and kept talking before Ross washed his hands of the truth like a modern-day Pilate.

"The truth is that Ararat is nothing more than a hole in the ground. There's nothing there."

Anger flashed across Ross's face, dissolving into desperation. "Nothing except a charge of espionage and my career. It's all gone if I don't do what Vogel says."

"It's all gone if you *do*. Especially if we have proof in our hands—literally in our hands—and don't act on it. If you don't treat what we just found like a scholar, you really *will* lose everything."

Ross stared into the dug trench as if looking into his own grave.

Graham sensed the threat draining from the shovel enough to slowly stand, shedding the posture of weakness. "It doesn't have to be this way. Listen to me, Isaac, there may be a way out of this for both of us." A glint of hope pounded against the suspicion in Ross's eyes. "You can tell Vogel that I got away from you somehow. You go back down to Şırnak. I'll go down the south side to Cizre. That way you can tell him that you tried to stop me, but I escaped. Did he really expect you to attack me with a shovel?"

"No. He wanted me to..." Ross reached behind his back, under his shirt, and pulled out a gun.

Graham's eyes widened with terror, morphing to confusion as Ross turned it in his hands, examining it as he kept the barrel pointed safely away.

"It's Şahin's," Ross said dully. "I can't shoot you, Graham. I don't want to. I've never even shot a gun before. I even took the cartridge out so no one would get hurt." He dropped it to his side. "I was sure there would be nothing here. That I wouldn't have to do anything, and it would all just work out. But now..."

"Ross, be reasonable. Think it through. This plan will work. It will protect you and still expose Vogel."

Warring emotions rippled across Ross's face as he considered it. "What about Akyol? If both of us don't come down, the PKK won't release him."

"Tell them I went to see the Sennacherib inscriptions and that you wouldn't go. Tell them you tried to talk me out of it."

"But then they will come after you."

"Yes, but by the time you explain it to them, I will be halfway down the mountain. It wouldn't be practical for them to chase me. Plus, if Akyol is right, then there are more PKK where I'm going than on the side we came up. Tell them I wanted to see the inscriptions at

Sah. Remember? Akyol said it was the first city built by Noah. That's where he said some of the inscriptions are. Tell them that's where I went, and I'll go down another way."

Ross let the shovel drop to the ground. "Why don't we both just go back the way we came. That way we can get Akyol back safe, and then we can get home, too."

"Because if Vogel sent Şahin to follow me to Van, what makes you think he didn't send Şahin to follow us to Şırnak? How do you know he's not there now? Or even somewhere behind us on the mountain?"

Ross looked back self-consciously at the suggestion.

"We have to be able to break Vogel's hold on us in some way," Graham said. "This way we each have cover. Şahin isn't following *you*. He won't know this conversation ever took place. You can tell him anything you want. Tell him I overpowered you or lost you on the mountain. It doesn't really matter. He's just a hired gun anyway. He has no real allegiance to Vogel except financially."

Ross nodded almost imperceptibly. "Okay, what about the PKK?"

"If you tell the men who are with Akyol that I went to Sah, then hopefully they will alert the fighters on the south side of the mountain. If they send people to look for me, then that will draw them away from the route I will actually be on."

"Which is where?" Ross asked.

"The shortest way I can find to Cizre. It's only fifteen miles away. From there I can hire a taxi to take me to Van."

Ross stared at Graham, then put a hand over his eyes and bowed his head as sobs rattled his body. He gasped as if he had been suffocated by his predicament and had just come up for air. "Please forgive me. I'm so stupid. I am so ashamed. Please forgive me."

Relief flooded into Graham, convinced the emotion was genuine, but was unsure whether to approach. "Ross, I understand. It's okay. Vogel put me in a position like this too. I get it. I really do."

Ross lifted the gun as he fished the cartridge from his coat pocket and loaded it, then extended it forward, slackly. Graham stared at the gun a moment before realizing Ross was handing it to him.

"Take it. You need it more than I do. You're still in danger even without me."

Graham reached out tentatively and took the gun, holding it as if it were poisonous. "Thank you, Ross."

FIFTY-NINE

As he followed the edge of the plateau of Cudi Dagh, Graham fixed his eyes on Cizre, hoping his plan had as much merit as he'd made it sound to Ross. The first obstacle he had to overcome was getting off the mountain, and Gertrude Bell's travelogue offered the answer—as long as he could figure out how to ask the question. Which canyon had the trail she used to reach the top?

He opened Google Earth on his phone and compared the satellite image to his perspective at ground level. Ross's revelation came back to him, reminding him that the satellite sleeve on the phone enabled Vogel to know where he was. But by the time Vogel figured out what was happening, the sleeve would be in a trash can in Cizre, severing the electronic tether. Hopefully. For now, it was a necessary risk. He consoled himself with the words of Joseph when he confronted his brothers who had sold him into slavery—the first step on his unlikely journey to become the second most powerful man in Egypt. "You meant to harm me, but God meant it for a good purpose." Spiritual judo, Graham thought, turning an attack against the attacker.

According to what he remembered from Bell's account, she had camped at Hasanah, near the second location of inscriptions. And to ascend the mountain, she went up via a gorge near the village. He wished Bell had included a map of the route, but at least she left a detailed description. She had paralleled the mountain before beginning the ascent, and he found the Hasanah waypoint at the foot of the gorge.

Like so many locations in modern Turkey that were formerly parts of Armenia or Kurdistan, its name had been changed. What Bell knew as Hasanah was now called Kösreli. He traced the image on the screen across the range to the east to the next gorge. It was about two miles from Sefinet Nebi Nuh, and a mile-and-a-half away from where he was now.

Graham could almost feel the touch of Ross's eyes on him as he hurried away, but he refused to turn around. Although he was still reeling from the betrayal, it was something he understood and even had some empathy for. The conflict and shame Ross couldn't hide revealed the good man Graham knew. And ultimately, Ross had done the right thing, a demonstration of repentance Graham admired.

The GPS indicated he had reached the top of what he inferred was Gabriel's Gate, and he hesitated before stepping over the edge. He was on a remote and barren mountain, trying to reach a town that was a terrorist stronghold on the Syrian border. He wasn't sure what frightened him more: being taken hostage or being lost in the wilderness. The question made him feel utterly alone. He had felt profoundly alone spiritually after Alyson and Olivia died, but this was different. He was literally, physically isolated. The realization almost made him thankful Vogel was tracking him, as if accompanying him from a distance.

The declivity of the gorge dropped two thousand feet in less than a mile, punishing his knees. More than once his feet slipped out from under him, sending him sliding down scree between plumes of scrub brush. Halfway down, the slope relaxed, finally depositing him in a basin at the top of a foothill.

Graham rested on a rock as he oriented himself with the satellite image, sighing when he saw that Kösreli was still another two miles west. Exhaustion—physical and emotional—weighed on him, and it took an effort of supreme self-discipline to stand back up. But he knew the longer he rested, the harder it would be to move on.

He followed a dirt track along the edge of the basin until the foothill dropped away, lowering him to the base of another gorge. Graham scanned the canyon and took comfort in discovering how much larger and more severe it was than the one he had chosen, affirming his decision.

According to the GPS, Kösreli lay half-a-mile south, around the bend in the stream coming down from the gorge. The satellite image showed a small village built among the ruins of a once-larger settlement. As many as two dozen obviously inhabited buildings sat in the midst of at least the same number of rectangular remnants of foundations and walls. Several plots included gardens large enough to make rows of plants. But as far as Graham was concerned, Kösreli's most interesting feature was that it was literally the end of a road leading to Cizre, and—hopefully—safety.

Before entering the village, he wanted to settle in his mind how to explain himself and how he came to need help. He also wondered how he'd recognize someone he could trust. He remembered both Akyol and Şahin saying PKK fighters put their cause above family. Graham assumed that meant they probably wouldn't be keeping large gardens in the middle of nowhere. On the other hand, their cause was to make a better life for their people, and the people they fought for lived somewhere. Graham wondered if one of those somewheres was Kösreli.

Akyol and Şahin also said the PKK had many offshoots. Graham had gotten lost in an alphabet soup of acronyms, each sounding like a distinction without a difference. He thought the best way to pick a house to approach would be to find one that had small children. If the PKK renounced having family, then kids would be a sign that the father was not himself a soldier.

As he studied the map to find a vantage point from which he could observe the village, he saw the location marker for the inscriptions an equal distance away from Kösreli, in the rocks high on the side of the hill facing the village. If he visited the inscriptions first, he might be spotted, and then his story of wanting to see them and not being able to hike back over the mountain might be more credible. And if he wasn't spotted, then he would be able to reconnoiter the village from there. Either way, it would enable him to see the inscriptions.

Ignoring the protests of his body, he started up the hill on the other side. From a distance, the hill looked almost smooth, stippled green with scrub brush. But once he was on its face, crossing it, he discovered it was rockier than he had expected. Near the top of the hill, he could see several rock outcroppings and thought—based on the images he'd seen of the inscriptions—it was the most likely place.

Two-thirds of the way up the hill, the layout of Kösreli began to resemble the satellite image. It occurred to him that without binoculars he didn't have a way to observe the homes like he had planned to. Given that this was supposed to be a day trip where he could visit the location and investigate it up close, he didn't think he needed to bring the binoculars.

Resigning himself to the failure of scouting the village, he walked the final leg to the rocks. The jagged crags were pocked with cavities and niches, making it difficult to be sure he was tracing all the possible surfaces.

Then he saw it: a vertical shadow too regular to be naturally formed, like a doorway cut into a rock that had been walled up.

The Assyrian king—Sennacherib—summoned Graham closer to the right half of the panel. As Akyol had said, the inscription on the left half of the panel was almost worn away. Cracks spiderwebbed across the slab, and the divots of time and weather imprinted the surface. Graham touched it, running his fingers over it as if confirming its existence. He stepped back and took several photographs before he became aware of another presence. He turned around and found someone watching him. A boy, no more than ten.

SIXTY

The boy was wearing blue jeans, a rib-necked sweater, and beat-up Adidas shoes. As the shock of his presence dissipated, Graham illogically conflated Bell's picture of the inscription with the boy, as if they were the same person. The impossibility of the idea was only a flash, like a subliminal frame in a movie, but it was enough to make Graham feel like the boy had been expected. He shook off the thought, smiled, and kneeled down.

"*Hoş geldiniz.*" As he sounded it out, the greeting he had always found to be an awkward way of saying *welcome* now seemed appropriate. *You came well.*

The boy smiled shyly as he gave the expected reply, which seemed even more appropriate. "*Hoş bulduk.*" *You found well.*

"*Tanıştığımıza sevindim.*" *I am glad to meet you.* Graham touched his chest to refer to himself. "*Benim adım Graham.*" *My name is Graham.* As he said it, he offered his hand to shake.

The boy took it timidly, letting Graham do all the work of shaking the limp arm, then touched his own chest and said, "Mattai."

Graham smiled and repeated the name. "*Mattai. İngilizce biliyor musunuz?*"

The boy answered with a shake of his head that he did not know English.

Mattai's name sounded from down below, carried up the hill by a man's urgent voice. Graham heard a tone of worry and warning as Mattai's eyes widened in recognition, spinning him around to look toward the village. Graham stood and spotted a man at least a hundred yards away, hooking his arm through the air repeatedly to gesture the boy to him. The man abruptly stopped as Graham came into full view.

He called Mattai's name again, this time with a voice that was more stern, rigid with an additional layer of concern which Graham took to refer to him, the stranger.

The boy made an expansive motion with his hands, keeping his palms face-down to the ground, as if he were trying to smooth the landscape, and gave Graham a serious look. "*There are many mines here.*"

"*Mines?*" Graham repeated the word for emphasis rather than a lack of understanding. A few moments earlier he had wanted to stay in motion, the faster the better. But the word had made a living statue of him, like a tableau vivant of the inscription he stood next to.

Mattai nodded. "*Mines.*" This time as he said the word, he brought his hands together, clapping violently, them yanking them apart to mime an explosion. "*I know where they are. Follow me.*"

Mattai began to pick his way carefully down the hill, meandering around unseen dangers, occasionally pointing to an innocuous looking place in the ground to avoid. Graham followed the boy's steps as precisely as he could, repeating the small stride as he looked futilely for signs of what might trigger the bombs. As they serpentined down the hill, the man called encouragements, needlessly reminding them to be careful. Graham didn't look up from the path picked by Mattai, but part of him envisioned his way up the mountain, and he wondered how he could have threaded his way through a minefield in ignorance. The thought was so nerve-wracking that it threatened to distract him, and he forced it from his mind to concentrate on getting down.

The bottom of the slope leveled out, and Mattai broke into a jog to cover the last twenty yards separating him from the man Graham assumed was his father. Graham raised his hand in a friendly wave as Mattai started talking animatedly, though not as if he had been in danger. The man glanced over Mattai's head at Graham during the report, then broke into a smile of welcome as he repeated a Turkish proverb.

"*Every guest is a gift from God.*"

SIXTY-ONE

Thirty minutes later, Graham was covering the rest of the distance to Cizre as a passenger in a decrepit truck belonging to Mehmet, Mattai's father. Mehmet looked like a grown version of Mattai, as if the father were a fulfilled prophecy of the boy's physical future. Against Mattai's protests, Mehmet left him behind to finish his chores.

Graham explained how he had come from Şırnak and had hiked to the peak from the north side of Cudi Dagh. After he reached the other side to see the inscriptions, he realized there wasn't time to return. Before he had finished, Mehmet offered to take him to Cizre, and from there he could take the bus back to Şırnak. Graham was thankful Mehmet was a testament to the area's reputation for hospitality, PKK notwithstanding.

Mehmet identified himself as Assyrian rather than Turkish, Kurdish, or Armenian. Graham remembered Bell had described Hasanah—now Kösreli—as being a village of Assyrian Christians. According to Mehmet, the Turkish government had forcibly relocated all the inhabitants in 1990, then planted mines in the area, especially around the inscriptions.

"*How can they do that?*" Graham struggled with the right words in Turkish and assumed he had misunderstood. "*I thought the United Nations had forbidden mines.*"

Mehmet arched an eyebrow skeptically. "*I have never seen the United Nations here. It was the Turkish government who said it had been mined.*" He said it as if *law* and *power* were synonymous. Twenty years after being relocated, those who wished were allowed to return to Kösreli and the other villages in the area.

Mehmet explained that he had grown up in the area and thought it would be safer than the cities. He was tired of being caught between the different factions and thought the village was remote enough to avoid being caught in the conflict. It was why he had left Mattai to his chores—Cizre was too unstable. But even in Kösreli, they still had to deal with the PKK, either directly, or because the Turkish soldiers would sweep the area looking for them.

Graham heard no bitterness in Mehmet, only resignation—a man who had adapted to survive circumstances he didn't like and were unfair. The realization convicted Graham, and he wished he faced his own unfair circumstances with as much grace.

Mehmet guided the truck over the Tigris River and into Cizre on the far bank. As they crossed the bridge, he pointed to the left, away from the city. "*That is Syria. This is the border.*"

The road followed the edge of the city to a roundabout, and they turned north to enter the city proper.

"*The bus station is here. There are taxis. You can return to Şırnak, no problem.*"

Or Adana, Graham thought—having Googled where the closest U.S. Consulate was. But that was a bus ride of several hours, not a job for a dolmuş. He could see the tour buses lining the road before they reached the depot. He was surprised to see that many of them advertised *Nuh* as a destination on their sides.

"*Why does it say, 'Nuh'? Do people come here to go to the mountain?*"

"*No, they come to see the tomb of the prophet Nuh—peace be upon him.*"

He'd forgotten about the traditional tomb in the course of the day's events. "*Is it far?*"

"*No, no. Very near.*" Mehmet turned into the lot for the bus station, and parked. "*We can walk there. I will show you, then you can go to Şırnak.*"

Graham hoped the detour was worth it as he walked alongside Mehmet, continuing down the main street, then branching into a neighborhood. Bullet holes pocked the masonry of most of the buildings, and rubble littered the streets. The debris of violence and disrepair gave Graham the sense that the unrest was too frequent to clean up after, that there was more to come.

At the first intersection in the warren of streets, Mehmet led Graham up a flight of steps into a plaza forming a small compound of half-a-dozen buildings. The main building—on their right—was a mosque, featuring a multi-domed roof and a pair of minarets flanking the entrance, towering over it like spiritual smokestacks. Three other buildings were also capped with domes, though none competed with the mosque. Apartment buildings rose six or seven stories high on the other side of the plaza, boxing it in, clothing it unceremoniously with laundry drying on balcony railings.

"*That is the tomb.*"

Mehmet gestured to the structure directly in front of them, a cube-shaped building two stories tall, crowned with a hexagonal dome. The building was covered in white tiles with a blue floral pattern, setting it apart from the beige and earth tone colors of the other buildings. Trapezoidal windows collected light in the upper half of the front wall. Below them, in the middle of the wall, two large tiles decorated with Arabic calligraphy identified the spot as the tomb of Noah.

As they walked toward the entrance on the left side of the building, English lettering caught Graham's eyes. The unexpected discovery of an English language plaque mounted in the plaza wall stopped him as he read it:

> *In the Gudi, Sumer, Akad, Elem, Assyrian, Epitaphs, and the Qur'an, Bible, and the Old Testament you can find a lot of texts about the flood. The man they told about is the prophet Noah. His real name is Abdul Gaffar and he is known as Noah, Nova, Nuh, Utnapastim in different languages. It's clearly written in the Qur'an that his boat stopped in the mountain of Cudi. He build his house in the top of the mountain of Cudi.*

"*Come. There is not much time. It is almost time for prayers.*"

Mehmet's prompt kept Graham from reading the rest, but it was interesting how in sync it was with all he had recently learned. He wondered yet again how he had been so unaware of the tradition. The reminder of prayers made him notice the waning light of late afternoon, and he hoped there was still time to catch a bus to Adana as he followed Mehmet into the building.

Although the building was two stories tall, there was only one story and one room. The left side of the room was sectioned off by a low, filigreed wooden screen supporting tall panes of glass. On the other side, an enormous coffin—at least fifteen feet long—was on display.

Graham studied the Arabic calligraphy embroidered on a thick green blanket, trimmed in gold, draped over the casket. The most remarkable thing about the tomb itself was that the coffin was as long as the room. Graham puzzled over the scale and odd proportions, wondering if any of the legends claimed Noah—Nuh—was a giant. Although he hadn't formed any expectation about what he would see, the possibilities did not include what looked like a salad bar or buffet that had been closed for the day. He worked to keep his expression reverent as he looked at his host.

"*Thank you, Mehmet. You are very kind to have taken the time to show this to me.*"

Graham led the way through the exit into the plaza and immediately froze, as if he had accidentally wandered into another minefield. Because he had. Five men stood in a semi-circle waiting for him, each with an AK-47 machine gun, their faces covered with masks.

SIXTY-TWO

THE SQUARE HAD GROWN MORE CROWDED, COLLECTING WORSHIPPERS for maghrib, the evening prayers. Graham turned cold with the realization that in order to suddenly be surrounded by armed men meant they—*he*—had been watched. As he abruptly stopped, Mehmet stepped past him before being checked by the sight of the weapons. The only motion he allowed himself was to pivot his head back and forth several times from Graham to the gunmen before settling on Graham.

"*What is happening? Who are you?*"

The mask in the center of the arc answered as if the question had been addressed to him. "*We are protecting our people.*" The knitting over his face distorted as the mouth behind it spit out sharp, accusatory words. The timbre of the voice made Graham wonder if the masks were truly PKK militants or young men—kids even—imitating them.

"*I am not here to hurt you.*" Graham hoped his own voice sounded calmer than he was. "*I am not your enemy. And this man did nothing but act as my guide. Please let him go.*"

Mehmet glanced at Graham in gratitude and confusion. The mask watched the exchange, then used his weapon to motion Mehmet away, ushering him into the crowd.

As Mehmet was removed, one of the other masks stepped forward and stripped Graham's backpack from his shoulder. He kneeled just out of reach of Graham and opened it.

"*I am a professor. I was hiking on the mountain and got lost. That man found me and brought me here so I could go home.*"

The second mask emptied the backpack, spilling the contents. The MacBook Pro clattered onto the flagstone, followed by the folded camping shovel and the portable chargers. Graham's heart sunk as the man held the bottom of the pack and shook it. Black granules fell from the inner pouch, joining the grit on the pavement. He continued to shake the backpack, apparently feeling the weight of an item that had not fallen out. The second mask reached into the bag and pulled out what had snagged on one of the webbed compartments: Ross's pistol.

Graham had completely forgotten about it, his look of horror the most surprised expression in the square.

The first mask jabbed his finger at the pistol. "*What kind of professor carries a gun? One who is also a spy!*"

"*No! No! That was given to me as I started climbing the mountain in case I needed to protect myself from—*" Graham stopped himself before he finished the sentence.

The mask completed it for him. "*From the PKK?*"

Graham's silence condemned him.

"*If you are a professor who has no fight with us, why would you fear the PKK?*"

"*I did not come to fight,*" Graham pleaded. "*I came to see the place where the prophet's boat landed. That is all. It was others who feared you, who feared for me and gave me the gun.*"

The mask looked around as he replied, speaking as much to the onlookers as Graham. "*We are demanding our land.* OUR *land,*" he repeated, pausing for effect. "*We are here to prevent the enemy from crossing into our areas. We are also here to prevent crime.*"

Graham nodded in understanding, hoping to convey he thought their position was reasonable. The mask waved his gun broadly, encompassing the surroundings, apparently cuing Graham to look around.

"*The enemy comes at us with heavy weapons.*"

Apparently, the mask wanted him to understand that the destruction and damage he saw had not been committed by them, but by Turkish soldiers.

"*All we have are Kalashnikovs.*" The mask raised his weapon to refer to his own gun as if it were almost insignificant. "*But when they attack, we will attack harder.*"

Graham nodded again, not knowing what else to do.

"*Tell them that in America. Tell your university.*"

Hope filtered through Graham's fear as the meaning of the words became clear. He was not to be the hostage, but the messenger. "*I will. I will tell them.*"

"*Tell your media the PKK are not terrorists. They say we are, but we are not. As long as they occupy our land, resistance will be our lives.*"

The mask stepped to one side, signaling the crowd to part and let Graham pass.

"*I understand,*" Graham said. "*Thank you for being merciful. I will tell them.*"

The mask dropped the backpack and kicked it to Graham, inadvertently scattering the granules as it skidded across the pavement. Graham watched helplessly as the material mingled with the rest of the dirt and debris, becoming dots he could no longer connect.

SIXTY-THREE

By noon the next day, Graham sat alone in a reception room at the U.S. Consulate in Adana as his story was checked out. He had told it three times now. It took an abbreviated account to get him in the door without an appointment, and he had given a detailed version twice. He used his laptop to show the diplomats the pictures he'd taken, partly as evidence to verify his story, and partly because they were fascinated by the sites.

He'd spent the overnight, four-hundred-mile bus ride asleep, but still fought to stay awake as he waited. He distracted himself cataloging and tagging images, a task he realized needed to be done as he explained what had happened. A chime interrupted his work, announcing a text from Steinmeyer.

Did you hear about Vogel?

Graham was instantly alert. *No. What happened?*

Steinmeyer took so long to reply that Graham didn't expect just one word.

Suicide.

A wave of nausea buffeted him, consuming all his oxygen, leaving him shivering and breathless. Even after playing him as a fool, sending him on a fake mission to provide cover for himself, Graham grieved the news. Part of him even felt responsible, as if finding a way to escape Vogel's influence left Vogel feeling as if he had no hope, no chance of redemption or forgiveness.

Graham's curser had activated the text field, creating an ellipse to indicate he was composing a response. He was at a loss for what to say and had typed and deleted several options when the phone rang, displaying Steinmeyer's name on the screen.

"I thought it would be easier to call since you seemed available to talk."

"Yes, thanks. So, what happened?"

"There was a fire in Vogel's library. When they recovered the body, they found he had shot himself in the head."

Graham pictured the magnificent collection that had been lost, adding to his grief. "I don't know what to say. How do you know all this?"

"The police came here to talk to me. They told me. They said there was a note. I did not get to see it, but apparently, he wanted the INTF to have his collection of biblical manuscripts."

"Like a will?"

"Something like that. But they wanted to know what our business was since it seemed to be the last thing he did. They were not executors, of course. And if they were, there was nothing left to bequest."

"Why did he start a fire if he was going to use a gun?"

"It is unclear, but the police think he may have been burning some documents in the trash can. They think that when he shot himself, he knocked the trash can over. He did not anticipate the possibility of the fire spreading to the rest of the library."

Graham made a mournful hum. "So tragic. Nothing is left?"

"Yours is the last and best document of his library's collection. Apparently, he did it because he had somehow gotten involved in espionage and was discovered."

"I'm afraid that is true," Graham said. "He told me the accusation was false, but I figured out he was using me to try to create a story to protect himself. He tried to use Isaac Ross the same way. He was forcing us, actually. But we found a way out of his plan. I guess he felt hopeless. It is so sad."

They ended the call with mutual promises to be in touch soon, leaving each other to process the news. Graham stared sightlessly at an image of Cudi Dagh as the phone rang again, this time with Ross's name on the screen.

"Isaac, I'm so glad you called. Did you make it down safely?"

"Yes. But I have been waiting to hear from you. I was getting worried. Are you okay?"

"I'm at the consulate in Adana."

"Adana? Was that your plan all along?"

"No. I was just trying to get to Cizre. Then I realized going to Şırnak might be just heading back into trouble. And I knew I had to get to an embassy or consulate. I didn't call or text because I didn't know if Şahin or Vogel might find a way to get to your phone. How is Akyol?"

Ross sighed, as if making room for the answer. "He was upset at first—understandably so. Almost as much as the PKK. But he calmed down once he saw they were not going to hold him. The PKK radioed to whoever else was up there and warned that you were on the mountain. Any trouble on your end?"

"I didn't see anyone else until I got to the village on the other side. That's where I got a ride into Cizre. But I did see one of the inscriptions. I'll send you pictures."

Ross ignored the promise. "Did you hear about Vogel?"

"Steinmeyer just told me. It never occurred to me that he'd hurt himself."

"Me either." Ross let a long pause hang between them before continuing. "Graham, I'm so sorry for what happened on the mountain. I am so…I'm deeply ashamed."

"I meant it when I said I forgave you. I really do. Honestly, so much has happened that I hadn't really thought about it much. We are all good."

"You're a good friend, Graham. Thank you."

Graham heard an uncharacteristic vulnerability in Ross's voice and felt a bond forming instead of a wall.

"By the way," Ross added, "you were right about Şahin. I saw him at the hotel in Şırnak. I don't think he knew I spotted him. But that's probably how the news reached Vogel so fast."

"Makes sense. Where are *you* now?"

"Just got to Ankara. Taking the next flight home. I don't think I'm getting back to Ararat this season. And this new place you dragged me to has given me a lot to think about. I'm still not quite sure what it was we saw."

"I'm not either," Graham agreed.

"It'll be interesting to see what the tests show."

"Unfortunately, I don't have the material anymore."

"Are you kidding? After I…you know, confronted you, I was too rattled to think about taking any. What happened? I thought you put some in your backpack."

"Long story." The door opened and Graham looked up to see one of the diplomats enter with a passport in his hand. "Gotta go. See you back in the states."

SIXTY-FOUR

Graham looked down into the ruins protected with a grid of plexiglass panes. The remains of Roman-era homes—two thousand years old—were displayed like an oversized ant farm. One of the houses was said to be where Saul of Tarsus—the apostle Paul—had lived as a child, though Graham thought the claim was doubtful. The association of Paul with the area was strong enough, however, for the ancient well adjacent to the homes to bear his name.

The site reminded Graham of the oldest physical description of Paul, a passage from a second-century apocryphal book called *The Acts of Paul*. According to the anonymous author, Paul was, "small in size, bald-headed, bandy-legged, well-built, with eyebrows meeting, rather long-nosed, full of grace." Graham had always thought it sounded like Yosemite Sam—except for the grace. And he guessed it was one of the oldest historical mentions of a unibrow.

It had been twenty-four hours since he had arrived at the consulate, and now he was twenty-five miles away, in Tarsus. Although Adana had an airport, flying from there would require a connection in Ankara or Istanbul. Given Graham's unauthorized entry into the country, the death of Sivan, his part in Akyol being held by the PKK, and the unusual nature of the passport, the safest departure would be a direct flight to America. And since that was only possible in Istanbul, an assistant trade officer was driving him ten hours across the country to catch a flight to Los Angeles. When he realized their route would take them through Tarsus, Graham had convinced the diplomat to take them six miles out of the way to see the historic sight, thinking he wouldn't ever visit it again.

Paul's story had always been a source of great comfort to Graham.

Saul—as he was known before his missionary work started—had been an enemy of God's who believed he was protecting God's law by persecuting Christians. But God pursued Saul, blinding him from all he could see, and opened his eyes to what he could not see on his own. And if God could transform such a committed, deluded enemy as Saul, it assured Graham there was hope for himself.

He had seen evidence of God's work in his own life when he was rescued from the darkness that enveloped him after Olivia's and Alyson's deaths. God didn't give him an understanding of everything that happened, but God's undeniable presence at Graham's most desperate moment was a foundation stone he could stand on with certainty when he was in uncertain circumstances.

Vogel had been in a similar dark place, but without the same hope Graham had in Paul's example. Graham wondered if Vogel would have felt as hopeless if he really had found evidence of Noah's Ark on Ararat, then decided it probably wouldn't have made any difference. Like so many others, the ark would not have saved him.

Graham walked back to the car and thanked the young diplomat as he settled into the front seat.

"Since we're doing the tourist thing, you have to see the other place." As he spoke, the trade officer passed the route back to the highway and nodded ahead toward an ancient stone arch. "Cleopatra's Gate. Used to be the gate to the city. She didn't build it, but it was named for her after she arrived here to form an alliance with Marc Antony against Octavian—you know, Caesar Augustus—thirty years before Saint Paul was born."

After failing to get a response, the driver maneuvered back to the highway.

"If you don't mind my asking, what was on the top of Ararat? And Cudi Dagh?"

A long, contemplative sigh said more than the words Graham found to respond. "I'm still trying to figure that out."

His thoughts took the question he had asked of Vogel and put it to himself: What would've happened had he found evidence of the ark on either of the mountains? Would a handful of bitumen granules truly have changed his life if they had been seven thousand years old? He replied to himself with words that could have come from Archimandrite Vardanyan. His faith didn't depend on finding anything, nor was it damaged by finding nothing. And yet, recovering artifacts to develop evidence was what he had devoted his life to. His faith did not come primarily from the evidence, but it was certainly buoyed by it.

He pondered about how he had almost lost his life on the peaks of both mountains, and how he had been preserved. One of his pastor's aphorisms played in his head: If you woke up this morning, God's not done with you. He hadn't wanted to waste his time and energy on an expedition he was unfairly forced to make, especially one that was a charade. But his trust was not in what he might find, but in what he already found. He hadn't climbed the mountains in search of a reason to believe. He climbed the mountain *because* he believed. What else was faith if not a journey into the unknown, through circumstances he couldn't control, trusting in God's past faithfulness to order the steps before him?

A chunk of wood at the top of the mountain wasn't going to change the value of the journey either way. For him, calling the landing site of the ark The Place of Descent was a misnomer. The mountain was a place of *ascent*, drawing him nearer to the one who waited on the other side, and who walked with him to it.

"Hope," Graham answered after an extended silence. "I found hope on the mountain."

AFTERWORD

Growing up in the 70s, I remember watching pseudo-documentary exploitation movies about Bigfoot, the Loch Ness monster, the Bermuda Triangle, UFOs, and Noah's Ark. My pre-adolescent imagination considered all these things possible (after all, movies had been made about them!). But Noah's Ark had the additional attraction of being proof corroborating the Bible. This was my earliest encounter—dubious, though it was—with the concept of what I would much later find was called apologetics. Thus, the quest for the ark has a kind of sentimental element to me, and for many years I treated it as a guilty pleasure.

That changed after I attended several sessions on ark research at a Near East Archaeological Society annual meeting. Dr. Randall Price of Liberty University gave a presentation on the state of his dig at the top of Mount Ararat. He had acquired subsurface RADAR data collected by a restricted satellite, and it indicated an anomaly near the summit of the mountain. Actually, there were two anomalies, both rectilinear, organic, and—taken together—approximately the size of the ark as described in Genesis.

At the time of the presentation, he was leading a team using chainsaws to cut a shaft to reach the object. Because the digging seasons on the peak of Ararat are so short, progress was slow. The mountain was closed to the expedition for various reasons, and in the interim, Price discovered a twelfth Dead Sea Scroll cave—the first in fifty years. Although Dr. Price's work is the basis for the fictional Dr. Ross's work in the book, Ross as a character is my invention.

Interestingly, one of the other presentations in that session was a minority report questioning the legitimacy of Mount Ararat's claim to be the biblical mountain. Bill Crouse, the scholar who presented the work, not only argued against the traditional Ararat, but made a historical case for Cudi Dagh. Crouse is a former advocate for the traditional mountain and had been a part of several ark expeditions in the 80s. His research included more than two dozen ancient sources from three different ancient cultures (pagan, Jewish, and early Christian) all of which speak of the mountain in ways that don't make sense of the traditional Ararat. He included a number of early Islamic sources to further buttress the case. He also cited several European explorers who visited Cudi Dagh and claimed the local traditions about the site were far older than the ones attached to Agri Dagh/Massis.

I'm very grateful to Bill for allowing me to pick his brain over the years, and especially for a long phone interview that helped me keep the plot as true to the facts as possible. To my knowledge, Bill is the only scholar who is an expert in the histories of both mountains. In addition to firsthand accounts of being on Ararat, the story about wood from the ark being used for the doors of Hagia Sophia and the information about the minefield near the inscriptions both come from him. He has also visited the cathedral at Echmiadzin and examined the fossilized wood allegedly from the ark by reversing a detached camera lens to use as a magnifying glass.

That NEAS meeting transformed my thinking about the ark from a sensational guilty pleasure to an object that could be legitimately studied. The two presentations (and others that followed the next year) were both so compelling that they created a quandary that has fascinated me ever since, and eventually became the inspiration for this book.

One of the more fascinating aspects of the search for the ark is the number of eyewitness claims over the last 200 years. Separating the hoaxes from the misidentifications (albeit well-intentioned) in order to get to possibly legitimate sightings is not an easy task, and invariably invites controversy. I chose to include the stories I found most interesting, many of which are also the most commonly appealed to.

The account of George Hagopian was taken from interviews with

Elfred Lee. Lee was also the artist who met with Ed Davis and produced the famous images of the ark with the raised catwalk air holes.

Ed Davis was interviewed on video about his encounter with the ark and served as my source for his story. Davis's polygraph test results were published by Don Shockey, and are faithfully reproduced, though edited to omit redundancy in storytelling. It was Shockey who first used satellite RADAR to identify a location for where to dig. His story on the mountain is told in his book, *Agri-Dagh (Mount Ararat) The Painful Mountain.*

The expeditions of Fernand Navarra are taken from his book, *Noah's Ark: I Touched It* Arthur Chuchian's account was documented in a report written by Bill Crouse who interviewed Chuchian for the newsletter, *The Ararat Report*, February 1990. Lloyd R. Bailey's *Where Is Noah's Ark? Mystery on Mount Ararat* proved an indispensable resource for vetting these claims, debunking the most well-known eyewitness claims from the point of view of a believer in the historicity of the ark. The strange story of the Smithsonian employee Robert Geist was found in Violet M. Cummings's book, *Noah's Ark: Fable or Fact?*

I have done my best to record these eyewitness claims as faithfully as possible. The photos, drawings, and maps described in the book all exist. The claims of missing photos are taken from real claims. In my view, the most startling photographs of an alleged ark on the traditional Ararat were taken by Eryl Cummings and Bob Garbe. The object Cummings captured ultimately proved to be a block of basalt, and Bob Garbe's photograph has never been unconfirmed. The basalt blocks on Ararat—some of them quite large and regular—could go a long way to explaining how so many people could claim to see the ark on Ararat and be mistaken.

As for Cudi Dagh, Gertrude Bell's quotes are taken from her book *Aramuth to Aramuth*, and from her diary entries housed at the University of Newcastle. She is the source for the legend of the pilgrim to the ark who was told by the Devil he couldn't go any farther and so built a dwelling near the peak of Cudi Dagh. The quotes from Bell's intelligence reports come from Robert Fisk's, *The Great War for Civilisation: The Conquest of the Middle East.*

Friedrich Bender published an account of his discovery of wood on Cudi Dagh, as well as the results of the tests he had done. Bender's find is made more interesting by the fact that he was not hunting for what he found, nor did he try to exploit it.

Although Ron Wyatt was able to bring a good deal of attention to the Durupinar formation, his identification of it as the ark has been largely dismissed. His quote about the lack of scholarly support was made to Elfred Lee, who included it in the chapter he contributed to *Explorers of Ararat*.

Daniel David Luckenbill's translation of the Sennacherib inscriptions at the base of Cudi Dagh are recorded here accurately.

The legends shared by the shepherds during the ascent of Ararat—the book of Raziel, the clamor of the people to storm the ark, the attack of animals, the maiming of Noah, the sacrifice, and what happened on the ark—are taken from the Babylonian Talmud. For these and other insights, I am indebted to the work of the eminent Talmudist Louis Ginzberg, who extracted the non-legal material from the Talmud, then organized it into the multi-volume *Legends of the Jews*.

History of St. Gregory and the Conversion of Armenia, a fifth-century work attributed to Agathangelos, is the primary source for many of the stories I included about Gregory and the Etchmiadzin Cathedral, the first Christian cathedral. Its mix of history with legend is a fascinating, though overlooked, part of the development of Christianity.

Flood stories from pagan cultures are well-known, and most predate the oldest books of the Bible. Although many have emphasized the differences in the stories, their common points are quite striking. The museum replicas in Vogel's study are only a small sample of the extra-biblical material for an ancient catastrophic flood.

The inscription at the traditional site of Noah's tomb in Cizre was edited for brevity but quoted verbatim with exception of substituting the alternate spelling Qur'an (rather than Koran) for the sake of consistency.

For the dialogue with the PKK soldiers, I repurposed their own words from television news footage of interviews done on the streets of Cizre. The hijacking of an explosives truck was based on a real PKK incident in 2014.

The University of Münster does indeed host the *Institut für Neutestamentliche Textforschung* (Institute for New Testament Textual Research). Its important work is essential for providing an accurate Greek New Testament that translations can be based on. It is partly due to their effort that many scholars question the authenticity of the pericope of the woman caught in adultery (John 8:2-11).

The discovery of bricks from the Etemenanki ziggurat in ancient Babylon is a real find. The ziggurat's identification as the Tower of Babel is not as widely accepted, but quite common.

The traditional sites in Tarsus as being associated with Saul/Paul are all actual places that can be visited (though not verified).

Lastly, the story about the rivalry between Sir Arthur Conan Doyle and Harry Houdini was an actual dispute. After Houdini's death, Conan Doyle published a book of essays called *The Edge of the Unknown* in which he claimed Houdini was a genuine medium who hid the fact behind the guise of a stage magician.

ACKNOWLEDGMENTS

I COULD NOT ASK FOR MORE ENCOURAGEMENT THAN WHAT I HAVE received from WhiteFire. Thank you, David and Roseanna, for being partners in this barn raising. Janelle Leonard's patient and careful eye once again restrained my written word from assaulting the English language. If only she could do the same for my speech!

Thanks to Dan Lynch, one of Graham Eliot's oldest friends, and a veritable idea factory for how to make more.

As usual, I am grateful to the friends who agreed to be guinea pigs for early drafts of the book. I'm even more grateful that most of them remain on speaking terms after turning the last page. This means you: Rick Altizer, Jamie Brandenburg, Boh Cooper, Mark Haggard, Jay Hollis, Cyndy McRae, and Eric Smith.

Love and eternal thanks to my wife, Jennifer, for letting Graham make such a large claim on my time and attention.

The Graham Eliot Books

The Well of the Soul
Among the Ashes
The Place of Descent